A
BRILLIANT
NIGHT
OF STARS
AND ICE

Other historical novels by
REBECCA CONNOLLY

Under the Cover of Mercy

Hidden Yellow Stars

A BRILLIANT NIGHT OF STARS AND ICE

REBECCA CONNOLLY

SHADOW
MOUNTAIN
PUBLISHING

For my dad,
a fellow history lover and bookworm,
for all of the encouragement, support, love, and laughter.
You're the best!

And for Bewley's hot chocolate,
a delightful Irish treasure quite fittingly discovered
on the adventure that inspired this book. Sláinte!

Interior images:
Map: Peter Hermes Furian/Shutterstock.com; Vector Tradition/Shutterstock.com
p. 301: Capt. Arthur H. Rostron, R.D., R.N.R., while serving as master of the Cunard liner
RMS *Carpathia* in 1912 / public domain / Wikimedia Commons
p. 302: Kate Connolly; https://static.wikia.nocookie.net/titanic/images/9/92/Connolly_k2_h
.jpg/revision/latest?cb=20151020082146

Visit us at shadowmountain.com

This is a work of fiction. Characters and events in this book are products of the author's imagina-tion or are represented fictitiously.

First printing in hardback 2022.
First printing in paperback 2024.

Library of Congress Cataloging-in-Publication Data
Names: Connolly, Rebecca, author.
Title: A brilliant night of stars and ice / Rebecca Connolly.
Description: Salt Lake City : Shadow Mountain, [2022] | Summary: "This historical novel follows the paths of Arthur Rostron, captain of the *Carpathia*, and Kate Connolly, a passenger on the *Titanic*, as the two ships converge on the night of April 15, 1912."—Provided by publisher.
Identifiers: LCCN 2021050307 | ISBN 9781629729923 (hardback) | ISBN 978-1-63993-248-1 (paperback)
Subjects: LCSH: Rostron, Arthur, 1869–1940—Fiction. | Connolly, Kate, 1888–1948—Fiction. | *Titanic* (Steamship)—Fiction. | Ship captains—Fiction. | Young women—Fiction. | Immigrants—United States—Fiction. | Irish—United States—Fiction. | Shipwrecks—North Atlantic Ocean—Fiction. | BISAC: FICTION / Historical / General | LCGFT: Historical fiction.
Classification: LCC PS3603.054728 B76 2022 | DDC 813/.6—dc23/eng/20211117
LC record available at https://lccn.loc.gov/2021050307

Printed in the United States
Lake Book Manufacturing, LLC, Melrose Park, IL

10 9 8 7 6 5 4 3 2 1

"We thank Thee that though in the ordinary
circumstances of life selfishness and greed seem to
be in the ascendancy, yet in times of distress and
peril, then it is that the nobility of soul, the Godlike
in man, asserts itself and makes heroes."

—PRAYER OF REVEREND HENRY COUDEN
in opening the US House of Representatives session,
Friday, April 19, 1912

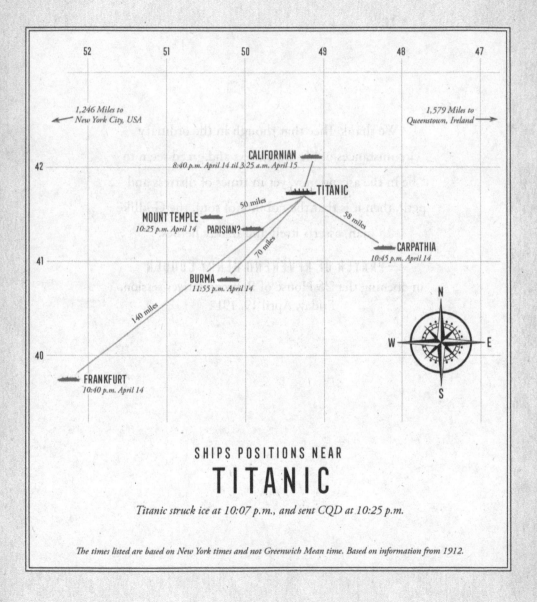

SHIPS POSITIONS NEAR
TITANIC

Titanic struck ice at 10:07 p.m., and sent CQD at 10:25 p.m.

The times listed are based on New York times and not Greenwich Mean time. Based on information from 1912.

CHARACTER CHART

CARPATHIA

Captain Arthur Rostron
Chief Officer Thomas Hankinson
First Officer Horace Dean
Second Officer James Bisset
Third Officer Eric Rees
Fourth Officer John Barnish
Harold Cottam
Chief Engineer Alexander Johnston(e)
Chief Steward Henry Hughes
Purser Ernest Brown
Dr. Frank McGhee
Dr. Vittorio Risicato
Dr. Arpad Lengyel

CARPATHIA PASSENGERS

Louis and Augusta Ogden
Carlos and Katherine Hurd
Reverend Father Roger Anderson
Father Albert Hogue

TITANIC

Second Officer Charles Lightoller
Third Officer Herbert Pitman
Fourth Officer Joseph Boxhall
Harold Bride

TITANIC PASSENGERS

Catherine Connolly (Kate)
Mary McGovern
Julia Smyth

Mary Glynn
Catherine Peters (Katie)
Katherine McCarthy (Katie)
Catherine Connolly (Kate)
Martin McMahon
Martin Gallagher
Margaret Mannion
Margaret Brown (Molly)
Noël Leslie, Countess of Rothes
J. Bruce Ismay
Sarah Roth
Sir Cosmo and Lady Duff-Gordon

LIFEBOAT 13

Ruth Becker
Dr. Washington Dodge
Elizabeth Dowdell
Ethel Emanuel
Helmina Josefina Nilsson
Artur Olsen
Marguerite "Margit" Sandström
Beatrice Sandström
Agnes Sandström

NEW YORK

Senator William Smith
US Steamship Inspector General
   George Uhler
Ellen Connolly McGuckian (Nellie)

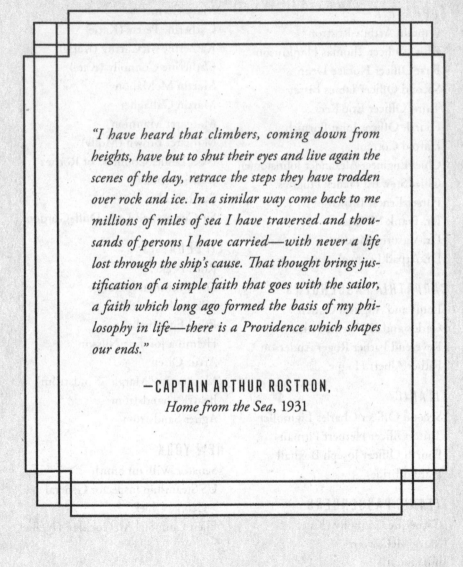

"I have heard that climbers, coming down from heights, have but to shut their eyes and live again the scenes of the day, retrace the steps they have trodden over rock and ice. In a similar way come back to me millions of miles of sea I have traversed and thousands of persons I have carried—with never a life lost through the ship's cause. That thought brings justification of a simple faith that goes with the sailor, a faith which long ago formed the basis of my philosophy in life—there is a Providence which shapes our ends."

—CAPTAIN ARTHUR ROSTRON,
Home from the Sea, 1931

CHAPTER 1

RMS *CARPATHIA* • APRIL 10, 1912

Arthur Rostron exhaled slowly, enjoying the last quiet moments he would have on the bridge of the RMS *Carpathia* before they were underway. The helmsman would soon join him, as would the pilot to take them out of port, but for now, he was alone on the bridge. He could hear the sounds of the deck from his present position, and he could almost see every action his men took.

He had a capable crew; more than capable, they could likely have taken the ship all the way to Fiume and back again without him having to issue a single order. But for this trip, they would be almost entirely full of passengers, which would keep the officers and crew on their toes. And their desire to prove themselves would mean they'd work with even more respect for his position than usual.

That respect had been well-earned during his long career, and while he appreciated it, he did not particularly care for leading his crew along when they were more than able to guide their own actions.

His mouth curved into a slight smile as he heard the sound of the horn blaring into the air. The day was fair and fine, the sun shone brightly, and the winds were minimal. He could imagine no better signs for a smooth passage than those, and he took encouragement from them.

A last call was issued to the embarking passengers, no doubt some only now straggling aboard. There were always stragglers. He did not turn to look at them, preferring to keep his attention toward the sea until they were underway. He would know them well enough shortly.

He'd have to mingle among his first-class passengers this evening as they dined, if for no other reason than to put on a show for them. With all the fuss the White Star Line was making with their new vessels, their older Cunard ship just wouldn't have the same appeal. The *Titanic* might have been fashioned with the latest finery, but there had never been complaints on what *Carpathia* could offer her passengers. The *Titanic* offered extravagance and ostentation, but the *Carpathia* had earned respect and admiration on her merits alone.

Nearly eight hundred passengers was no small thing when she was almost a third the tonnage of *Titanic*, yet no one would have called their experience upon *Carpathia* cramped. She was a good ship, and a fair enough vessel for any sailing upon her. She still had plenty of life in her, and what she lacked in finery, she made up for in experience.

And Arthur had decades of expertise captaining such a ship.

Not even *Titanic* could claim both finery *and* expertise.

He couldn't, and wouldn't, blame Captain Smith for taking on *Titanic* rather than retiring, as some had expected. Why not have one more glorious voyage across the sea, and make history while doing so? Edward Smith was the envy of more than one seafaring man, many of whom longed for the opportunities and energy that now seemed allotted only to the young.

But Arthur was happy with where he was. *Carpathia* was far more his style and taste; she was steady and capable, inconspicuous and unassuming. She had nothing to prove to the newspapers or the public, and he had nothing to prove while captaining her.

The sea was his great love, and he'd continue to sail her as long as he could.

And so long as his wife would let him.

He chuckled softly at the thought of her and her wry view on his love for the sea. Ethel didn't seem to mind when he was away at sea, and she properly appreciated his presence when he was home in Liverpool, but would she have complaints if he stayed with the sea until he could no longer remain upright of his own strength? He'd have to inquire when next he was on land.

She called the sea his "other great love," and sometimes his "other wife," but always with affection. He was fortunate she was so understanding of his passion, and so capable without him. With their four children to care for, she had mastered the art of management and organization, and there was a reason the children utterly adored her. There had never been a situation at home while he was at sea that she had not managed, and the longer their marriage went on, the more in awe of her he became.

A wistful smile crossed his lips as the image of her rose in his mind—her warm, dark eyes containing all the laughter in the world in their depths while somehow also holding everything he adored about home. Perhaps there was something to be said for the weary sailor returning to his home port, and the comfort such a homecoming aroused.

"We're ready to push out, Captain, whenever you please," came the voice of his first officer, Horace Dean, a promising man with a good head on his shoulders. He grinned as he approached Arthur. Flanking him were three other officers, their black uniforms crisp, their gold buttons glistening.

Arthur smiled back at them. "Very good, Mr. Dean. Are you ready to see Fiume again?"

Dean chuckled easily, his dark eyes crinkling. "Yes, sir, and to feel her warmer climate again."

"You've been away from England too long, Mr. Dean, if you're finding the weather at present to be too cold." Arthur nodded at the younger man on Dean's left. "Mr. Bisset, what's your report?"

The second officer stepped forward with a crisp click of his heels, grinning eagerly and adjusting his cap over his dark hair. "All's well, Captain. I've checked with Mr. Cottam in the radio room, and he's well settled."

"At his age, he should be well settled anywhere," the burly Scotsman on Dean's right grumbled good-naturedly, his mustache twitching with his grin. "Naught but a wee pup, he is."

Arthur couldn't argue that; he nodded, still smiling. "Aye, but I'll take the youngest graduate to date from the Marconi school as our operator any time, don't you agree, Johnston?"

The Scotsman returned his nod, the white scattered among his ginger hair catching the light. "Aye, Cap'n. An' besides, who needs bells and whistles, like some other ships have, when we've clearly got the best crew?" He gestured to the deck, and the men all turned to survey it briefly through the vast opening from the bridge overlooking it. A faint breeze wafted in and carried the scent of damp wood from the New York City docks.

Arthur grunted softly to himself. There wasn't much point in addressing Johnston's comment as none of them would miss the reference. Bitterness had been wafting through several seamen over White Star's recent extravagances, from her own people as well as others. The fame and attention that both *Olympic* and *Titanic* had garnered had made things uncomfortable for anybody not associated with them.

Not to mention the potential passengers who wanted a piece of that exciting new experience.

Earlier today, before passengers had begun to board, Arthur had spoken with all of his officers and crew, reminding them of their value and the opportunity before them, but it might be worth reminding them again. Encouraging them. Expressing his confidence in them.

Value could not be placed only on the loudest voice or the brightest star, no matter how it attracted such.

Arthur looked beyond the three officers to the fourth and final man who had joined them, his trusted chief officer, Thomas Hankinson. They had not been sailing together long, but the stout man knew the sea like a beloved friend and had sailed her longer than Arthur had himself.

The chief officer was an unobtrusive man of few words, but he nodded in greeting, a glimpse of his smile visible beneath his thick but neatly trimmed mustache.

Hankinson could have captained the ship as capably as Arthur, there was no mistaking that, and he was grateful to have the man among his officers and overseeing the deck.

"If I may, sir," Bisset broke in, his voice hesitant.

Arthur nodded, instantly on alert. "Proceed."

Bisset dipped his chin briefly. "Cottam did mention hearing some increased chatter about ice."

The tension ebbed from Arthur's chest and shoulders in a breath, and he found himself smiling at the young second officer. "It is April, Bisset. Ice happens, and rumors are bound to follow."

"Not rumors, Captain," Bisset insisted, unfazed by Arthur's teasing jab. "Reports. I am not an alarmist by any stretch, but the facts are the facts. The amount of ice drifting down is considerably heavier than usual."

Arthur took that in for a moment, giving his young officer an assessing look. "Mr. Dean, would you explain to the second officer why this isn't a concern for us?"

Dean, well-used to being Arthur's right hand, barely blinked. "Because *Carpathia*'s course takes us more than eighty miles south of the westbound routes that see dangerous ice. We shouldn't see anything."

"Precisely." Arthur nodded and returned his attention to Bisset. "I am not worried, given our course, but rumors, reports, and what have you, are not to be discounted. Have you a keen eye?"

"Yes, sir," Bisset replied. His mouth curved ruefully. "I've even been told it's a weather eye, for whatever that might be worth."

Appreciative chuckles came from the group, and Arthur patted Bisset's shoulder. "Then you can be our eye for ice, eh?"

"Just as you please, Captain." Bisset nodded and stepped back, raising his chin.

Another promising lad, and the future to match, if he kept at it.

Arthur slid his glance to the Scotsman once more. "All is right in your area, Johnston?"

He received a firm nod in response. "Aye, Cap'n. The boys below are more'n ready. Sound the word, and we'll have this old girl giving us all she's got."

"Not that old," Arthur pointed out, raising a brow. "Barely twelve years."

Johnston snorted softly. "Ancient, Cap'n, in this day and age. She's got life in her yet, but she's no spring chicken."

There was no denying that.

"Hankinson?" Arthur asked, returning his attention to the chief officer.

"All set, sir. We are ready when you are."

Arthur eyed each of his officers present, then cleared his throat. "Right then, we'll get our passengers where they need to go, and before they know it, too. About your work, men, if you please. Push forward, keep her steady, and get us some distance from New York."

"Yes, Captain," they said as one. Bisset and Johnston left to see to their duties, Hankinson moved out to oversee the deck, while Dean stepped forward next to Arthur on the bridge.

Arthur barely glanced at him, hiding a smile. Dean had unconsciously, or perhaps consciously, mirrored Arthur's stance and position as he'd taken up his post. A bit of ambition there, perhaps?

"Are you really not concerned about the ice, sir?" Dean asked in a much lower voice, his eyes on the horizon, which was perfectly clear with the midday sun high above them.

Shaking his head, Arthur squared his shoulders. "I'm really not, Dean. Yes, it's a bit cooler than normal this year, but we're well south of it. It's the northern ships that ought to have concerns, not us."

Dean grunted in acknowledgment. "Very true, sir. A friend of mine with White Star got a position on the *Titanic* and is sailing with her now."

"Indeed?" Arthur made a face, impressed in spite of himself. "And under Captain Smith, no less, a fine position. What's his name?"

"Charles Lightoller, sir. Old friend. I was the best man at his wedding."

Arthur chuckled. "Well, don't get any ideas about leaving us to join him and the White Star, First Officer. I envision a bright future for you here."

Dean grinned, hands clasped behind his back. "Thank you, sir. Believe me, Cunard and *Carpathia* are enough for me."

"Very good. Eyes on the bridge, Dean. I'm going to check our course."

"Yes, sir."

Arthur nodded, then turned from the bridge, heading into the chart room.

Diagrams of the ship hung on the walls, but those were not of interest now. Nor were the details of other ships sailing presently and their courses, though he'd had them prepared thoroughly enough. He moved directly to the maps pertaining to *Carpathia*'s present course, piled at least three deep on the table, as per the usual. Their course was simple enough, and certainly smooth enough, but he was a careful, cautious seaman. Those traits had served him well, and he would continue to rely on them until he could no longer sail.

Bisset's words about ice were stuck in his mind, despite his years of experience sailing in the North Atlantic. Ice wouldn't be a concern for them, not even with the cooler weather of late. The route was too warm, and their path clear of any trouble spots. Still, he would keep the warning in the back of his mind until they were well free from any such reports. He was not the kind of man who would put the ambition of the voyage above the safety of his passengers and crew.

Leaning over the maps, tracing the course with compass, ruler, and pencil, and quickly making the calculations, he nodded to himself. Even if they did hit trouble, it would be minor at worst, and the ship was more than capable of making up for any difficulties. She had been tested at a top speed of fifteen knots five, even at her age, but there would be no need to get anywhere close to that speed.

Steady, calm, and sure. That was his way, and that was *Carpathia*. There was no need for anything more.

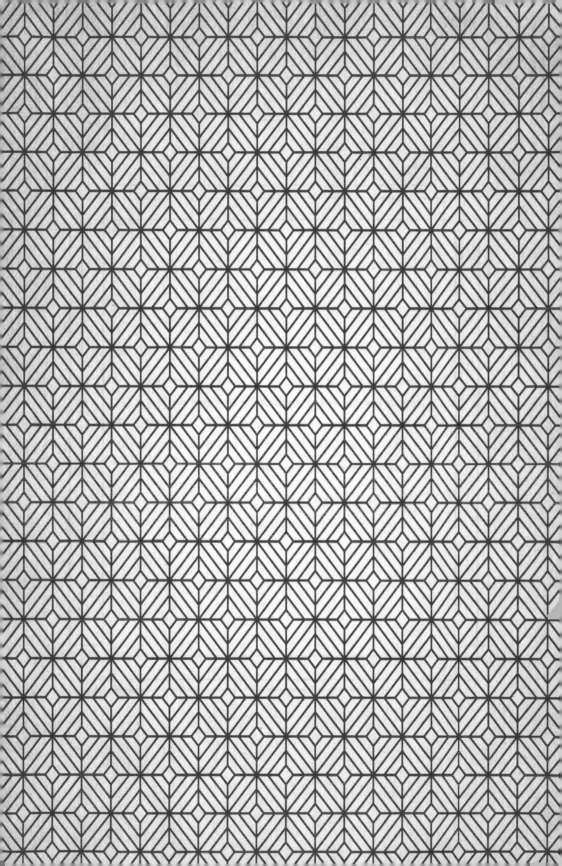

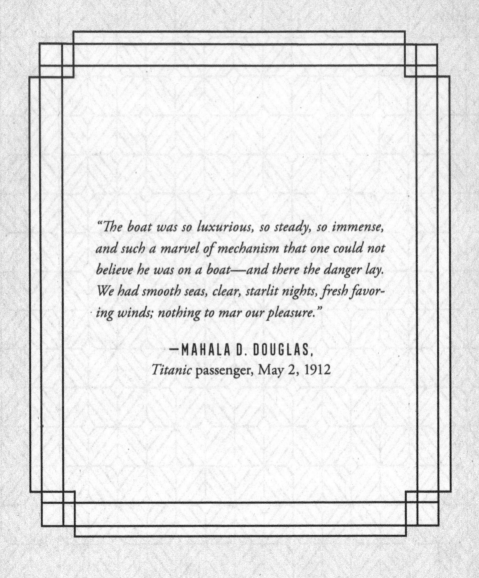

"*The boat was so luxurious, so steady, so immense, and such a marvel of mechanism that one could not believe he was on a boat—and there the danger lay. We had smooth seas, clear, starlit nights, fresh favoring winds; nothing to mar our pleasure.*"

—MAHALA D. DOUGLAS,
Titanic passenger, May 2, 1912

CHAPTER 2

"Mary! Kate! Hurry yourselves up. I've found the way to our cabins!" Julia called out.

Catherine Connolly chuckled and glanced behind her at her friend Mary McGovern, who seemed equally amused as they made their way through the crowd and along the white-paneled corridors of steerage. "Julia will think she's discovered El Dorado aboard and not our cabins, Mary. How difficult is it when we board on the third-class gangway and there are signs to guide us?"

"True enough," Mary replied, holding her carpetbag tightly in one hand and her straw hat in the other. She grinned broadly, her blue eyes bright. Tendrils of her light brown hair fell from her bun. "Difficult discovery, was it, Julia?"

"I'll thank you both to save the cheek," Julia Smyth shot back over her shoulder, green eyes dancing, as they usually did. "And there will be no fuss when I have first pick of the beds."

Catherine—or Kate as she liked to be called—choked on another laugh. "We're in third class, Julia, right at the stern of the ship, and for all we know, we're sharing a cabin with someone who boarded in Southampton. The first of the beds might not be free."

"I'll still have the first pick of the beds that remain then." Julia lifted her chin, her copper hair catching the light, and continued down the pristine yet narrow corridor of rooms.

"With all your siblings at home," Kate added, "it wouldn't surprise me if you fought our cabinmate by hand for the best of them overall. I daresay you're used to it."

Julia didn't respond, not that it mattered.

And Kate wasn't particular about the beds, no matter how she teased.

The farewells to her family had been difficult and more painful than Kate had expected, but the promise of joining Nellie in America was a good consolation. Her sister and her husband had promised to help find her a position once she was settled there. The prospects were better than in Ireland, at any rate, and that was the point. She needed more opportunity than Ireland held for her, and even her mother understood that.

It hadn't stopped her tears, but she understood.

Julia and Mary were seeking similar opportunities in America, and the three of them, all from the same home county, had banded together for this grand adventure. How they had managed to find passage onboard *Titanic*, of all ships, was a mystery, something providential or simply good luck, but there was no helping the excitement.

It was everywhere on the ship, on every level, even down here, several stories below the strolling elite. After the glory and success of *Olympic*, everyone wanted to be part of *Titanic*. She and her friends had boarded in Queenstown, and Kate had seen that excitement spread from the children heading to second class to the fine ladies already in first class. And here in third . . . Well, with the number of Irish who had come aboard with them, there was no doubt a great deal of merriment would commence once they were underway.

"Here we are!" Julia called in delight, turning toward their cabin and shuffling inside. "Oh! Good morning to ya, dear. Prepare for an invasion."

Kate and Mary followed, grinning at their rambunctiously optimistic friend.

A girl sat on the lower bunk as they entered. She smiled timidly at them.

"And who might you be?" Kate asked, setting down her things.

"Mary Glynn," came the soft response, a clear Irish lilt accompanying the words. She blushed, the color in her cheeks a stark contrast against her fair complexion. Her deep brown eyes were wide, staring at them all, and her equally dark hair was braided and piled atop her head. "From County Clare."

"Well, now we've got two Marys in a berth," Julia said as she tugged the pin out of her hat. "And if you don't mind sharing the room with three girls from County Cavan, we'll be a merry party all the way to New York."

Mary grinned and gestured to the cabin. "I don't mind at all. Settle in, and let's explore the ship!"

"I'm Julia Smyth, that's Mary McGovern, and that's Kate Connolly. Perhaps we should call you 'Mary-from-Clare,' and this one 'Mary Mac'!"

Kate smiled as she removed her coat and set her things on the bunk nearest her. She already felt at home with her roommates, glad that they were all roughly the same age—early twenties—though Mary-from-Clare might have been closer to eighteen.

Kate looked around the small space. It was a sparse cabin, but with clean, white walls, salmon-pink floors, and sturdy bunks with more overhead space than she'd had in her bunk at home. A sink for washing adorned one wall.

She'd heard some cabins could house up to ten passengers, but this one was designed for just four. She was glad of it; small numbers could make for a far more pleasant journey. It did mean, however, that their cabin was rather tight quarters.

There wouldn't be much need for exploring down here. For all the finery rumored in *Titanic*, there was not much of it in steerage. Oh, it was better than other ships, she had no doubt, possibly a great deal so, but cramped berths were cramped berths, and that wasn't going to change. Just because *Titanic* had more of them than other ships didn't make it any more impressive. Cleaner, perhaps, and it still smelled of fresh paint, but hardly awe-inspiring.

She pressed her hand against the pillow on her bunk gently, surprised that it was actually fairly downy. Perhaps steerage on *Titanic* would be finer than she expected.

Not that it mattered, all things considered. She was still going to America, and the newness of the ship made even being in steerage more appealing. The crossing would be pleasant enough, and in a few days, she would be in New York. She could be cramped for a few days.

She looked around, half-listening to the enthusiastic chatter of the other girls in the cabin. The room might have been small, but the promise of what lay ahead of them was enormous.

She ought to make the most of the experience while she could.

"What in the world have you got in there, Mary Mac?" Julia pressed with some insistence as they began to open their bags and arrange themselves.

Mary blushed a little and held up a small parcel. "It's Saint Mogue's earth. You can never be too careful."

"What is Saint Mogue's earth?" Mary-from-Clare asked.

Julia turned with a smile. "A parcel of Saint Mogue's earth is said to protect against fire or drowning. My nan kept a small pot of it in her kitchen her whole life." She glanced at Mary Mac. "You're not afraid of drowning on this ship, are ya? It's laughable."

Mary shrugged. "You can never be too careful," she said again.

"I think a little exploration might be good for me," Kate announced, changing the topic. The less time spent cramped together, the better, no doubt. "Who wants to venture? Marys? Julia?"

"I do!" Mary-from-Clare stood and brushed at her simple cotton twill skirts, her hair slightly disheveled amid her braids.

The other two declined, so Mary and Kate headed out together.

"What's waiting for you in America, Mary?" Kate asked as they moved through the corridor, following the signs toward the public rooms and maneuvering around other passengers seeking their cabins. A few children darted by, laughing merrily. "Sweetheart? Family?"

Mary laughed once, a surprisingly musical sound, despite the derision in it. "No sweetheart. Not even leaving one behind. Perhaps I'll find one in America, but it is what it is. I'm going to stay with my cousin in Washington DC. What are you doing?"

A screaming child prevented Kate from immediately answering, and the harried mother scurried passed them, her cheeks flushing. Poor woman.

"Kate Connolly, would you slow down?"

Kate turned in confusion, scanning the corridor and the scattered passengers in it. The only people she knew on this ship were Mary at her side and her companions back in the cabin. Who could possibly be calling for her by name?

"I'll keep whatever pace I like, thank you," a brisk Irish voice replied to the question, startling Kate even more.

"Surely there's not another Kate Connolly aboard *Titanic*," Mary murmured behind her, laughing.

Kate shook her head, blinking as she stared up the corridor, wishing she could see through the people to the source of the new voice. "I shouldn't think so, but there are Connollys everywhere in Ireland, it seems."

A trio of women approached, laughing together with their arms linked, which was unusual given the press of people in the corridor, but the trio adjusted for any obstacle. Their simple clothing suggested they belonged with Kate and her companions in steerage, but their confidence and energy seemed better suited to strolling the first-class promenade deck.

Kate straightened as they reached her, smiling quickly. "Did one of you call for Kate Connolly?"

"I did." The girl with dark hair and the palest eyes Kate had ever seen tilted her head at another in the trio. "This is Kate Connolly. Why?"

"*My* name is Kate Connolly," Kate admitted, gesturing to herself. "From County Cavan."

The trio laughed, and the other Kate Connolly, who was a trifle older than her companions but bore the same energy, grinned and held out a hand. "Pleasure to meet you. My compliments on your fine name."

Kate inclined her head in what she hoped was a gracious nod. "The same. Whereabouts are you from?"

"County Tipperary," the other Kate told her. "And Katie Peters and Katie McCarthy are from there also." She gestured to her two friends at her side.

"My, my, aren't we a confusing bunch?" Kate gestured to Mary. "This is Mary Glynn."

Nods went around the group.

"Sorry to dash," one of the Katies said; she was fair-haired with bright green eyes and a sprinkling of freckles across her cheeks that gave her an impish air. "But we've got to track down Katie's sweetheart,

Roger Tobin. She's got a dreadful fear he'll find another one while on the ship."

"Hush, now," the blue-eyed Katie replied. "I have not." She smiled at Kate and Mary. "I'm sure we'll see you both around the ship as we go. Third class can't be that immense."

The trio moved on, leaving Kate and Mary to look at each other in stunned amusement.

"You'd be hard-pressed to find another Kate Connolly on Irish land, yet here we find one on Irish water?" Mary shook her head, exhaling roughly. "What are the odds of that?"

It was an incredible coincidence, to be sure. But the trio of girls was nice enough, and despite what blue-eyed Katie had said, there were bound to be lots of passengers in third class. Kate had heard a rumor that there were more than five hundred passengers just in steerage alone, and she believed it. They'd likely not have reason to mingle, or even to cross paths, with the trio while on board. And once they got to America, they'd all go their separate ways.

Still, she'd like to sit down to lunch with the other Kate Connolly, learn about her life, see if they were alike in ways other than their names.

When would she have another chance?

"The miracle of *Titanic*, I suppose," Kate replied softly. She smiled at Mary. "Right. Shall we continue? The public rooms shouldn't be far."

Mary nodded, and they continued on their way, the corridor filling with more and more people coming aboard.

The size of the ship was astonishing. Though it was only the size of a few city blocks, once on board, it might have been the size of a full country, and it could likely carry all the people of one. Utter madness, in Kate's opinion.

And unnerving, if she thought about it too long.

Languages of all kinds filled the air, and, enclosed as the passengers were down here, the sounds echoed and magnified. Kate knew some of the languages, but there were many she was sure she had never heard before. Various accents accompanied them, as did the wide variety of clothes the passengers wore. It felt as if all the world's cultures were on display in one place. Kate's travel experience was severely limited, so she couldn't tell one culture from another, but the bright colors and patterns fascinated her. Children giggled and dashed about the corridor, much to the exasperation of their parents. There was no difference between cultures and traditions there.

Stewards called out various directions, attempting to organize the masses of new passengers, but few people paid them much attention.

"Yes, down that corridor, sir!" one steward called, his polite tone taking on an exasperated note. "No, ma'am, keep going."

"Oy! Don't kick the paneling!" another steward shouted at a mischievous pair of boys, his pristine white coat making him seem somehow more puffed up.

"Come along, now, ship's about to leave!" cried yet another.

Their voices echoed as well, but the lack of response echoed more.

Kate smiled at that.

All in all, it was madness, and Kate took Mary's hand in hers as a precaution, especially as the last of the passengers crossed from the gangway at a dead run, making the cramped corridors even more so. How would any orders or instructions reach any of them?

They turned into a large room with several tables and plenty of chairs to line them. Wood panels decorated some sections, but for the most part, the same white paint that was everywhere else was on the walls here as well. And, ironically, posters of other White Star Line ships were on display. It was a bright room, which she approved of, with plenty of light streaming from several portholes.

It was a sight better than many other dining rooms in steerage, she imagined, though she couldn't say for sure. She'd heard the most awful tales from her cousins and uncles from their travels—of rats skittering across floors, not enough chairs for mealtime, and feeling claustrophobic in dining rooms. There was room for exaggeration, especially in her family, but there would be some truth as well. Luckily, she saw no rats, and there was certainly plenty of space for meals.

"Not a bad space, considering." Mary shrugged, still smiling, and glanced over at Kate. "I don't suppose it matters so long as we eat."

Kate grinned at her, then gestured for the door. "Let's see what else we can find. Do you think there's a room for dancing?"

"Dancing?" Mary tossed her head back on a laugh as the two of them left the room. "Do you really think we'll hold a ball or something while we're on here? We're not fine folk down here."

"What of that?" Kate demanded. "The fine folk will have their dinners and parties—why shouldn't we? I daresay one or two of the Irishmen aboard will have brought their fiddles, and we don't need more than that to dance a jig. Give us a bit of spirits, and we'll be up and at it in no time at all."

Mary shook her head as they rounded a corner, smiling cheekily at a passing steward who eyed her with interest. "One or two Irishmen likely brought their own spirits aboard as well."

"Undoubtedly."

The girls linked arms and strolled along the ship, finding the men's Smoking Room, which was already in use by a few guests, the small but well-situated General Room, which appeared as unremarkable as its name suggested, and an area aptly named the "Open Space" that could be used for a great many things, especially the dancing and music Kate was imagining.

All in all, Kate's opinions of the ship improved with every room she saw; even in steerage, the ship was impressive in its size, scale, and finery. The temptation to find a way into the upper classes sprang to life within her, though she knew the odds of seeing the sights of the first-class accommodations were slim.

Except for the sounds of the engines and the slight rattle to the walls, one would never know they were on a ship at all. Of course, they hadn't left port yet, so she might feel differently once they were underway.

Nellie had told her she had been miserably ill on her journey to America; the seasickness had not abated until she had fully reached her destination. But Nellie had not traveled on such a fine ocean liner, and Kate had heard her brothers talking a few nights ago about how the size of a ship could diminish the effects of sickness.

She hadn't thought to ask how they knew any such thing.

"Mary Glynn, is that you?"

Mary slowed a step, her arm tensing in Kate's, as a tall, attractive young man came into view. He was fair-haired and broad-shouldered, and he swept the cap off his head as he approached them.

His eyes were solely on Mary, and his grin was infectious. "I thought that was you. What are you doing here?"

"What does it look like I'm doing?" Mary quipped, her voice trembling with just a touch of excitement. "Sailing to America, same as you."

"Aye, that you are, and a fine thing to be doing the same with you." His smile spread, and his blue eyes flicked to Kate. "Pardon me." He bowed a little. "Martin McMahon, at your service. I'm from County Clare, same as Mary."

Kate offered a friendly smile. "Kate Connolly, County Cavan. Not to be confused with the Kate Connolly from Tipperary, also on board."

Martin raised a brow. "Must be a blessed ship for there to be two of you on it."

"And you're not going to flatter either of us away, I promise you that," Kate informed him lightly.

"Sure look it, she says such a thing wi'out dancing with me first," Martin teased, returning his attention to Mary. "I dance well, don't I, Mary?"

"You're grand," Mary said simply, her lips twitching shyly at the edges. "If I recall."

Kate watched her new friend with fascination, wondering at the history between the two. "There's bound to be dances aplenty once we're away, won't there?"

"If not, I'll make it so," Martin said, still fixed on Mary. "And remind Miss Mary of my dancing abilities, as she has so clearly forgotten. What do you say, Mary?"

Mary's smile was small, but it was there. "I might be persuaded."

"Might is grand." He grinned freely, then seemed to recall Kate was there as well. "And I won't say no to a dance with you, Miss Kate, once we have one."

Kate nodded in amused pleasure. "I'm no great dancer myself, Mr. McMahon, so I'd be pleased to have you teach me the way."

"Right, and it'll be my pleasure to do so." He replaced his cap and nodded at them both. "Until next time, Miss Connolly. Miss Glynn." His eyes lingered on Mary, and then he walked past them.

Mary exhaled slowly.

Kate tugged her friend back to walking. "I thought you said you had no sweetheart on board, Mary."

"I don't," she replied. "Martin McMahon has that effect on every girl in County Clare. It's not particular to me."

"It looked particular from here." Kate hummed in playful consideration. "Perhaps by the time we get to America, you will have a sweetheart after all."

"Sure look it, Kate Connolly, and mind your tongue. Let's find the deck for third class, shall we?"

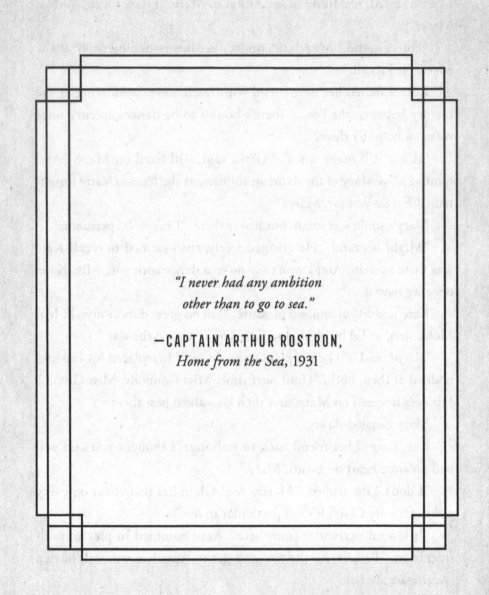

*"I never had any ambition
other than to go to sea."*

—CAPTAIN ARTHUR ROSTRON,
Home from the Sea, 1931

CHAPTER 3

RMS *CARPATHIA* • APRIL 12, 1912

"Ah, there's the captain now."

Arthur hid a wince, then turned to face the voice, forcing a polite expression for whoever it was. His walk along the deck had been a whim after the sun had risen. The morning was brisk, and the weather promised to be a fine day, so he had been in a fair mood because of it.

He thought he could escape notice, given the earliness of the day, but it was not to be. Passengers often wanted to meet with the captain during the voyage, and as much as he disliked being social at sea, it was part of his duty to accommodate them.

His expression became a little less forced as he saw his very young, very bright, third officer, Eric Rees, accompanying a couple headed toward him. His uniform was spotless, and his white hat contrasted brightly against his dark hair and eyes. His warm smile and cheerful demeanor made him the perfect officer to engage passengers socially. If he was bringing this couple to Arthur for a greeting, it would be a worthy interview.

"Good morning, Mr. Rees. Giving a tour this morning, are we?" As the couple drew closer, he realized he knew them. "It's about time you had one, isn't it, Mr. Ogden?"

Mr. Ogden chuckled. He was a regular passenger of *Carpathia* and known to nearly the entire crew. "I'd say so, sir, though I'd wager we could find anything on the ship we wished to now."

Arthur nodded. "Undoubtedly. A few more trips, Mrs. Ogden, and you'll know her better than I do."

Mrs. Ogden, a little less congenial than her husband, smiled, folding her furs more tightly about her. "Highly unlikely, Captain. Your job is to know her best, is it not?"

He bowed his head in acknowledgment. "I suppose it is, madam. And how have you found her?"

"Marvelous," Mr. Ogden boasted with a pat on Rees's shoulder. "Your third officer here has done a fine job of showing us around. Knows the ship backwards and forwards."

"He ought to, if he is my third officer," Arthur said with a wry look at Rees, who grinned back.

"But Captain," Ogden went on, "we've just seen third class for the first time. Rees here says their dining room extends the full width of the ship and seats three hundred passengers? And the walls . . . paneled polished oak and teak dado?"

Arthur raised a brow. "Yes, what of it?"

Ogden's brow furrowed. "Well, that is extraordinarily generous for third class."

"It is, indeed," Mrs. Ogden chimed in. "Why bother? We are not *Titanic.*"

No, they weren't, and he was growing weary of the comparisons.

Arthur maintained his smile, his eyes still on the elderly couple. "Mr. Rees?"

Mr. Rees stepped forward as though called upon in school. "We of the Cunard Line like to accommodate all of our passengers, Mrs. Ogden. They have a smoking room and a ladies' room as well. We hope any passenger on the *Carpathia* will be comfortable."

"Precisely." Arthur nodded at the officer, who stepped back. "One does not have to be *Titanic* in order to be fine and comfortable."

"Indeed not, I should say," Ogden boasted as though he, too, were part of the crew. "Very fine." He looked at the lifeboats and davits, tapping the nearest one with his walking stick. "And what might this be, sir?"

Arthur gestured to his officer. "Mr. Rees."

"Sir." Rees nodded and stepped forward again. "This is a davit, Mr. Ogden. It is a crane used to swing out and lower our lifeboats, which, as you see, are presently only sitting on the deck and fastened in place. Attached to the davit"—he paused and indicated the pulleys and ropes—"you will see the falls, or lines. These are hooked to the lifeboat and provide the means by which we can safely lower lifeboats to the water."

"Marvelous," Mr. Ogden said in awe, grinning at them all. "And what is the capacity of these fine lifeboats, hmm? They seem rather large."

"They safely fit sixty or so, sir," Rees replied. "They were tested with a good deal more people than that to ensure safety. I've heard as many as seventy men were in the lifeboat without any danger at all."

The answer delighted Mr. Ogden, whose demeanor lit up with childlike wonder. "Absolutely magnificent. How many do we have? Are they all here? What is the speed of hoisting them up and lowering them?"

"You should have been a maritime man, my dear." His wife laughed, clearly familiar with her husband's enthusiasm.

Another couple approached, their attention on the small group. Arthur did not know these passengers, but they were both slender and smartly dressed in coordinating suit-sets, his of deep brown, hers of plum, though neither would outshine the Ogdens. Neither smiled either, yet Mr. Rees brightened at seeing them.

"Mr. and Mrs. Hurd, what a pleasant surprise," Rees said.

The Hurds did not share his joviality. It was clear they had been making a study of the ship themselves, and while not displeased with her, Arthur suspected they were not entirely impressed with her either.

Clearly, they would have felt better suited to *Titanic*.

More's the pity.

The trim Mr. Hurd looked Rees up and down, his wide, dark eyes narrowed in appraisal. "Ah, yes, it's Third Officer Rees, isn't it?"

Rees was unflappable. "Yes, sir. Have you met Mr. and Mrs. Ogden?"

"No. A pleasure, sir. Ma'am."

"And our captain," Rees went on. "Captain Rostron. As fine a captain as the sea has ever known."

Arthur smiled slightly. "That'll do, Rees."

Mr. Hurd eyed Arthur, his gaze lingering on the gold braids at his shoulders. His small mustache twitched. "Carlos Hurd, Captain. My wife, Katherine."

Arthur nodded to the lady in turn. "Ma'am."

She barely responded, her hand still resting comfortably on her husband's arm. She sniffed faintly, and a feather from her expansive hat waved in the breeze as if to answer for her.

"And what do you do in America, Mr. Hurd?" Ogden asked without hesitation. "Your profession, that is?"

Hurd glanced at him. "I'm a newspaperman, Mr. Ogden. New York."

Mr. Ogden's expression did not so much as twitch. "And is there money in newspapers?"

The Hurds both seemed to stiffen at the question. "Some. Good day to you both. Rees. Captain."

They moved on, eying everything on the deck with a hint of speculation, from the davits to the lifeboats, from the red-and-black funnels towering above to the smooth planks beneath their feet.

Arthur watched them go, then looked up into the clear, bright morning sky with a smile. "What say you, Rees? Is this as fine a crossing as we've ever had?"

"Near enough, sir. A bit brisk, but fine indeed. Quite comfortable, come to think." Rees clasped his hands behind his back, inhaling deeply. "Altogether, very fine."

"A bit of a cool breeze doesn't bother me so long as the weather is fair," Arthur told the group. "Far better than the alternative."

Mr. Ogden nodded fervently. "Right you are, Captain. A fair wind and a following sea, isn't that the saying?"

Duty pulled at Arthur, along with an urgency to resume his work. He nodded politely to them. "Indeed, sir. If you will excuse me. As you were, Rees." He tapped the brim of his hat, moving down the deck and letting his features relax into a more natural expression.

Other passengers were on the deck, but none seemed interested in approaching him. He smiled politely to all, watching their expressions and manner. From what he could tell, they all seemed pleased with the ship and their voyage.

That said something, for sure.

The ship's speed was quick and steady, though no one would accuse them of racing. All was well below decks and above, and that was all he could ask for from his ship.

The sea was another matter entirely, but thus far, she had been kind.

He continued to walk, knowing that those passengers who rose early would be finishing their breakfasts and would more likely than not take a stroll along the deck under the morning sun. He had learned long ago that seeing the captain, having a chance to greet him, did a great deal to encourage confidence in both himself as their captain and in the Cunard Line.

But he would much prefer being on the bridge or checking their course, being engaged in the action of his position, rather than the politeness of his position. Ethel teased him incessantly about his lack of social interest, but he had always assured her that she was sociable enough for them both.

A pang of fond loneliness filled him, as it sometimes did on the long stretches of his voyages. He'd thought about bringing his wife along with him on one or two of these trips, but the idea of bringing his two loves together had never given him complete comfort. What if they quarreled, and he had to choose between them?

Perhaps it was a foolish whim. They had done well enough with their present arrangement, and coming home to Ethel somehow made the going away worth it all.

His attention shifted to a young officer coming toward him, striding eagerly. "Captain Rostron, sir."

Arthur nodded in greeting. "Mr. Barnish. How are you finding things?"

Barnish fell into step beside him, matching his pace and his manner. "All perfectly well, sir. First Officer Dean and Second Officer Bisset are on the bridge, and Mr. Cottam from the radio room has just delivered a batch of messages to them. Says he's been in touch with his friend on *Titanic*—a Mr. Phillips, sir—and the man is having the time of it."

"I'd wager he is," Arthur remarked, looking toward the horizon without much attention. "Though I don't know how much enjoyment a Marconi man gets aboard any ship. All the noise from the wireless and all those messages? It's enough to make any sensible head ache.

Still, *Titanic* is large enough for two men on the Marconi, I hear. Poor Cottam—all alone on poor *Carpathia*."

"I don't believe he's complaining, sir." Barnish laughed. "He's pleased to work alone and is amusing himself by taking down as many messages as he can for other ships and sending them on. Perhaps he'll become a relay station, sending messages from land to ship or ship to ship for the rest of his days."

Arthur grunted once, wondering how in the world such a thing would be of any use on a ship and not a physical station on land. "If it suits him to do so, and does not interfere with his tasks, I suppose I shall not object."

"Also, the Marshalls keep him occupied, sir."

"The Marshalls?" Arthur shook his head, thinking back. "I don't believe I've met them."

Barnish's mouth curved into a lopsided smile. "First-class passengers, sir. They have nieces on *Titanic*."

"Fortunate girls."

"At any rate," Barnish went on, ignoring the comment, "they've taken to sending messages to each other. Cottam indulges them, and it's not an extensive amount. I think it actually lifts the Marshalls' spirits to do it."

Arthur would have to consider that. He'd always considered the Marconi as more a tool of necessity than one of amusement, but perhaps his passengers or crew felt differently.

The times were changing; there was no doubt about that.

He glanced behind them at the group he'd just left and gave the man next to him a pitying look. "Barnish, do Rees a favor and in five minutes, tell him he's needed on the bridge. Make something up, if you have to."

To his credit, Barnish did not even blink at the odd request. "Yes, sir. Right away. Erm . . . in five minutes, that is."

"Very good, Barnish. That'll be all."

Barnish nodded and strode away.

Arthur paused on his stroll to breathe in the brisk sea air. He believed it was the clearest air to be found anywhere, and on all his voyages, a moment's reflection and deep breath had always given him the clarity he sought, whether he was wrestling with inner turmoil, spiritual strife, or something far more temporal and even nautical.

He had become rather good at taking advantage of any moments he could discover, even if the timing might not always be ideal.

A turn at the watch in the middle of the night. Stealing a breath in the early morning before any of the dining rooms had opened for passengers. Slipping away at meals before he'd be missed by passengers or crew.

Even locking himself in the chart room had helped at times, though the air there wasn't nearly so refreshing.

Arthur continued to walk, heading up to the bridge to check on his officers. He'd take a moment with the maps, recheck their position and their course.

And then, perhaps, he'd check in with his young, ambitious Marconi man. Just in case any of his accruing messages were of any interest.

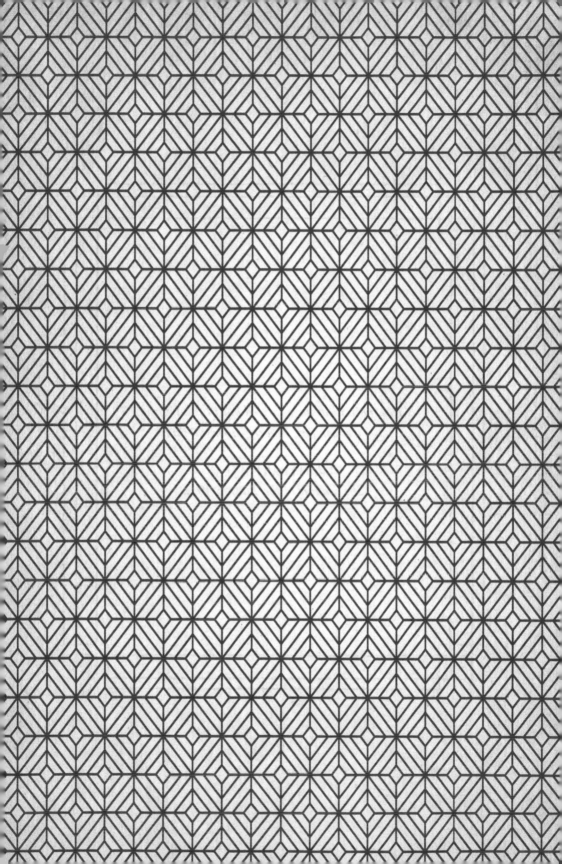

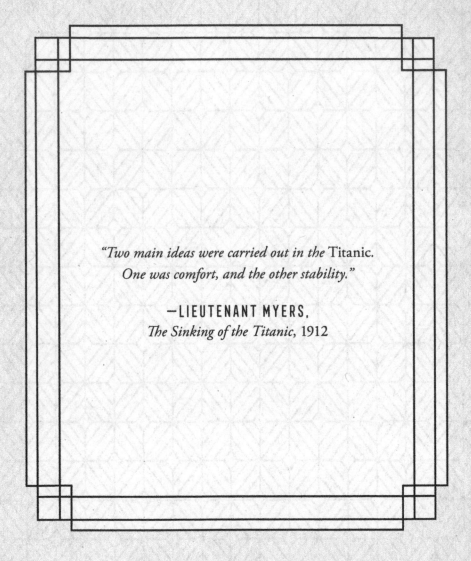

"Two main ideas were carried out in the Titanic.
One was comfort, and the other stability."

—LIEUTENANT MYERS,
The Sinking of the Titanic, 1912

CHAPTER 4

RMS *TITANIC* · APRIL 14, 1912

The room was full of people, and that was putting it mildly.

In truth, it was rather difficult to move, let alone enjoy the company and the music.

Why they had decided to have a party in the General Room rather than use the Open Space had not been made clear, but Kate supposed that was of relatively little matter.

What mattered was the spirit of merriment and the excitement that pervaded the room. Cultures and languages mixed and blended into an entirely new concoction. Drink and dance would do that to a room, and nobody seemed to mind the closeness of the crowd. Most people were going to America to start a new life, and there was something thrilling about sharing that promise, that future, and those wishes.

Kate smiled as she looked around her, skilled musicians filling the air with song. It was just as she had predicted: men had brought fiddles, and they played them with gusto and glee. Laughter and cheers accompanied the music, breathless giggles and encouraging whistles.

The air smelled of beer, of perspiration, of that unidentifiable scent of several perfumes blending together. Kate knew the combination well.

It smelled of any given dance in Ireland.

A jolt of longing laced through her breath, though it was gone again in an instant as she forced herself to continue smiling. Her cabinmates danced and laughed, their hair becoming more and more disarrayed with every subsequent dance. She'd done her share of keeping time to the music, too, though she now took a moment to breathe.

Leaning against the wall for comfort and support, she considered the days they had been aboard this ship. She could barely tell the ship was moving. She'd never felt so much as a twinge of discomfort from being on the sea, and the faint hum from the engines had become a comfortable, lulling sound.

Their days on *Titanic* were not particularly exciting, but she had enjoyed some time in the Open Space to herself. She'd chatted in the General Room from time to time with other passengers, meeting families and ladies and, in some cases, eager young lads from all parts of the world.

Kate glanced around the room again. Though they were technically steerage, nothing about their accommodations felt particularly lacking.

Some of the passengers had been on other liners before, and they spoke of the crowding, the feeling of neglect and lack, and being expected to bring their own food and provide their own meals. On *Titanic*, at least, they were fed three times a day, and not from their own stores. Meals were provided for them in the Dining Room, and though the food was simple, it was hearty and filling. Only that morning, they'd enjoyed options of oatmeal porridge and milk, smoked herrings, jacket potatoes, bread and butter, marmalade, Swedish bread, tea, and coffee for their breakfast.

Luxury was the theme on this ship, no matter on which level one was housed.

There was a piano in the General Room, and someone was nearly always playing it at any given time of day. The music delighted the children, as Kate had witnessed that morning.

The children on board had been quite restless, weary of being confined. Some of the younger women had attempted to entertain them, which the weary mothers had appreciated, and, for a while, it had worked. Some of the *Titanic* crew members had come through on a break and amused the boys with exciting tales of their tasks, promising each that they, too, could one day work on so fine a ship.

Kate wondered how many of the children understood the level of work and effort these men engaged in. They were not officers, nor even stewards, for the most part. They were the engineers, the firemen, the seamen, and the stokers. One or two might have been quartermasters, but none were in a position that would ever receive recognition.

Yet they were very much alike to the people in this room, and Kate wondered how many of the stewards and seamen and crew working among the higher-class passengers had come from below. Were they comfortable up in those heights? Did they feel out of place? Did they envy those they served?

Did they miss the comfort known below?

"You look entirely too pensive for this atmosphere, Miss Connolly."

Kate smiled at Martin McMahon, with whom she had already danced once. "I was only thinking of *Titanic*."

His brows rose, and he looked around them pointedly. "What about her? This is *Titanic*."

"I know that." She laughed and shrugged. "Sure'n, she's a grand ship, but she's almost the world, is she not? Classes and ranks, privilege and none, but we're all riding her to get where we need to go."

"Tha's too philosophical for me, Miss Kate." He shook his head, whistling low. "We're not without privilege here, are we? We have drinks, we have music, and we have beds for when too much of either makes us ache."

Kate chuckled and curtseyed in a show of acknowledgment. "I do believe you are Irish, Mr. McMahon."

He winked, thumbing his cap back a bit. "So I've heard." He watched the dancing for a moment, and Kate watched him as he did so. His expression held little by way of answer, but something—or someone—held his attention enough that he barely blinked, and his lips formed the slightest smile.

"Would you allow me a bit of impertinence, Martin?" she asked, folding her arms.

"I would," he replied. "I'd encourage it, even."

"Do you fancy Mary Glynn?"

Generations of Irishmen would have been proud of Martin's composure as he simply continued to watch the dance, treating Kate's question the same as if she'd asked for the time. "Aye. She is a fair girl and sensible as cotton. Naught to find fault in. Trouble is I fancy plenty o' girls, and Mary knows it."

Kate laughed in surprise. "Why not pick one over the others? Mary, for example. You're both on this ship, both going to America. Take a chance on her, Martin. Why not?"

Martin nodded, seeming to consider the notion, though he still didn't move. "Maybe I will, Katie-girl. I'll need another pint before I do, though." He winked again and pushed away from the wall, leaving Kate to shake her head after him.

When the song finished, Julia joined Kate, her copper hair barely contained in her crown of plaits.

"What are you about, Kate?" Julia asked. "You're not pining after that one, are you?"

"No!" Kate laughed and pushed a lock of hair from her face. "He fancies Mary Glynn, though I'm not sure he's brave enough to do anything about it."

Julia made a face of either disappointment or disgust, perhaps a blend of both, and sighed heavily. "All the more reason to get to America. She'll want someone who is brave enough to do something about it. Where is the girl anyway?"

"Amply entertained, it seems." Kate gestured toward a group of laughing men and women not far from them. Mary-from-Clare was in the midst of them, a strikingly handsome man at her side. He had the look of the dark Irish about him, and when he smiled, he showed the most perfect teeth Kate had ever seen.

"Some girls have all the luck," she said quietly.

"And some make their own." Julia seized Kate's hand and tugged her along, heading directly for the group.

Several sets of eyes shifted to them as they approached, leaving Kate to laugh about their bold, unexpected arrival.

Mary, however, wasn't embarrassed at all. "Julia, Kate, meet the Galway Gang."

The group erupted into laughter, leaving Kate and Julia to look at each other in confusion.

"A gang we are not," the handsome man replied, still chuckling, dark eyes dancing, "but welcoming we are." He bowed with a flourish. "Martin Gallagher, ladies. And I do, indeed, hale from Galway." He indicated the pretty girl to the other side of him. "This is my sweetheart, Margaret."

"Not so lucky, then," Julia muttered for Kate's ears alone. "As if we aren't Irish enough, we've got a *second* Martin to contend with? What do we call them—Galway and Clare?"

Kate giggled, shushing her friend.

Margaret nudged this Martin hard. "Don't call me your sweetheart unless you're prepared to back that up." She gave Kate and Julia a playfully exasperated look, then proceeded to introduce the rest of the group, all of whom had perfectly common Irish names and perfectly welcoming smiles.

Stories were shared, certain parts repeated at increasing volumes over the jubilant sounds of fiddles and laughter, and it was clear after a few moments that, while there may have been flirting among the group, there was nothing particularly romantic taking root here. They were jostled a handful of times when the dancing got too close, which made them all laugh more. No, there was only warm entertainment and the arms of friendship from those who called the same blessed shores home.

And tonight, that was enough.

"Why are you not dancing still, Julia?" Mary Mac asked as she joined the group, breathless and bright-eyed. "I'd have thought you the sort to dance all night, and yet . . ."

Julia raised a brow, never one to be bested in teasing by friends. "Mr. Gallagher, isn't it fascinating that Miss McGovern here brought a talisman against drowning on board the *Titanic*? An unsinkable ship, and she fears drowning?"

"Indeed?" Martin looked at Mary with interest. "What did you bring?"

Mary's cheeks flushed. "A parcel of Saint Mogue's earth."

To Kate's surprise, Martin looked impressed. "I've heard of him."

"I thought you were from Galway," Mary Mac said, seeming as thunderstruck as if the man had said he invented whiskey.

"I am," he replied easily. "But I know my way around the saints of Ireland in other counties." He smiled at Mary Mac and nodded. "Better to have a saint on your side than not, aye, Miss McGovern?"

Had Martin Gallagher not had a sweetheart at his side already, he could possibly have found one in Mary McGovern in that moment.

Her beaming smile bordered on the blatant, and Cupid himself would have thought her obvious.

"Are there any saints who might help me sleep more soundly?" Kate teased with a playful yawn. "Not that I'll need it tonight, but when our days are more sedate . . ."

"My feelings exactly," Mary-from-Clare said, rising from the seat she had claimed and stretching. "I'm so fatigued, I may sleep the rest of the way to America."

"Can we go, then?" Mary McGovern asked, breaking her adoring gaze away from Martin and taking Kate's arm. "I've been looking for you for ages, and I may walk in my sleep to my bunk."

Julia shook her head at the lot of them. "Well, I refuse to be left out when the three of you have settled on something, but I must say, this is a disappointing way to end the evening. And at barely eight o'clock? Shameful."

Martin Gallagher laughed. "Don't be too hard on them, Miss Smyth. Traveling is arduous, and tomorrow may be full of new adventures."

"I hope not," Kate replied drily. She waved with fondness to her newfound friends. "'Til tomorrow, all."

They made their farewells, and Kate's small group headed out to the corridor to make their way back to their cabin. They passed other passengers who had not been dancing, some more pleasant than others: surly looking men smelling of strong drink and cigars, a young woman walking with a fussing infant, a pair of elderly ladies strolling together with content smiles, and a young couple silently walking with their hands entwined.

Kate smiled as they passed the couple, restraining the urge to sigh.

"Mary-from-Clare," Julia suddenly asked, "did you dance with Martin McMahon tonight?"

Mary looked at her in bewilderment. "No. Was I supposed to?"

Julia shook her head but gave Kate a despairing look.

Some sweethearts they would have been. Poor Martin, and poor Mary.

"Good evening, ladies." A man in an officer's dark uniform headed toward them, his hat under one arm, his smile cordial and fine set against a strong jaw.

"Luck be kind," Julia murmured behind Kate and Mary.

Kate barely contained her laugh.

"Good evening, Mr. . . . ?" Mary McGovern prodded.

"Pitman," came the smart reply. "Third Officer Pitman, ladies. At your service." His soft British accent somehow sounded musical when accompanied by his smile. "I heard there was a party down here this evening. Have you enjoyed yourselves?"

"Oh, very much," Julia gushed with a nod. "Are you going to step in there yourself, Officer? They'll go on for hours, if able."

Officer Pitman chuckled easily and brushed a hand over his dark hair, his dark eyes crinkling with his laughter. "No, I'm afraid not. I'm just seeing to the last of my duties, and then I will retire. We don't get much sleep on these voyages as officers, so we must take advantage where we can."

Mary-from-Clare tsked. "All work and no play, Officer."

He bowed. "I must agree, miss, though a dull officer is better for the ship."

He winked at Kate, but she sensed it was less flirtatious and more friendly, which, somehow, set her perfectly at ease.

"While I have you lovely Irish lasses here," he said, "is there anything I may report back as to how the crew of the *Titanic* can make your travel more comfortable?"

Kate raised a brow at him. "Well, we could do with some more pillows, if we are talking true comfort. And perhaps some cake."

"Aye," Julia echoed behind her. "And another washroom. Do you have any idea of the inconvenience of only having two, given the number of ladies and children, Officer?" She shuddered playfully.

Officer Pitman grinned. "I will see what I can do, though adding a washroom mid-Atlantic may prove beyond my abilities."

"There is a first time for everything," Julia pointed out. "Other than that, everything's grand."

"Glad to hear it." He nodded and stepped aside, gesturing them forward. "Enjoy the rest of your evening, ladies, the sad lack of excess pillows aside."

Mary McGovern heaved a sigh as they started to pass. "We shall try, Officer Pitman, though it will likely be a theme in our reviews of the ship."

"Then I shall attempt to remedy the oversight for you all tomorrow," he replied, a playful smile curving his mouth.

"Nicely done, girls," Julia praised in a low voice as they moved toward their cabin. "Mass flirtation with authority. It would not surprise me if we do find extra pillows and cake at our disposal tomorrow."

Kate made a face, shrugging slightly. "I'd trade the cake for a stroll about Second Class with Third Officer Pitman myself."

"Catherine Connolly!" one of the Marys cried amid giggles.

Kate only grinned, the mixture of fatigue and exhilaration making her giddy, if not entirely silly. Or perhaps it had been the drink of the night, though she'd had very little.

Whatever it was, her spirits were light, and she was grateful for it.

"Adventures may await tomorrow, indeed," Julia teased. "Let us hurry to sleep and see what happens!"

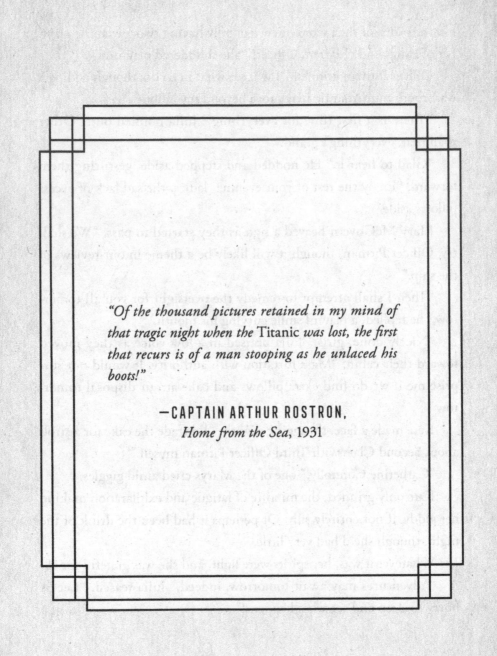

"Of the thousand pictures retained in my mind of that tragic night when the Titanic *was lost, the first that recurs is of a man stooping as he unlaced his boots!"*

—CAPTAIN ARTHUR ROSTRON,
Home from the Sea, 1931

CHAPTER 5

"Messages, sir."

Arthur turned in mild surprise to see Harold Cottam, the young Marconi operator, standing behind him and holding out a few slips of paper. He and Officers Hankinson, Dean, and Bisset had been chatting on the bridge about the day's events and what they anticipated for tomorrow, just as they did every evening before Arthur retired, and he hadn't expected anything else.

He'd forgotten all about the messages received over the radio.

He smiled at the young man. "Ah, thank you. Anything good?"

Cottam shrugged. "Ice warnings from the *Mesaba* and *Californian*. Passenger messages otherwise. The Marshalls will be delighted; their nieces are on *Titanic* and sent them a line or two."

"And how are things on *Titanic*?"

"Apparently quite perfect, sir."

Arthur grunted once, shaking his head. "As is to be expected, no doubt." He paused, looking over the papers. "Gentlemen, consider the ice warnings from *Mesaba* and *Californian* noted, but they are all well to the north of our course."

The stoic Hankinson gave a brisk nod.

"Yes, Captain," Dean replied.

"Noted, sir." Bisset also nodded his affirmation.

Arthur nodded at his officers—excellent men, all of them—and then turned to Cottam. "Did I hear that you know the Marconi man aboard *Titanic*?"

Cottam seemed surprised by the question and nodded. "Yes, sir. Jack Phillips."

Arthur tapped the messages received into the palm of his hand, but Cottom offered no more information. He raised a brow. "Well, be sure and greet him from all of us while we're in range of them."

"Thank you, Captain. I will." Cottam dipped his chin, turned on his heel, and moved down the ladder back the way he had come.

As simple as that. Cottam would send the message—likely now, as it happened. Would the marvels of the world never cease?

Arthur glanced at his second officer, smiling. "Wonderful thing, wireless, isn't it?"

Seeming to understand his amusement, Bisset nodded. "Indeed, sir."

Dean scoffed a laugh into a fist, but said nothing.

"Now, then," Arthur said, feeling the length of the day setting in. "Bisset, it is just after eight. You have the watch until ten. Dean, you're on after. Hankinson, you are relieved for the night. I'll walk the deck, mark our course, and then retire."

"Right you are, Captain." Dean clipped a firm nod, as though the action accompanied the weight of command in the captain's absence.

One day, in the not too distant future, Dean would bear the weight of command fully, Arthur had no doubt about that.

He turned from the bridge and leisurely made his way out to the promenade deck, the cool night air greeting him as an old friend. A few couples strolled along the deck as well, looking out at the brilliant night sky and its reflection in the ocean.

Arthur felt far more relaxed and at ease than he had for days, and he paused to fully appreciate the view around him. It was a clear night, and such a sight was magical on the open sea. That was something he hoped never to grow accustomed to, no matter how many nights he spent upon the waves. The sound of the ship parting the water and the occasional wave slapping against the ship were the most soothing sounds in the world. Though the steamships were large enough that the roll of the water and the tide was almost never felt, every now and then, Arthur missed the sensation.

He greeted a few of the couples and families politely as they passed him, though none stopped for conversation.

He was glad of it. This moment was for him and for the sea, though there was never an opportunity to enjoy true serenity while in command. Duty, responsibility, honor—they called on him first. Only when the ship was near to its destination would he fully relax, fully be at ease, and fully feel able to breathe.

Yet he loved the command as well.

There was no rest in it, but there was satisfaction.

Which was, in itself, a kind of rest.

Here, on the sea, he knew his place and his course. He knew clarity, and he knew his abilities, both of which allowed him a dignity essential to his position.

All for love of the sea. Respect for her, and patronage of her. Never mastery, only navigation.

She was a fickle creature, the sea.

And how he adored her.

All too soon, he was alone on the deck, and the lateness of the hour pressed upon him. He turned to retreat to his cabin, touching the brim of his hat at a passing couple making one more venture into the night.

He removed his hat the moment he entered his cabin, tossing it onto the desk filling one side of his room. It was a neat, tidy room, hardly better than the cabins his officers enjoyed, aside from a bit more space and the connection to the chart room. His cabin was also more conveniently located to the bridge, but beyond that . . .

Well, an able seaman only needed a proper place to lay his head when he took his rest.

Arthur quickly undid the buttons of his jacket and shrugged out of it, hanging it in the bureau. He brushed at the fabric, though it was still as pristine as it had been that morning. Somehow, it never seemed to tarnish as they day went on. He worked at the buttons of his waistcoat next, followed by his white shirt. Collar, cuffs, and tie were pulled off and set on his desk with his hat.

He stared at the pieces of his uniform, then exhaled the weight of a full day's work before moving to his bed.

He set his pocket watch on the bedside table, as usual, then picked up his Bible. He never slept right without reading some verses to set his thoughts heavenward, and he never dared make his account of the day without the proper perspective.

When he couldn't manage to read another word, let alone write one, he completed his undressing and donned his nightshirt. Murmuring a few words of prayer, he laid his head down on his pillow, closed his eyes, and welcomed his sleep.

———

"Captain!"

The door to Arthur's cabin was thrown open, and thundering feet entered, light bursting into the small space with nearly as much urgency as the people accompanying it.

He squinted, fumbling for his pocket watch, the numbers blurring before his eyes.

Half past twelve, was it?

Who the dickens was the cheeky beggar coming into his cabin at this time of night—and without knocking? They were about to get a quick lesson in ship etiquette they would not soon forget.

"Sir!"

Groaning as the lights in his cabin suddenly flicked on, Arthur closed his eyes, trying for patience in spite of his weariness. "First Officer Dean, knocking before entering is generally—"

"It's the *Titanic*, sir," Dean interrupted, his voice nearing a frantic pace and pitch. "We've just received an urgent distress message. She's struck ice and is sinking fast. She requires immediate assistance."

It was *what*?

Instantly alert, Arthur sat up and swung his legs over the bed. He stared at his first officer. Dean was by no means an alarmist, but he looked as terrified as though they themselves had struck ice.

The same horror, the same cold depth, suddenly sank into Arthur's stomach.

And that decided everything.

"Mr. Dean, turn the ship around, steer northwest. I'll work out the course for you in a moment."

Dean nodded, already darting out of the cabin.

How far were they from *Titanic*? Northwest was the general direction, he knew, but what was the range? How soon could they get there?

How bad was it?

So many questions. And decisions upon decisions would need to be made very shortly.

Arthur pushed to his feet and turned, spotting Cottam, whose eyes were as wide as the moon herself.

"Mr. Cottam, are you sure it's the *Titanic*?"

Cottam swallowed. "Yes, sir."

"You are *absolutely* certain?"

A nod. "Quite certain, sir."

"And you are equally as certain that she needs our assistance?"

Cottam squared his jaw. "I am, sir."

Arthur held the lad's eyes for a moment, assured by the certainty he saw there more than the words he heard. "All right. Come with me, I need to plot our course. Message them and tell them that we are coming as fast as we can."

He moved into the chart room adjacent to his cabin, waving for Cottam to follow, which the lad did, nearly stepping on his heels. Arthur quickly moved a chair out of their path and shoved the top two charts out of the way, finding the one he needed beneath them.

"Right." Eying the charts, Arthur's mind began to spin, calculating the course, his heart pounding. "Were you given a position?"

Cottam thrust a slip of paper into Arthur's hand. "Here, sir."

Arthur glanced at it, his heart beating a thunderous tempo. He read it twice more, committing the position to memory.

41°46' N, 50°14' W.

"Who calculated this?" Arthur asked, flicking his eyes to Cottam. "Did they say?"

Cottam shrugged, the motion tense and angled. "An officer, sir. That's all I know."

Arthur's eyes darted back to the chart, marking his position in relation to the *Titanic*'s with a stub of a pencil. They were not as close as he would like to be, not nearly close enough, but he wasn't about to let that stop them. Other boats would have heard the call and replied to her message as well, so all he had to do was get his ship there as fast as he could and be prepared for whatever they might face.

He ran his fingers over the positions again, double- and

triple-checking, nodding to himself before turning to Cottam. "Very good. Tell them we're on our way. Tell them . . . tell them four hours."

Cottam rushed from the room, leaving behind an eerie silence broken only by Arthur's racing heart.

It thudded anxiously against his chest, each beat bringing with it more pressure.

Arthur found it almost difficult to breathe, but there was no time to think about that.

His hands flew across the familiar charts again, details and figures appearing and forming with an ease he had rarely known before.

There was no time for questions, hesitations, or doubts.

Only action.

"Four hours," he murmured, shaking his head. "I'll make it less if there's any way."

But whether there would be any way was another matter altogether.

He nodded to himself and hurried back into his cabin, flinging off his nightshirt and tugging back on his uniform. He did up the buttons as quickly as his shaking fingers could manage, doing his best to steady his breathing. He tugged on his jacket and reached for his hat, pausing for a moment.

Bowing his head, the words fled from his lips.

"Father God, let us get to them. Guide our hands and our feet, our ship and our hearts. Let it be enough."

He swallowed, the action harder than he would have liked. The scope of this undertaking grew in his mind by the second. But there was no time for doubts, no time for fears. It was all up to faith and action now. "Amen."

Placing his hat on his head, he strode out to the bridge, a new fervency accompanying his pulse. All thoughts of sleep or peace were erased from his mind.

There would be no peace for anyone tonight.

"My husband awakened me at about a quarter of 12 and told me that the boat had struck something. We both dressed and went up on the deck, looked around, and could find nothing. We noticed the intense cold; in fact, we had noticed that about 11 o'clock that night. It was uncomfortably cold in the lounge. We looked all over the deck; walked up and down a couple of times, and one of the stewards met us and laughed at us. He said, 'You go back downstairs. There is nothing to be afraid of. We have only struck a little piece of ice and passed it.' So we returned to our stateroom and retired."

—HELEN BISHOP,
Titanic passenger, April 30, 1912

CHAPTER 6

RMS *TITANIC* · APRIL 15, 1912 · 12:45 AM

Kate's legs shook as she sat on her bunk, her knees bouncing up and down in a furious pounding that she had absolutely no control over and minimal awareness of.

Her jaw began to tremble in the same helpless manner.

"Would you stop it, Kate?" Mary Mac barked without looking at her. "You're shaking the entire bunk."

"Sorry," Kate snapped, forcing her legs to still, which only made her chest and arms quiver instead.

If possible, her heart felt like it was shaking inside of her as well. An ominous feeling had settled on her, something she couldn't shake off, and the longer she sat, the more the feeling grew.

Waiting was possibly the worst of all things.

They'd heard a loud, unusual sound only a few minutes ago, and then the strangest sound of all: the engines had stopped.

After days of a continual hum, the silence was eerie.

Something was wrong.

They'd all woken, and in the dark of their cabin, whispered to each other about what might have happened. How could the engines have suddenly stopped in the middle of the night? Was there a problem? Was there danger?

Mary-from-Clare had changed quickly, flipped on the light, and gone out to see what had happened. After she'd left, the rest changed as well, and then they just sat there.

Waiting.

"Ugh!" Julia exclaimed, slapping her legs and rising from her bunk, pacing the small space. "This is utterly maddening. Why won't anybody tell us anything?"

"Perhaps nothing is wrong?" Mary Mac suggested hopefully.

Julia paused and shook her head. "Mary would have been back by now if it was nothing. They would not stop the engines for *nothing*. Something is wrong."

The door to their cabin opened, and Mary-from-Clare returned, scowling. "That was utterly pointless."

"What was?" Julia demanded, hands going to her hips.

"Asking anyone about anything," she replied. She squeezed her eyes shut and covered her mouth with one hand, almost trembling.

"What happened, Mary?" Kate asked as gently as she could while still shaking, her fear growing by leaps and bounds.

"They laughed at me. Apparently, we're in no danger." Mary opened her eyes and looked around at them, tears shimmering in her eyes. "But I don't believe a jack of them. Please, can we leave? Go inquire of someone else, or go up on deck, or something?"

"I think we should pray," Mary Mac whimpered as she sat beside Kate. "I don't like it."

Kate didn't like it either. Something was completely and absolutely wrong, and apparently there were no answers at all. Less than an hour ago, the ship had begun to shake, almost tremble, and though the disturbance did not last long, it had woken them all. They had heard sounds of confusion echoing up and down the corridor beyond their door, so clearly something was amiss.

But apparently, they were fools for being afraid.

"What exactly did they say?" Julia demanded as she continued to pace. "And who were *they*?"

"I don't know," Mary-from-Clare said, her teeth chattering with her anxiousness. "Men that were around. They only said naught was amiss, that I was silly and to go back to my bunk."

Kate looked around at her friends, her stomach twisting within her. "We should go. To the common areas, at least. We should hear more there than we will here."

Nods rippled throughout the room, and they grabbed their coats, hurrying out.

The main corridor was an increasing sea of fleeing masses. Other passengers found the situation fearful as well, and, like the girls, they had come to see what was wrong. Some were only curious, others utterly terrified, but the feelings of the passengers fed into the sense of *wrongness* that filled the air.

Increasing numbers spilling into the corridor increased the panic, and soon the current of the crowd bordered on a frenzy, a rogue wave carrying them all toward the common area without a care for bodies or bonds.

Young men darted forward, jostling other passengers. Children stumbled in confusion, pulled by worried parents who clutched their hands.

There were those who only stood in confusion and still others who mocked the fear, just as they had with Mary-from-Clare.

And no one was getting any information.

The pressure of the swirling mob ripped Kate's hands away from her friends, and, try as she might, she could not see any of them as she craned her neck, searching for a familiar face.

"Back to your rooms," a voice called from somewhere ahead. "There is nothing to worry about. We will inform you if there is."

Kate frowned at the patronizing tone. If passengers were afraid, why was the crew not doing anything to assuage those fears? Why were there no explanations?

Surely, they weren't restraining people and forcing them to stay in their cabins, not with this concern. Something *had* to be wrong. Why else would any of them be so worked up?

She rose up onto her toes but only saw people piling upon each other as they attempted to mount the nearest stairs.

Mad. Completely and utterly mad.

But what else could be done?

Kate was suddenly bumped to one side, sending her crashing into another passenger, who turned to her with fear and trembling. The woman began rambling in panicked tones, the language as unfamiliar to Kate's ears as the woman's face was to her eyes. She had beautiful skin and the darkest eyes Kate had ever seen, but no words she spoke even remotely resembled words Kate knew.

She had no way to help her.

Kate took her hands and squeezed them hard. "Keep going," she whispered, praying that somehow the terrified woman would understand. "Keep going. Don't stop."

The woman's eyes searched Kate's, and then she nodded and placed a gentle hand on Kate's cheek. Nothing was said, but amid the growing chaos, there was a moment of peace.

Then Kate was jostled forward, away from the woman, and back into the sea of confusion that swept her along with the rest of steerage.

She had to get to the General Room. With no information, and no one seeming to help, she needed a place to breathe and gather with her friends. If nothing was wrong in truth, all the passengers rushing here and there would be sent back to their cabins.

If something was wrong, however . . .

Well, being in the General Room would surely be closer to safety than their cabin was, located so near the propeller and engines at the stern of the ship. But how would they get to a safe place, if needed? Safety was surely above, and there was no direction for any of them to move besides up to the third-class deck anyway. But there were no lifeboats on the third-class deck; those were located at least four stories above where Kate and her friends were now.

All these people could not fit on the third-class deck, if that was the answer.

So where would they go?

She forced her desperate thoughts away and focused on moving forward.

At last, the General Room neared, and Kate breathed a sigh of relief at the sight of it. She managed to slip inside, her breathing unsteady as she searched for her friends.

One by one, they emerged from the corridor, along with many of the sea of passengers.

"Are they keeping us down here?" Kate demanded of the others, though none of them would likely know.

Julia shook her head, her hair pulling free from its braid. "The gate wasn't closed. But whose voice was that, telling us all to go back?"

Kate shook her head, looking around for any sort of sign, hint, message, or familiar face. Children cried, voices rose, and all the languages that had only hours ago filled the air in a delightful blend now sounded an angry, discordant storm—the terrifying sound of fear.

The power of it was deafening.

"Mary!"

Both Marys turned, but it was Mary-from-Clare whose arm was grabbed.

Martin McMahon looked at them all, eyes wide. "We've struck an iceberg. I've just spoken with a chap from engineering. He says to get life belts."

"From where?" Mary shook her head. "Where are we supposed to—?"

"In the rooms," Mary Mac interrupted, her eyes brightening. "I noticed them when we first came in, and I saw them again as we left."

"How are we supposed to get them?" Julia demanded, flinging a hand toward the mass of passengers in the corridor. "We've only just gotten through that."

"I can help," Martin said firmly. "I'll get you through."

Kate sniffed once, nodding to herself. "We need those life belts. We don't have a choice; we have to get them."

Mary Mac took a deep breath. "Kate and I will go get them." She turned to the others. "Stay here."

Martin turned with them toward the entrance. "I'll help you fight the tide to get there. I'm after my own as well."

"Be careful, Martin," Mary-from-Clare called after them as they hurried back out into the raucous mass.

No word for her or Mary Mac, Kate noted, not that it mattered.

Perhaps Mary-from-Clare had a soft spot for the lad from her fellow county after all.

Staying close to the walls, Mary, Kate, and Martin headed back toward their cabins. Kate was surprised by the comparative ease of their passage. They were still jostled and bumped, and more than once, Kate felt an elbow jab into her stomach, but it was nothing like before. And this time, she was not letting go of her friend's hand. Not for anything.

They turned off the main corridor; the people there were no less worried, but fewer in number.

Martin stopped and nodded at the girls.

"All right, then?" he asked, his words clipped, his tone short and anxious. "Can you find your way back?"

They nodded.

"Hurry, Martin," Kate insisted.

"You, too." Then he was gone, and the girls continued on.

There was only one more turn of the corridor before they would reach their room, but the short distance seemed somehow impossible to cross.

Mary suddenly seized Kate's arm. "Kate, is that . . . ?" She broke off, her finger trembling as she pointed ahead. "Is that . . . ?"

Seawater was slowly creeping up the corridor ahead of them. The water was almost sluggish and barely covered the pink floor, but it was there.

It was there.

The *Titanic* was sinking.

Not only that, it was sinking quickly. There had been no water on the floor when they had left the cabin.

There was no time.

"Mary," Kate whispered, her eyes burning as she stared at the approaching seawater. "Run."

They bolted down the corridor toward their cabin, the endless expanses of white walls feeling to Kate more like a cage, each wall seeming to close in on them as they ran. She could not hear the sluggish approach of the water, yet in her mind, there were suddenly crashing waves and towering icebergs.

She had to escape.

Gulping in air, Kate quickened her pace, and she and Mary reached their room before the water was beneath their feet. Once inside, Mary turned and stretched up to reach the life belts stored above the door, handing each one to Kate in turn.

Kate slid one over her head, then shoved the other two under her arms. She looked about the room in a moment of panic, wondering what she could take that she might need.

The answer, of course, was nothing.

There was nothing of value in her cabin. Nothing she would risk her life or safety over.

Not one thing.

Mary put on her own life belt and took one of the other belts from Kate, nodding firmly. "Ready?"

Kate swallowed, but returned the nod. "Yes."

Without looking back, the pair of them tore from the cabin and raced back up the way they had come. Their pace would fuel the energy and panic of the other passengers, but Kate did not care. She needed to get back to her friends, and, somehow, they needed to get up to a higher deck.

But how? The way was so crowded and full, and chaos was everywhere. There was no good direction to take, and misinformation in abundance. And what about Martin? Had he retrieved his life belt and come back?

Cries filled the air, and the wailing of terrified children increased. Grown men shoved each other aside, others bellowing for women and children to get ahead of the rest.

How would they survive this? How could they hope to get anywhere when the water was already coming through?

Titanic was sinking.

How could that be?

"Put your life belts on," she told the family near them, who had, mercifully, brought them from their cabin. "All of ye."

The terrified mother nodded, helping her children despite the little one's crying, sleepy complaints.

Pray God, none of the wee babes remember this, Kate thought to herself. It would be bad enough for the adults, but the children?

She wanted to scoop up as many as she could and rush them to the top decks herself.

If only she knew the way up.

The General Room was filled with more people now, all of them terrified and anxious. Some clung to each other, some sat alone in silence, and some watched the madness in the corridor as though it were a strange phenomenon they could not understand.

"Shouldn't we try to get out of here?" Mary Mac asked as they rejoined their friends, handing out the life belts. "Go up to the boat deck, at least."

Before anyone could respond, a small group entered the General Room, somber and shaking their heads. "No use," one of them muttered. "The ship is too large. We'll never find it."

Kate watched them sit on the benches, dejected, and her heart pounded with a new, unsteady cadence.

Julia swallowed hard, then looked at Mary with almost vacant eyes. "How? Getting anywhere in that melee would be a miracle, and that is the fourth group that's come back without any luck. Nobody is interested in saving third class, even if we could get up there. Have you seen any *Titanic* crew down here to aid us? I have not."

Kate stared at her friends silently, horror and fear and apprehension filling her. Even if they could fight their way through the crowds, and even if they found the boat deck, the class distinctions would undoubtedly be preserved.

Julia was right. No one in authority was telling them how to get where they needed to go, or that they needed to do so at all. There were too many passengers in third class for a rapid and careful evacuation, especially when the wealthier passengers would be at hand first. A few passengers might take up the charge and lead some others up, but they would have to know the way as well. Did anyone here know such a thing?

Closer proximity to the lifeboats would give those passengers more time to escape.

Third Class had to ask for directions to even have a chance.

Tears threatened to choke Kate. They washed across her face, and her lungs tightened. She swallowed hard, desperate to force the lump in her throat out of the way, and failing. She settled for clearing it twice.

She looked at Mary Mac, her eyes swimming. "I think now would be an excellent time for a prayer, Mary. If you can."

Mary blinked, then nodded and immediately knelt on the floor.

Julia, Mary-from-Clare, and Kate joined her in kneeling, taking each other's hands, bowing their heads.

"Our Father," Mary Mac intoned, her voice quivering, "which art in heaven, hallowed be thy name . . ."

"Thy kingdom come"—Kate and the others joined in—"Thy will be done, on earth as it is in Heaven."

Words faded from Kate's voice, though her lips continued to move in fervent recitation.

No, not recitation. The words were familiar, well known, but these were not simply words she had uttered or read in her life. This was the cry of her heart.

From the depths of her soul.

A hand suddenly settled on her shoulder, gripping tight.

Kate turned with a gasp that startled the others out of prayer.

Martin Gallagher stood there, his other hand clinging to his sweetheart, Margaret. He leaned close, his expression firm, and whispered, "Come with me, girls. I'll get you up to the boats."

"*A sailor has his faith; he lives so close to nature, there are times when he feels in touch with the infinite.*"

—CAPTAIN ARTHUR ROSTRON,
Home from the Sea, 1931

CHAPTER 7

"Mr. Dean, Helmsman, new course: North fifty-two West."

"Yes, Captain."

Arthur nodded at the helmsman, who was already turning the wheel, clearly having been given enough instruction from Dean to have no doubt.

"Engine room. Full speed ahead!" Arthur said.

Mr. Dean moved to the engine order telegraph, or EOT, shifting the handles on the dial to the correct positions three times, the signal for urgent action in the engine room below.

Everything would be urgent now.

Arthur looked at Dean. "I need to see all officers in the chart room at once. Send for the surgeons, the pursers, Chief Engineer Johnston, and the chief steward."

Dean snapped a sharp nod, already moving to obey. "Yes, Captain."

Arthur turned toward the chart room but paused at seeing the quartermaster and the watch heading out to wash the deck.

He moved at once to head them off. "Ho, there!" he called.

They stopped, looking at him with wide eyes.

"Captain?" the quartermaster asked.

He lowered his voice as he approached. "Knock off all work, and get our lifeboats ready for lowering. Don't make any noise about it."

The men exchanged confused looks, alarm clearly setting in.

"Don't get excited, men," he assured them in a moderately calmer tone. "We're going to another ship in distress."

Relief washed over their faces, followed by somber determination.

Whatever he asked of his men, they would see it done.

Arthur nodded, which they took as a cue, scattering to set about their work. He watched for another moment, then moved back down the stairs to the chart room.

Once there, he looked over the chart again, his fingers drumming anxiously on the table while he waited for the men he'd requested to gather.

What had happened to *Titanic*? How bad was it?

What would they find when they arrived?

His heart held the faint hope that everything they were doing now, everything he was about to put into action, would be too much. Would be an overreaction. Unnecessary.

But next to that hope lay a heaviness that told him those hopes weren't to be met. And in answer to that, he could only continue to pray that what lay in his power would be sufficient.

So, what lay in his power?

He moved to a desk in the corner and pulled out a loose piece of paper, scribbling down every item currently running through his mind.

A few minutes later, his officers and senior crewmen assembled in the chart room, tired but alert, all eyes riveted on him.

Arthur inhaled slowly, glancing down at the list in his hand. "The *Titanic* has struck ice and is sinking fast," he told them in low tones. "We are en route to offer assistance, and I require your very best efforts to see that we arrive with all preparedness and that all aboard is kept in perfect order."

He looked each man in the eye, one by one, the severity of the situation setting in more firmly upon him as they stared back. Furrowed brows, tense frames, but full attention.

He raised his chin a touch as he looked at his chief engineer. "Johnston, I need more speed than the *Carpathia* has ever mustered. Call the off-duty watch to the engine room, and rouse every available stoker to feed the furnaces. Cut off the heat and hot water to passenger and crew accommodations, and put every ounce of steam the boilers make into the engines."

With each item, Johnston nodded his agreement and approval. "Aye, Cap'n. It shall be carried out at once." He left quickly, not waiting to be dismissed or to hear what anyone else was assigned.

Arthur took a great deal of satisfaction in that.

He shifted his attention to the remaining men. "Chief Officer Hankinson, you will oversee the deck. Give orders to stop all work and have the men prepare the lifeboats. Take out spare gear, and have the boats ready to turn outboard. First Officer Dean, you are to assist, and will be in charge of the bridge."

The older man nodded, eyes alert. "Yes, Captain," he replied, his voice clear, his Canadian accent ringing out.

"Yes, sir." Dean clasped his hands behind his back, dark eyes clear, his jaw set.

Waiting.

Arthur eyed his two most senior officers for a moment, grateful for their commitment and vigilance, their dutifulness without question, before resuming the review of items on his list. His notes had started simply enough, though the end of his list had become far more specific and detailed, the manner almost frantic.

"I need Dr. McGhee and assistants to be stationed in the First Class dining saloon. Dr. Risicato and assistants in Second Class. Dr. Lengyel and assistant in Third Class. Any passengers requiring medical attention will go to their respective dining saloons so as to keep order and avoid confusion." He glanced up to see all eyes on him, then continued. "Each doctor will have supplies of restoratives, stimulants, and everything on hand for immediate needs of probable wounded or sick."

Arthur gestured to the head purser, who stood even more at attention, if such a thing were possible. "The purser, along with the assistant purser and chief steward, will receive the passengers at each gangway, controlling our own stewards in assisting *Titanic* passengers to the dining rooms and other necessary rooms. I would also ask that you get the Christian and surnames of all survivors as soon as possible to send by wireless."

"Survivors?" the purser asked, his brows rising. "Do you think it's as grave as all that?"

"A great deal may happen between now and then. I aim to be prepared for the worst."

The purser nodded firmly. "Yes, Captain."

Arthur nodded without looking at him. "The inspector, steerage stewards, and master-at-arms will need to control steerage passengers of *Carpathia* and keep them out of the Third Class dining hall, as it will be a medical area. You will also need to keep them out of the way of the crew, and off the deck to prevent confusion while the relief efforts are taking place." He raised his eyes, tapping his list with one hand. "There isn't enough space for the lot of them in one space while the dining hall is in use. Kindly explain that to them."

Nods bobbed all around.

"Chief steward," he said next, eyeing the man who stepped forward.

"You will need to ensure that all hands will be called and that coffee and other needs are ready to serve to the crew. We will need coffee, tea, soup, and other basic foodstuffs in each saloon. Stock blankets in saloons and at the gangways, as well as some for the boats. And you will see that all the rescued are cared for and their immediate wants are attended to."

"Of course, Captain," the chief steward replied. "It will be done."

Arthur paused in thought. "And perhaps some additional stewards should be placed in each alleyway to reassure our own passengers should they inquire about noise in getting the boats out, or the working of engines, or any other activities related to our recovery efforts."

"Excellent thought, sir." The chief steward nodded in approval and clasped his hands behind his back, ready for additional instructions.

Good man.

They all were.

He turned to his officers, praying his orders wouldn't venture into madness.

"All the hands on board will need to be called from their beds," he instructed. "They will be allowed some coffee and anything else they need to suffice, but there is no time to linger. The first task will be to prepare and swing out all boats. All gangway doors will be opened. A chair sling will be needed at each gangway for handling the sick or wounded. Boatswains' chairs, pilot ladders, and canvas ash bags from storage should be at each gangway."

"The ash bags to carry the children up, sir?" one of the officers asked.

"Exactly," Arthur replied. "We have no way of knowing how many people will need help, or what equipment the other ships will have, so make sure we have plenty available."

He marked that item off the list before moving on.

"Cargo falls with both ends clear, bowlines in the ends, and bights secured along the ship's sides, for boat ropes or to help the people up," he rattled off quickly. "Heaving lines need to be distributed along the ship's side, and gaskets handy near gangways for lashing people in chairs, if needed. The forward derricks need to be topped and rigged, and steam on the winches."

After spending far too long hearing his own voice drone on and on, Arthur paused for a breath, looking around at the others in the room with him.

Their attention was still fixed on him, not a man among them seeming overly burdened, apprehensive, or even remotely fatigued, despite being roused from sleep.

It was all he could have wished for, and, though what lay before them was terrifying in its magnitude and intimidating in its uncertainty, in this, at least, he had comfort.

"My cabin and all officers' cabins are to be given up," Arthur told them. "The smoking rooms, library, and dining rooms all are to be utilized to accommodate the survivors. All spare berths in steerage need to be reserved for *Titanic*'s passengers. Get all our own steerage passengers grouped together, as much as we can. I don't believe they'll mind when they are aware of the circumstances."

Heads nodded all around, each of the officers caught up in what needed to be done.

Arthur's throat closed with new and belated emotion, untimely though it was. He cleared his throat and swallowed. "In all of this, gentlemen, we must have order, discipline, and quietness, and we must avoid all confusion. We must be better sailors, better crew, and better men than we have ever been."

More than one man straightened at these words, a new fire in his eyes.

Somehow, Arthur felt it, too.

"We are running up through ice, so we will double the lookouts."

He focused on his second officer. "Bisset, I teased you about your eyes before, but we need them tonight."

Bisset nodded immediately. "Of course, Captain. Whatever you require."

Glancing down, Arthur noted the last items on his list completed. He folded the paper and wrapped his fingers around it as he clasped his hands behind his back, looking at his men yet again.

"We will fire the company rockets at 2:45 AM, and again every quarter hour after to reassure *Titanic*." He shook his head, exhaling heavily. "Again, we must have silence, order, and discipline. There is no telling what we will face tonight, but I trust in each of you to see to your duties as we venture into the unknown."

His words hung there, somehow instructing himself as well as those under his command.

He nodded at them all, and for himself. "See to it."

"Yes, Captain," they replied as one before filing out of the room at a quick pace.

Arthur released another rough exhale from the center of his chest, and he took a moment to steady himself. He closed his eyes, breathed slowly, and fought through the scattered items in his mind for clarity.

Had he said all he needed to? Should he have encouraged more? Had he omitted anything important from his list of orders?

He shook his head, scolding himself for self-doubt at a moment like this. His officers and crew were capable men. If there was anything that needed to be done that he had not ordered to be done, surely God would inspire one of them to make it so. They were on an important mission now, one that could either save many lives or bear witness to a loss of catastrophic proportions.

They could not achieve this task without heavenly assistance.

And heavenly assistance would need mortal hands to exceed expectations.

Arthur set his jaw and strode up to the bridge, pausing a moment after he entered. He lifted his hat from his head, just an inch or two, and closed his eyes.

His lips moved with words he did not give voice to, the cries of his heart needing to take wing before he could again take his place. Before he could lead. Before he dared move another step.

A warm wave of calm rolled through his being, and his next breath was an easier one. Murmuring an amen, Arthur replaced his cap and opened his eyes.

His officers stood there, eyes on him, as witness to his invocation. Rees had also removed his hat and now crossed himself.

"Bisset," Arthur said first, "take your post on the starboard bridge wing. Shout out if you see anything."

"Aye, sir." He moved past Arthur to take up his new post.

Arthur looked at Dean. "Well?"

"Chief Officer Hankinson asked me to address the men, sir, and I am about to do so. Would you care to accompany me?" He gestured toward the deck, and Arthur saw the bustling seamen already working, though there were some who, it seemed, did not understand the urgency of the situation. They moved with their usual speed, laughing and joking among themselves as they might have done on any other day.

He nodded at Dean. "Yes. You address them, though. If you would."

"Of course, sir." Dean moved out to the upper deck and called out, "Come on, come on, look lively."

The men hustled over, all of them attentive and nearly eager for their instructions.

Arthur stayed some paces behind Dean, taking careful note of this band of men before him.

"Listen to me, men," Dean began, his voice ringing out clearly.

"There has been an incident with the *Titanic*, and we are answering her distress call. We have been told she is sinking fast. You are to swing out all the lifeboats and have them readied for lowering. We have no notion what condition *Titanic* or her lifeboats will be in, so *Carpathia*'s boats must be ready to assist them."

A burly seaman near the front frowned in confusion. "Shouldn't we wait, sir, to see if that is the case?"

Dean immediately shook his head. "The time spent clearing and swinging one of the lifeboats out might be the difference between life and death for any poor souls struggling in the freezing water. We will not watch them freeze to death before our very eyes, will we?"

"No!" the men shouted, their chorus seeming somehow ten thousand strong.

"Swing them now!" Dean ordered, matching their roar in his own voice.

The crew sprang into action, those who had been laughing before now as serious as the others. The men worked together like Arthur had rarely seen a crew do before. There was much yet to be done, but at least he could be sure the deck would be in readiness.

Dean watched the action for a moment, then turned to him.

Arthur swallowed a lump of emotion. "Well done, First Officer." He nodded toward the deck. "On my orders, have each officer report to me personally on the bridge to ensure we have all in readiness. I'll see to our course and address our communication with *Titanic*."

"Yes, sir."

Assured for the moment that all that could be done had been done, Arthur returned to the bridge, sparing a nod for the helmsman, and focused his attention on the dark sea before him.

The water reflected the brilliance of the stars in the sky with almost eerie clarity. The waves were calmer than he had seen on many occasions, though they would soon be cut through as the ship sped toward the disaster. The sky was perfectly clear, and there was no moon, lending all possible brightness to the stars alone. The air was cold and crisp, the water would be more so, and such a calm, silent night could mean death for so many.

Four hours, he'd said. In less than four hours, they would be to the *Titanic*.

He prayed she could remain afloat that long.

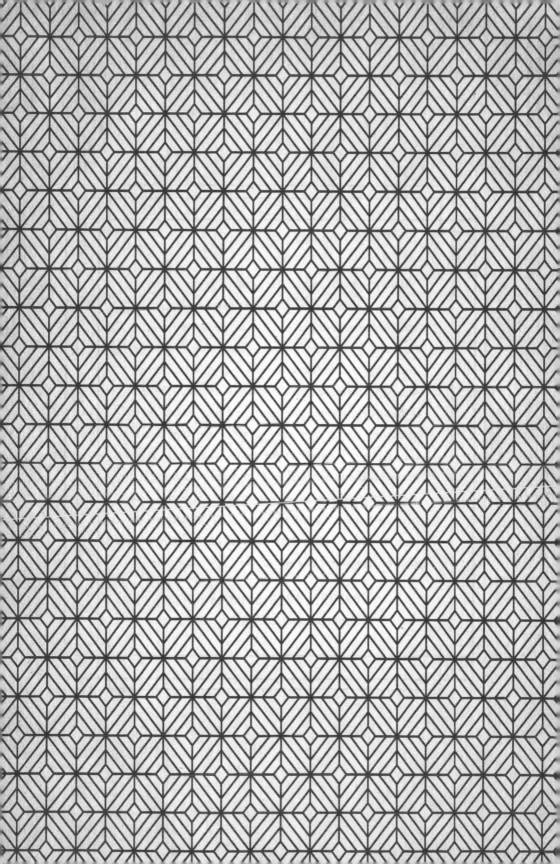

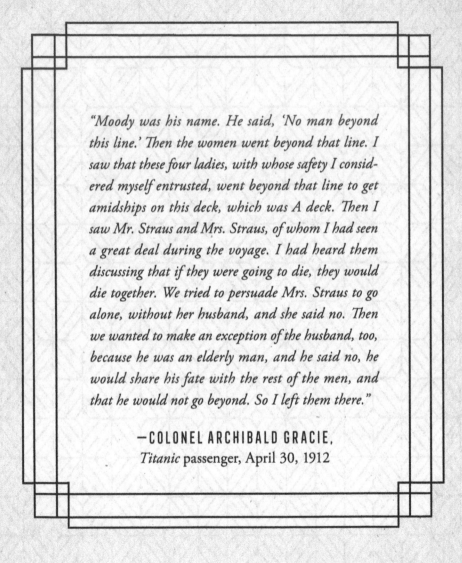

"Moody was his name. He said, 'No man beyond this line.' Then the women went beyond that line. I saw that these four ladies, with whose safety I considered myself entrusted, went beyond that line to get amidships on this deck, which was A deck. Then I saw Mr. Straus and Mrs. Straus, of whom I had seen a great deal during the voyage. I had heard them discussing that if they were going to die, they would die together. We tried to persuade Mrs. Straus to go alone, without her husband, and she said no. Then we wanted to make an exception of the husband, too, because he was an elderly man, and he said no, he would share his fate with the rest of the men, and that he would not go beyond. So I left them there."

—COLONEL ARCHIBALD GRACIE,
Titanic passenger, April 30, 1912

CHAPTER 8

RMS *TITANIC* • APRIL 15, 1912 • 1:15 AM

The boat deck on the second-class level was nearly as chaotic as the corridors of third had been. Jostling, bumping, shoving, bruising, and that was only as Kate and the others emerged onto the deck itself. Families were calling for each other, children were crying, and barely audible over the sounds of all that were the shouted orders of the officers and crew.

"Women and children only!" one of the officers bellowed. "Get back now! I said women and children only!"

"Oh, thank God," Kate breathed. "There are boats left!"

"But how many?" Julia asked no one in particular as they moved farther out onto the boat deck. "Did anybody count the boats earlier? I heard some of the men in the Great Room talking about how the lifeboats aren't meant to be holding vessels; they're meant to transfer passengers to another ship. There cannot be enough of them for this. Not for all of us."

"Does it matter?" Mary Mac replied, quickening her pace.

No, it didn't matter. If there was even one boat left, that would be enough.

Provided they could get on it.

It felt like a miracle that Martin had somehow led them up to the frigid, crowded boat deck, moving past the frightened passengers with competence and confidence, to give them even this small chance at rescue.

"Women and children! You heard me!" the officer called out again.

"As long as he's bellowing that, there's a chance," Martin assured them all, smiling with good humor that was beyond Kate's ability to summon.

Kate shivered in the cold, night air and fastened the buttons of her coat as they hurried forward. She looked up at the sky. How could it be so clear and the stars so bright when they were fleeing for their lives? Why was it not storming and gloomy? Yet the cold might have been enough of a reflection, numbing their senses and their thoughts while they tried to find a few inches of open deck space.

Martin guided them around various groups of people. Some were crying, while others were running, darting off in one direction or another. There was no rhyme or reason, and there was very little order at all.

"Where do we go?" Kate heard a woman cry. "Where's a free boat?"

"I believe there are a few aft, madam," came the stuffy reply from a man in full dinner dress and top hat, looking as though he had been going for a stroll. "Allow me."

Kate started to turn to follow as they passed, but Martin grabbed her arm. "Where are you going?"

She gestured after the man in the top hat. "He said some boats were aft."

Martin shook his head. "Was he wearing an officer's uniform?

Because if he wasn't, I wouldn't trust his directions to the lavatories. Come on." He released her arm and continued forward with the rest.

There wasn't anything to do but follow, especially as Martin's point was a good one.

Everything was madness, but at least there were apparently boats for them. Provided they would be allowed on.

A break in the crowd revealed the edge of *Titanic*'s deck.

There was no boat.

Kate went up on her toes and tried to peer over the heads of others, though it was difficult to see anything through the crowds.

She saw another lifeboat about midway down the ship's deck, and air rushed from her lungs in a wave of relief. Her shoulder bumped against someone else's, and she turned to apologize, but the woman had already moved on, rushing past several people toward another boat.

"There are so few boats left," Mary Mac said from Kate's right. "And they're nearly full already."

Kate had noticed the same thing but hadn't dared vocalize it. She and her friends continued on, still hoping to find room in a boat. Various women and their children were loading into lifeboats, and the remaining crowd surrounding them was chiefly made up of men, a few of whom pressed forward in an attempt to enter a lifeboat.

"Women and children!" a crew member called, shoving the men away. "Get back! Women and children only!"

"What is that?" Mary-from-Clare asked. "Does anyone hear music?"

Kate glanced at her. "I don't hear anything."

"So long as it is not the heavenly angels calling us home," Julia ground out, "I do not care."

"There are a few spaces up there," Martin told them, gesturing them forward. "Hurry. Go!"

"Come with us!" Mary-from-Clare insisted.

He gave her an exasperated look. "Women and children only for now. I'll be along when able. Go!"

Kate's heart sank as she realized Martin would have to stay aboard the sinking ship until the officers and crew were satisfied that all women and children had boarded. There were so few boats, and if more of their fellow third-class passengers should come up, or if more passengers from the other classes appeared, it was entirely possible Martin and many of the other men might not have a chance for a lifeboat.

Kate paused, hoping to thank Martin for getting them out of Third Class, for seeing them safely to a boat, for everything.

She found him stealing a moment with Margaret behind a cluster of passengers waiting at a lifeboat. She didn't dare interrupt, knowing that this moment with his sweetheart might be the last, should the worst happen.

"Come on," Kate ground out to the others, taking Julia's hand and leading her friends around the male passengers lingering by the nearest boat. "Here!" she called out to the crew member.

He saw her and nodded. "Come on, miss. Into boat thirteen. Hurry now."

Kate barely paused at the deck's edge before jumping into the boat, Julia right behind her. Mary Mac and Mary-from-Clare entered with more grace, but no hesitation.

A shot from a pistol rang out, causing a few people to shriek.

Kate gripped Julia's arm, staring at the people nearest them on the deck.

"Women and children only!" the officer shouted again.

Two more shots rang out, and then a young woman and a girl approached, carried by a few crew members through the crowds to their lifeboat.

Mary Mac immediately held out her arms. "Here, here. Give the lass to me."

The little girl, perhaps six years of age, was crying desperately and had no interest in leaving the ship, nor any preference for the man carrying her. Mary took the girl from the crew member, trying to shush the child as she sat back down, rubbing her arms.

"Don't cry, Ethel," the young woman pleaded as she started into the boat. "I'm here. I'm here."

The little girl reached for her, and Mary Mac gave her over willingly.

"Men cannot go into the boats, sir," a crew member ordered.

"I know," an accented voice returned, his words choked with emotion. "My boy . . ."

There was silence for the briefest of moments amid the chaos. "Bring him here, then," the crew member said.

Kate's eyes filled with tears, her lower lip quivering, as she watched a man carry his young son to their boat.

"Here," Julia whispered, patting the open place beside her. "Set him here, sir."

He nodded his thanks and sat the boy beside her. He took his son's face in his hands, then leaned over and kissed him. "His name is Artur," his father told Julia, keeping his eyes on the boy. "Artur Karl Olsen. Please . . ."

With tears streaming down her face, Julia nodded and put her arm around the boy. "We will take care of him, sir. All of us will."

He patted his son on the head, not acknowledging Julia's words as more passengers were loaded into the boat. The man stroked his son's cheek and stared into his eyes with such solemn intensity that Kate's heart broke.

It was as though he knew he would never see his boy again. As though this were truly the end.

"It may be a long, long time before I see you" he told his son, his voice breaking. "Be a good boy, Artie."

Then he stepped back, disappearing into the crowd of men. The boy, possibly seven or eight years old, clearly did not understand what was happening and stared silently at the place where his father had gone.

"I can't bear it, Kate," Julia whispered as she glanced over at her. "I can't."

Kate bit her lip and took her friend's hand, squeezing tightly.

"Ruth!" a woman cried. "Ruth, get into that one! I'll be in this boat with your brother and sister!"

Frowning, Kate strained to see what was happening.

A girl of perhaps twelve calmly approached the officers and asked, "Can I board this lifeboat?"

Without a word, she was lifted up and nearly tossed in, a pair of fair-haired young women with Nordic accents seated behind Kate situating her between them.

"More women!" the officer nearest them called. "Any more women?"

No other women came forth.

"All right," the officer said. "A few men, then. Dr. Dodge, if you please. And a few of the victualling crew to manage the boat. Come on, men, fill it up. Quick now."

Kate and the others squeezed closer together, the chill of the night air whipping around them.

There were perhaps forty or fifty people in boat thirteen at present, but they could easily take more without overfilling. Quietly, a few men began to join them in the boats, though without any of the frantic fuss that had pervaded the area only moments earlier. No squabbles, no fighting, nothing but a calm acceptance from both those entering the lifeboats and those who remained on deck, hoping for more boats but knowing there were not.

The expressions of each man were the same, whatever his fate.

As though there were no real victories here.

How could that be?

"Right then," the officer said to the crewmen at the levers. "Lower away."

"Wait!" a voice bellowed.

Through the crowd, a steward appeared, clutching the hand of a young woman with a babe in her arms and another girl trotting behind her.

"Make room," the officer snapped to their boat. "Get them in. Get them in."

Kate released Julia's hand and reached for a child. "Come here, little one."

The mother gestured for her daughter to climb in, and she did so, going to Kate without a moment's hesitation. The men in the boat aided the woman and her baby into the boat, and even allowed the steward accompanying them into the boat as well.

"No more room here," the officer called out. "Lower away!"

The lifeboat shifted, rocking from side to side as it began to be lowered toward the icy water.

Kate held the little girl in her arms closer, shielding her face from the cold and so the child wouldn't panic at seeing the height from which they were being lowered. Though they were being lowered evenly, so to speak, the boat deck was so very, very far from the water below. Kate herself was woozy at the sight of it, and she knew she would not be easy until they had settled on the sea.

The girl's mother sat across from them, shushing her baby and looking up at the deck of *Titanic* in apprehension.

"Steady," voices from above called as they continued to lower the lifeboat. "Keep her steady now."

"That's Martin Gallagher," Mary-from-Clare whispered from behind her.

Kate looked up but could not see him from her vantage. "Where?"

"There. By boat fifteen. He's . . . he's praying the rosary. Why will they not let him in the boat?"

Kate looked harder and then she spotted him. His rosary was out, his fingers tight on the beads, his lips moving rapidly. As though he could sense her attention, his eyes flicked to hers. She could see something in his eyes. Finality? Resignation?

There had to be more boats, emergency ones somewhere, surely . . .

Martin's mouth curved into a sad smile, and he dipped his head in a very small nod.

Something cracked in Kate's chest at that nod.

Squeezing her eyes shut, she held the little girl in her lap more tightly. She couldn't bear to look at Martin any longer. She couldn't bear to think of what would shortly happen to Martin, to Artie's father, to the very crewmen lowering their boat at that moment. She did not want the memories of their faces haunting her life forever. She did not want to feel anything at all but the cold of the night and the warmth of the little girl on her lap.

Anything else was too cruel and too horrifying.

The girl whimpered, and Kate smoothed her hair. "Come now, darling," she murmured. "Your mama has to settle your sister first, and then, I think, you can sit with her. Can you wait for that, lamb?"

"Tysta ner, Margit," her mother urged in her native tongue, her voice trembling as she tried to smile at Kate. "Det är okej, älskling."

Kate returned a smile to the woman, assuming the little girl she held bore the name of Margit. Little Margit seemed to settle with her mother's words, curling herself closer to Kate and quieting.

"No," a voice from the boat suddenly cried. "No, I can't. The ship is safer. I can't—"

"What are you doing?" another lady shrieked. "Come back down!"

Kate turned quickly to see a young woman gripping the ropes and attempting to climb back into *Titanic*, though she had quite a way to go.

"Stop that. It's too late!" one of their crewmen said firmly, tugging her back into place. "The ship is sinking. We have to get away!"

"Don't!" a different voice called from above, drawing Kate's attention there.

A young man stood where another lifeboat had once been, staring down at the sea without expression. His eyes flicked to those in boat thirteen, and Kate felt a wash of despair when their eyes locked. She did not know him, she had never seen him, but the emptiness in his eyes matched the hopelessness raging within her. He took a breath, his shoulders sagging further, and then jumped from the edge of *Titanic*.

Kate gasped, along with others in their boat, as the man's body hit the water, immediately lost amid the splashing and swimming of others.

Had he been wearing a life belt? Would he come up? How long would he last in the water before he froze or drowned? Would any lifeboat have room to pick him up?

How many others would choose to jump?

The sound of lapping water met Kate's ears as their lifeboat settled on the sea with an awkward roll, the rocking from side to side more pronounced.

"I can't." The young woman had let go of the ropes and was curled into herself, squeezing her eyes shut, and whimpering. "We're going to die. We're all going to die."

Kate turned away, wishing she could shut her cries out. She might have been right, there was no denying the danger they all faced, but the abject fear and desperation in her voice was too close to the cries of Kate's heart to hear aloud as well.

She couldn't bear it, and for the children to hear it as well . . .

It was too much.

"Ho there!" a voice from the rear of the boat suddenly shouted. "Whoa! Stop lowering! Stop!"

Screams and cries broke out, and Kate whirled in her seat in fear.

Their lifeboat had not been completely released from its lowering ropes yet, though the few crewmen assigned to their boat had started working on them, but the next lifeboat was being lowered steadily and swiftly directly above them. If boat thirteen remained where it was, the other boat would crush them in a matter of moments.

The men in the back of their boat rose to their feet, waving at those on the deck or reaching up as though they could somehow push boat fifteen away, could somehow prevent it from smothering them all by sheer force.

A few other men sprang up and began to cut at the vast number of ropes instead of working on the hooks connecting them.

"A knife! I need another knife!" one of the men bellowed.

"Get those falls cut!" another barked to the rest. "Get them cut now! Cut them!"

Kate eyed the ropes that still connected them to *Titanic*, realizing with horror that their boat could go nowhere until the ropes were severed.

"Lord have mercy," she whispered as she clung to Margit, looking at the approaching hull so near them.

"Stop!" the men called again. "Thirteen is not loosed!"

"Stop! Stop, please!" a few of the women cried.

A terrified scream ripped from Kate's throat as the hull of the other lifeboat continued toward them.

"No!" Julia yelled, rising to join a group of perhaps twenty people who were attempting to press the approaching boat away. Ten or so men were still frantically struggling to cut the ropes and free them.

The occupants of boat fifteen were beginning to cry and scream as well, looking over the side at Kate and the others as the two boats drew closer and closer.

More of the men in boat thirteen joined in to help with the ropes while the others still attempted to push boat fifteen away from them. Impossibly, it seemed as though the descent of boat fifteen was slowed while they did so.

The ropes snapped free, and the boat rocked.

"We're loose!" the men in boat thirteen shouted as others took up the oars and rowed them away from the sinking *Titanic* as fast as they could. Their strokes were awkward and uncoordinated at first, then gained strength and rhythm.

People were everywhere in the water, swimming desperately in their life belts, trying to get away, trying to find bits of furniture or wreckage to cling to or float on. Anything to get out of the icy water.

One of the swimmers—a young man—looked at her, and seeing the panic in his eyes made Kate's stomach clench with sudden pain. He bobbed beneath the water briefly, sputtering as his head appeared again, his breath coming in short, frantic bursts.

Kate forced herself to raise her focus higher, to push away the guilt she felt at seeing so many in the water while she was being safely rowed away. She did not know much about boats and seafaring, but she knew they could not pull anyone from the water aboard the lifeboat. The panic that would ensure, the floundering of their boat, the potential to capsize them all . . . And they were already near to capacity, if not at it. There was nothing they could do for those poor souls.

Nothing.

As the rowing smoothed out, the rocking of the boat became a lulling, soothing motion that ought to have settled Kate's body, if not her mind. The waves were pushing them away from the ship, aiding their retreat.

Still Kate could not breathe easy.

"I feel as if I can still hear the music," Mary-from-Clare announced softly. "Can you hear it?"

Kate strained to listen for any notes that might give her comfort or consolation, but between the gentle, splashing sounds of the sea and the oars as they moved through the water, the panic on the ship above them, and the distant cries from people in other lifeboats, there was nothing resembling music left to hear.

"What is it?" Kate begged her friend. "What do you hear?" She looked at Mary-from-Clare who sat with her eyes closed, her brow creasing.

"I think . . . I believe it is the hymn 'Nearer, My God, to Thee.'" Mary opened her eyes and managed a weak smile. "I wonder how many of us have heard it tonight. How long do you think they'll play?"

Kate could only shake her head.

Once a safe distance away, the rowing slowed, and Kate and the others in the lifeboat watched as their ill-fated ship appeared to tilt forward, toward the bow, sitting low in the water.

The screams and cries of those still aboard *Titanic* somehow seemed to echo more loudly upon the water, ripping through the night air worse than the chill of the wind.

There she was, the majestic monarch of the seas, still alight with her finery, slowly sinking before their very eyes. The rows of portholes in her body were now at an angle, those near the bow on the lower levels no longer visible, though those on the upper levels, and on every level near the stern, were still above water. The upper levels shone as brightly as they might have done for a party, though the rooms would now be all but empty.

Kate suspected the water had by now completely submerged the corridors of Third Class, where she had been not so long ago.

How many people were still down there? Or had they all found their ways up to the boat decks? The lifeboats were probably gone now. How many souls would be left with neither boat nor raft, and would instead have to wait for rescue in the freezing water rather than upon it?

She watched her breath curl into clouds in the cold air before her, and she shivered as the reality of the night and its dangers struck her. The icy depths of the ocean, colder still than the air about them, would show no mercy and offer no hope. Those set adrift would have only their fellow floating companions to console them.

She couldn't imagine what sounds would fill the air then.

Did a body create noise as it froze? What pain would someone experience? Would the water be cold enough to make death painless, or would the suffering be slow and agonizing?

Somehow, the future before her was suddenly more terrifying than anything she had endured in the last few hours.

"It was supposed to be unsinkable," a young Irish voice murmured from behind her. "They said it was unsinkable."

"No ship is unsinkable," uttered a lower, more cynical voice. "They were wrong."

"Do you hear it?" Mary-from-Clare whispered through tears. "They're still playing—as if for their own funeral. And everyone else's." She sniffed and buried her face in her hands.

Mary Mac wrapped an arm around her and leaned her head on her shoulder.

Shivering more from her thoughts than the cold, Kate adjusted Margit more securely in her arms. "Hush now, Margit," she murmured, though the girl had made no sound. "Shall we try for some sleep, hmm?"

"Kall," the little girl whimpered, her small body shivering.

"Me too, my lamb," Kate told her, assuming the word meant *cold*, and doing her best to wrap her coat around Margit as well. "Me too. Close your eyes, and stay close to me. I'll keep you warm."

Margit did so, and Kate looked over at the ship once more in despair. The vessel was somehow still majestic despite her descent, the scattered lifeboats, and the cries and screams of passengers all around her.

Somehow still a wonder. Somehow still marvelous.

But not, as it happened, unsinkable.

The lights on *Titanic* blinked several times, rippling up and down the expanse of her, and then, with one last flicker, went out for good.

And with it, the flicker of hope.

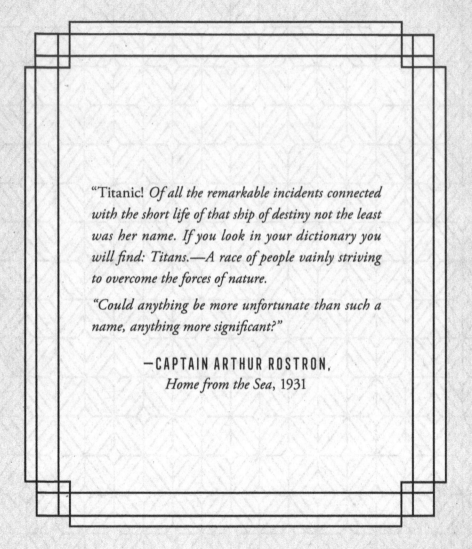

"Titanic! *Of all the remarkable incidents connected with the short life of that ship of destiny not the least was her name. If you look in your dictionary you will find: Titans.—A race of people vainly striving to overcome the forces of nature.*

"Could anything be more unfortunate than such a name, anything more significant?"

—CAPTAIN ARTHUR ROSTRON,
Home from the Sea, 1931

CHAPTER 9

Waiting had to be the worst of all things when one was desperate for action.

Though Arthur knew that all that could possibly be done was being done, he could not escape the nagging feeling it was not enough. That there should be more. That standing on the bridge while they raced northward in the cold did not serve anyone, least of all him.

But the bridge was where he needed to be. Stoking the furnaces might have satiated his urge to act, but that task fell to others. Swinging out the lifeboats might have given him satisfaction, but he could not go out and work alongside his men.

He was the captain, and there was more to do in that role besides the obvious physical preparations.

Maddening though it was.

He fixed his eyes on the horizon, though it was barely visible in the dark night. The stars blurred from the sky into their reflections, only the slightest rolling of the water identifying which was sea and which was sky. A night like this made the task of lookouts and watchmen more difficult. Once his favorite time of sailing, the night was now his enemy.

Drumming his fingers, he glanced at the gauges, mentally noting their readings.

With a nod of satisfaction, he looked out at the deck, seeing the bustle and feeling the energy among his crew. They were preparing everything he had asked and everything Mr. Hankinson and Mr. Dean had asked, and they were doing so without complaint.

All was being done, he reminded himself. He was seeing it happen before his eyes.

Why, then, would this nagging, impatient feeling not leave? He was unsettled, and he did not like it.

His attention shifted as Officer Rees entered the bridge.

"Lifeboats ready, sir," he reported, out of breath.

Arthur nodded absently. "Good, good. Excellent, Rees."

Rees stepped aside, heading out for the deck again as the head purser came behind him.

He clipped a quick nod. "Gangways near to ready, sir."

"Thank you, Brown." Arthur straightened, his mind working on an additional item or two. "Be sure you and the others ask which class the passengers are in so they may be directed appropriately. It will make the organization and identification easier."

"Yes, sir."

Arthur looked at the clock on the wall, though he knew the time well, having marked it regularly. "I calculate we will arrive at 4:00 AM. There can be no accidents due to darkness. Find some of the crewmen and string up cables and lamps to the liner's hull above the gangways."

Mr. Brown clasped his hands behind his back, nodding. "Excellent idea, sir. Mr. Hankinson recommended some slings and heavy canvas be strung up as well to lift any survivors unable to move with ease."

"Yes, yes, so directed. See to it."

"Yes, Captain."

The head purser left, and Arthur removed his cap, wiping perspiration from his brow.

It was all getting done. They were racing to *Titanic*, and they would be ready to aid her when they arrived.

He shook away his foreboding thoughts, then proceeded out to the deck himself. If he could not participate in the action, he needed to feel the energy of it at least.

A young lady in a nightgown and wrapped in a shawl approached him almost at once. "Pardon me, Captain, what's the trouble? The very walls of the ship are vibrating, it's freezing in the rooms now, and there's such noise. The steward near my cabin said—"

Arthur restrained a sigh, irritation adding to his impatience, though he knew other passengers would have the same questions, the same concerns. They deserved an answer, too.

"The *Titanic* has struck an iceberg and is sinking," he told her. "The walls shake because we are going as fast as we can to her aid. I pray you will excuse the rest; it is necessary for the rescue."

The woman's eyes widened, and she swallowed hard. "I see. I shall do my best to assist, sir."

"Thank you." Arthur managed a brief nod, then turned to the officers and men on the deck who had noticed his presence and paused in their work.

They stood there as though awaiting further instructions, as though this was simply some special request on a typical voyage.

As though they did not understand what was at stake.

Arthur's rising unsettled state roared within him. "Great God, men!" he barked, surprising even himself. "Get ready to save those poor souls! There must be twenty-five hundred on board!"

They moved quickly, shouting encouragement to each other and working in tandem as though fire licked at their heels.

He supposed that, in a way, it did.

Dean and Rees came to his side shortly, and the three of them compared notes on the tasks completed and those yet to be done. Hankinson had remained on deck with the men to oversee their work. So far, everything was in order, and all he had asked was being accomplished. He could ask for nothing more, and yet . . .

Arthur looked up, spotting Bisset posted where he'd ordered him, watching for ice. He eyed the deck, surveying the work there even as his officers discussed its operation.

"Captain!"

Their group turned at the urgent voice, and Arthur saw Mr. Cottam dashing onto the deck. "Cottam?"

He panted as he came to a stop before them. "*Titanic* tells *Olympic* she's sinking fast, sir."

Arthur exhaled sharply, almost groaning at the update. "Anything for us?"

The lad looked completely run-down, his eyes nearly lifeless, weariness etching lines onto his young face, yet he appeared no less determined than any other man on the ship. "No, sir, not yet. I've told her we're on our way, but she's calling out to anybody in the vicinity now. She's putting her passengers into lifeboats."

"Not good." Arthur pressed his lips together. "Why aren't ships closer to her position aiding her as well? Surely there must be some in a better proximity than we are."

Cottam met his gaze squarely. "No one else in the vicinity is responding, sir. *Olympic* is farther than we are, and even with her speed, we will arrive first." His voice shook, and he swallowed hard.

Arthur exhaled a short, confounded breath, nodding. "Very well. Keep me updated, Cottam."

"Aye, sir." Without so much as a nod, Cottam turned and ran back to the radio room.

Arthur shook his head. "Not enough, Dean. We're doing everything possible, but it's not enough."

"No, sir." Dean scanned the deck, his brow furrowing. "Where did the stewards go? I know the chief steward had them out here."

"He wanted to speak to them, Mr. Dean," Rees broke in. "Thought they might work better and with more motivation if they knew the reason."

Arthur grunted. "Not a bad idea. Many of our men would do the same, I daresay."

The chief steward's voice then reached them from somewhere deeper in the ship, raising in volume and in power. "Every man to his post, and let him do his duty like a true Englishman. If the situation calls for it, let us add another glorious page to British history."

With that rousing speech, the stewards and stewardesses began to stream back onto the deck and into other parts of the ship, renewed in vigor and full of determination.

Dean made a sound of consideration beside Arthur. "I should have had the chief steward make my speech. The man has a gift with words, I daresay."

"If it will help us do our duty," Arthur murmured, "and motivate our crew and passengers, I'll let the chief steward make the same speech over meals, over the pulpit, and have it written out for every set of eyes on board this ship." He sighed and looked at his officers. "Latest speeds have us at fifteen knots. Johnston assures me we can get more."

The other two nodded.

"I'd say we're nearing sixteen now, sir," Rees commented with a careful look around the ship. "I think she'll be shaking more than she already is."

"Sir!" Cottam raced up to them again, this time with a message in hand. "I finally got *Titanic*."

Arthur took the message and read it aloud. "'Come quick. Our engine room is flooded up to the boilers.'"

Dean swore beside him, running a hand over his face.

Arthur read the note again, blinking and praying the words might change. He looked at his Marconi man, swallowing with some difficulty. "Tell them we're coming, that our boats are ready, and to have theirs do the same. We have a double watch in the engine room, and we're making fifteen, sixteen knots. Tell them we're coming, Cottam."

Cottam nodded, bolting back down to his office.

Silence fell among the three of them as they stood there, words seeming unnecessary and impossible.

If the engine room was already flooded, the *Titanic*'s passengers weren't going to make it.

They would not make it.

A tightness squeezed in Arthur's chest, the dark reality of the situation seizing control of his lungs and increasing the beating of his heart.

"I'm going to the bridge," he managed to tell his officers. "Keep at it."

"Yes, Captain," they replied, but he was already moving.

He could not lose composure, lose confidence, lose anything in his bearing in front of anyone under his command. The sequence of events would lose relevance when all was said and done, but it was all he could think of at the moment.

Was there another way to draw more power and speed from the engines? Could anything else be sacrificed to get to *Titanic*'s position more quickly? He knew all would be in readiness when they arrived; he'd been over his list a dozen times now, and it was as thorough as any orders he had ever seen. But in getting there . . .

They needed the wings of eagles to fly to *Titanic*'s aid in time.

He'd never been inclined to curse a ship before, but the words were on his tongue. He did not dare speak, of course, being just superstitious enough to avoid risking it, but the feelings were there, real and raw. A twelve-year-old liner streaking northbound, undoubtedly into ice-strewn waters, in the hopes of being of some use to a newer, stronger, sleeker ship that even now was sinking into the depths of the sea.

It was impossible.

Surely there were other ships in closer vicinity that could do more.

It would not change his mind or his course, but a feeling of futility seeped into his soul.

Arthur shook his head, banning such negativity from forming into concise thoughts. He gestured to a passing steward and requested that Chief Engineer Johnston come up to the bridge.

If anyone would know how to get more out of *Carpathia*, it was he.

Arthur surveyed the deck, pretending at calm while he waited, his frame almost perfectly still, hands clasped behind him. By appearances, he was the picture of a serene captain. Yet his hands tapped against each other, revealing his real impatience, though no one but the helmsman would see.

Johnston arrived at the bridge, coal-dusted and sweaty. Had he been working alongside his men in the engine room? Or was it simply part of the atmosphere that no one could escape?

"All hands are below deck, sir," Johnston informed him as he strode in. "They're doing all they can. Some of the stokers, having heard the nature of our mission, came directly from their beds wi'out changing first." He grinned and shook his head in disbelief. "I'd say they're mad, but I dinnae think they are."

The image of such behavior made Arthur proud and did much to ease his fear. "Nor do I, Johnston. Excellent." He looked at the gauges, checking the current speed of the ship.

"I think we can get her to sixteen-five, Captain, if not seventeen outright," Johnston said without any hint of boasting. "With the men working as they are, it shouldn't be too difficult."

Arthur nodded. "Most excellent. See to the men, Johnston, and keep their spirits up. They are the backbone—if not the heart—of this ship. Give them my thanks, as well."

Johnston grinned, clearly carrying a great deal of pride in his men. "Yes, sir. Gladly."

Johnston turned to leave, nodding at Cottam, who hesitated just outside, poised to enter the bridge.

Arthur immediately crossed to meet him. "What does *Titanic* say?"

Cottam stared at him, pale and nearly shaking, his eyes wide. His throat worked once, then again before he even opened his mouth in an attempt to speak. "She . . ." He broke off, swallowing hard. "Nothing, sir."

All air in Arthur's lungs vanished, and he blinked. "Nothing?"

Cottam shook his head. "Nothing since the last. Never acknowledged our last message to her. She was sending out nothing but CQD, over and over again, and then she . . . she cut off mid-CQD." His mouth worked, his cheeks somehow losing more color.

"Just the distress call?" Arthur reiterated, unable to believe it. "Nothing more?"

"Just the CQD, sir," Cottam said again. "And nothing since . . ."

No. No, it wasn't possible. It couldn't be, not yet . . .

"Can't you get her?" Arthur demanded, his voice rising in pitch as panic lanced him.

"No, sir." Cottam shook his head again, finally seeming to come to his senses. "She doesn't answer anyone, sir. She doesn't send anything either."

The two men stared at each other as the gravity of the situation settled on both of them.

"She's going down," Arthur muttered to himself, the truth of the situation reflecting back to him in Cottam's eyes.

"Pardon, sir?"

Arthur was moving at once. "She's going down!"

He whirled toward the EOT while Cottam raced off the bridge. *"Full speed!"* Arthur bellowed as he signaled down to the engine room himself.

For a moment, he thought he could hear a roar from the men down below, the sound like a charge into battle.

Whether it was real or imagined, he supposed it did not matter. This was a battle now, and they would continue to sound the charge so long as they had the power to do so.

"Our boat was managed very well. It is true this officer did want to go back to the ship, but all the passengers held out and said: 'Do not do that. Do not do that. It would only be foolish if we went back there. There will be so many around they will only swamp the boat.' And, at the time, I do not think those people appreciated that there were not sufficient lifeboats to go around. I never paid any attention to how many lifeboats there were. I did not know."

—GEORGE HARDER,
Titanic passenger, May 3, 1912

CHAPTER 10

It was unbelievable. If she were not seeing it with her own eyes, Kate would not have thought it possible.

Titanic, nearly full dark now, was sticking high out of the water at an impossible angle, propeller in the air. The screams of those still on board ripped through the air, a sound worse than any ghost story could have ever spun.

The sea was a dark, cavernous thing now that no lights shone upon her, and the deep, guttural sounds she uttered were unearthly as she slowly consumed what had once been a mighty vessel.

Kate covered Margit's ears as best she could while she held the girl close, praying that somehow Margit wouldn't remember anything of this. Even Kate did not want to remember any of this.

"I don't know what to pray for," Mary Mac whispered behind her. She was curled against those nearest her for warmth. As they all were. "That the screaming will stop or that the voices will grow stronger."

It was harrowing to think on, but Kate understood completely. The bloodcurdling screams would likely never leave her memory, but when she considered what silence would mean, she shivered from more than the cold.

Nothing good would come out of this. No good alternative, no hopeful side, no bright spot to consider.

There was only darkness, cold, and pain.

A deep groan seemed to rise up from the water itself, rolling out across the ripples and waves like roaring thunder. With it came the tell-tale metallic rumbling of *Titanic*, though the darkness hid any specifics of what was occurring.

Little Artie clamped his hands over his ears, and the other passengers in the boat seemed to huddle closer together.

"What's happening?" someone asked over the sound.

"The ship is breaking apart!" another said. "Can't you see it? She's split in two!"

Kate buried her face against Margit. She did not want to see the dark mass of *Titanic* breaking apart, nor watch it sink. She was numb, losing the ability to feel and the desire to think. Perhaps it was more merciful this way.

Anything else was too horrific to live in her memories. Reside in her mind. Haunt her dreams.

Screams tore through the air, accompanied by loud splashing and the endless groaning of the ship as it creaked and crashed. The cacophony of it, the brutal wall of sound, slammed into each of them, stripping them of whatever warmth and peace they had managed to cling to.

Worst of all, were the cries of children.

She could have gone her entire life without hearing such a sound.

And then there were the other voices. Names were shouted across the sea as people searched in vain for friends and loved ones, praying to God that they were not alone in this icy hell.

Kate found herself praying as well, whispering incomplete invocations, stammering words and thoughts in a stream of near-babbling. Surely heaven would hear her heart regardless of what her lips could utter.

A baby in their boat began to fuss and cry, protesting in a way that so many of them undoubtedly would like to.

"Papa," Artie whispered from Julia's side. "Where is Papa?"

Tears sprang to Kate's eyes, hot and furious, as her chest squeezed with emotion. She hadn't known she had any tears left.

Dear God, she prayed with a fervency she'd never known, *let this nightmare end*.

Another loud rumble rent the air, and the screams increased in pitch, as did the splashing.

"She's going under!" someone bellowed behind Kate.

The water beneath their lifeboat rolled and pitched, the passengers clinging to the sides and each other for support.

"How far away are we?" one of the stewards asked from the back.

"Half mile or so, I reckon," another replied.

"Nay, less than that."

"Look at her . . ."

The hushed statement silenced them all, and Kate could no longer resist looking.

Barely visible through the darkness, past the scattered, floating lifeboats and their silent occupants, the bow of the great *Titanic* sank lower and lower into the blackness of the sea. It was both horrifying and riveting to see such a great beast swallowed up almost effortlessly.

Moans and cries became muffled, gagged in places, and the disparity of sound shook Kate to her core.

"What's happening?" she asked of her fellow passengers.

"The suction of the sinking ship," one of the crew replied in a flat tone. "It pulls them under, draws them in. Even the strongest swimmers cannot escape it."

The breath in Kate's lungs vanished as she imagined not only an icy death, but a suffocating one. The idea of being dragged to the bottom of the sea while still conscious was horrible. She could only hope their deaths were quick and merciful.

"Hail, Mary, full of grace," a soft Irish voice murmured behind her.

And hers was not the only voice lifted in prayer.

Soon their entire lifeboat was awash with various pleas, some from the rosary, some from the soul, and some begging with heaven for some sort of rescue.

Had any kind of message been sent out before the disaster had become too great? Was anyone coming to their aid?

Could anyone have even known their rescue was needed?

Kate stared out at the water beyond them, away from the bodies, the wreckage, away from other lifeboats, letting the dark waves rock and sway her body, safe in a lifeboat, even as it froze the bodies of others less protected. A comfort and a curse at once.

If the Lord can calm the raging sea, why could His hand not stay this thing?

She shook her head at the doubting thought, the cruel question that had no answer.

"That's the last of her," a man in the back announced in a hushed tone. "She's gone."

Silence filled their group, hearts sinking as quickly as the ship had. The magnitude of such a statement was unfathomable, the weight of it even more so.

How could it have happened? How could such a marvelous ship now be on her way to the bottom of the sea? The unsinkable ship had done the impossible, and all of the hopes and dreams she'd represented were lost.

Lost along with the lives of those who had once hoped and dreamed aboard her.

Faces flickered across Kate's mind. Faces she had seen in steerage on the way to her cabin, faces alight with joy and revelry only hours ago. Faces without names that were suddenly bright as the sun. Faces from the day she had boarded and from Sunday services. Old and young faces. Faces of laughter and love and terror and tears. Faces upon faces, all gone, their lives cut short.

Had anyone she recalled made it to a lifeboat? Were any of them now in the water struggling for breath and life?

Had the family she'd insisted wear life belts listened to her? Were they together?

Martin McMahon had helped them get life belts. Was he gone?

Martin Gallagher had led them to the lifeboats. Had he been permitted to enter one at the last?

What of the other Kate Connolly and her friends?

What of Officer Pitman and his cheerful politeness?

How many people had been trapped inside *Titanic* herself as she went down?

How many were in the boats, like her, awash in guilt, in fear, or in grief?

What would become of any of them now?

The baby in their boat wailed in the chilled night, his mother tearfully shushing him to no avail.

Strange how such cries did not seem to bother any of them, and Kate felt that this sweet infant, crying out in distress, might have been the voice of them all in this night. Free with his tears, open in his pain, vulnerable without fear.

She might have wished for him to cry all night, but the cold was increasing, and the sounds of the baby's agony must have been distressing to his mother. Kate could not wish for the woman's pain to be compounded as well.

But, oh, what comfort there was in that cry for a time.

"There now, wee one," a man murmured. "It's no wonder you're upset, what with your toes peeking out. If we tuck you in a bit more, your ma can keep you warm and safe, hmm?"

Kate's tears spilled at the tender note in his voice, though all were strangers here.

"Thank you," the mother replied.

"Not at all. What county in Ireland are you from, then?" the man asked in a weak voice.

Her response was just as fragile. "County Tipperary. Do you know it?"

"I do, actually. I have friends in Clonmel."

"Who are your friends? Perhaps I know them."

The normalness of the conversation seemed almost foreign to Kate's ears, given all that had transpired, and while their voices were not entirely at ease, there was a genuine tone to it that warmed her.

"Artie!" Julia suddenly cried, reaching for the little boy beside her as he leaned over the side of the boat.

The man behind her grabbed the boy's arm.

"My hat," Artie said with a sniffle, pointing to the water. "My hat."

The man patted Artie's shoulders gently. "Your pa taught you to take care of your things, I reckon. It's all right, lad. It's all right."

"Here," another man said, shucking off his outer coat. "Is very cold out. Please, for the boy."

Julia took it, nodding with tears in her eyes as she wrapped a now-sniffling Artie in its depths. Mary Mac rose and carefully, awkwardly, stepped between passengers to sit beside Artie, lifting him onto both hers and Julia's laps.

"Both of us will keep him warmer," Mary Mac explained, turning the boy so he could face their shoulders and be shielded from the slight wind. "Is that better, Artie?"

He whimpered in response and buried his face between them.

"Please," a feminine voice called from nearby. "Please, help."

Kate and the others looked around, but saw no one.

"Where?" one of the men called. "Where?"

A weak cough replied, and then, "Here, sir."

"There!" Mary-from-Clare called, pointing over Kate's shoulder to the water.

Kate gasped as she caught sight of a woman struggling in a life belt. She swam closer to them but seemed weighed down and near to drowning.

"Get her in!" one of the men ordered, and those at the oars began to turn the boat in her direction. "Closer!"

The woman sobbed. "Sir," she pleaded suddenly, "let go of me."

Her words made little sense, but then a head popped up near her left shoulder, the skin pale as snow.

"I will not," he insisted through chattering teeth and barely moving lips. "If I do, I will drown." He slipped beneath the water again, pulling the lower half of the woman with him.

"He's hanging onto her!" a woman shouted. "Lord above, he'll drown them both!"

"Help me!" the swimming woman begged, choking on water. "Help—"

Kate scooted to the other side of the boat as much as she could, trying to give the men plenty of room to reach her.

They rocked to and fro as they jostled positions, reaching down into the water. They had the woman by the arms but couldn't move her much given the added weight of her passenger.

"Let go of her, man," someone barked. "You'll kill her, and capsize the rest of us!"

"I can't," he panted, clinging to her. "I can't."

The woman whimpered, pulling on the arms of her would-be rescuers.

"For pity's sake, just let go long enough to let us get her in!"

There was a long pause, and then the man let go of her at last.

"Heave!" With a mighty groan, a few men pulled the woman aboard, while others fought to stabilize the boat for the sake of the others.

The woman crumpled onto the bottom of the lifeboat.

"Blankets!" another woman called out. "Please. Blankets, coats, something!"

Layers of fabric were gathered from all parts of the boat, and the men wrapped them about their new passenger.

"Pardon me. Excuse me," a man said, pushing gently past Kate. "Please, let me through. I'm a doctor."

The crowded passengers parted as much as possible and made room for him to tend her. "Madam, my name is Dr. Washington Dodge. May I help?"

She nodded, the motion frantic and oddly mechanical as he began to check her.

The men turned to the water again. "Right, sir, now—"

Silence was the only response.

Kate looked at the water where the woman had been pulled from, but there was no one else waiting to be saved.

"Saints preserve us," someone breathed, and several crossed themselves. Slowly, each man moved back to their seats, not another word among them.

The woman cried as she shook with the cold. "I didn't even know his name," she managed, a slight Nordic accent to her words.

"Hush now," an older woman murmured, crouching near her and covering her soaking dark hair with someone's coat. "Not another word."

"I didn't know him." Her pale eyes stared up at them, pleading for understanding. "I've been swimming for ages, and he was clutching to me half of that time. I would have saved him, if I could . . . but I am so tired . . ."

The older woman shushed her again. "Darling girl, you cannot carry his burden, too. Hold on, now. Help will come for us." She rubbed the girl's back through the blankets and coats, humming softly.

Help would come, she'd said. But from where? From whom?

And when?

The cries of the other poor souls in the water filled the air, and the humming in boat thirteen could not drown out the sounds—or the pain.

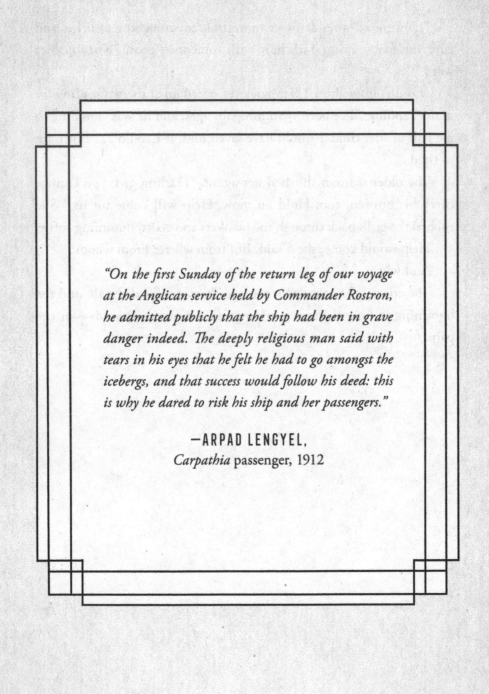

"On the first Sunday of the return leg of our voyage at the Anglican service held by Commander Rostron, he admitted publicly that the ship had been in grave danger indeed. The deeply religious man said with tears in his eyes that he felt he had to go amongst the icebergs, and that success would follow his deed: this is why he dared to risk his ship and her passengers."

—ARPAD LENGYEL,
Carpathia passenger, 1912

CHAPTER 11

"We need to be prepared for every eventuality," Arthur said with a sigh, finishing yet another speech in a short space of time.

It was becoming a miserable habit, this rambling on of his.

Dr. McGhee, the ship's surgeon, nodded as the pair of them conferred on the bridge. "I quite agree. I've conferred with the other doctors, and all is nearly ready."

Arthur patted the doctor's shoulder. "Good. Thank you, Doctor. But as for the state of mind of the passengers, I don't—"

A green flare suddenly appeared in the sky ahead of them.

"There!" Arthur pointed, racing forward. "There's *Titanic*'s light! One point off the port bow. She must still be afloat!"

A faint cheer from the deck made its way up to the bridge, and, for a moment, all was well in Arthur's heart.

But the longer he looked, the weaker the feeling became. He peered more closely at the flare. "Seems far, doesn't it? Still a long way off, I'd wager."

Dr. McGhee joined him, eying the flare himself. Though he was a medical man, he was also an experienced sailor. "Undoubtedly," he said with a nod.

Arthur frowned as the light faded entirely. He heaved a slow exhale. "Thank you, Doctor."

The doctor returned to his duty, and First Officer Dean took his place beside Arthur. "The flare, sir?"

"Far," Arthur admitted, not needing to pretend at optimism with his first officer, "but encouraging all the same."

"Ice ahead!" Bisset's voice sounded around the deck and into the bridge, cracking through the murmur of workers.

The lookouts soon echoed the officer's cry, sending Arthur and Dean striding forward in synchrony.

"Where?" Arthur demanded, scanning the dark sea and seeing nothing.

"Two points on the port bow!" the call came back.

He and Dean looked where he indicated, and a flicker of bright starlight reflected off a surface on the water.

That was sign enough.

"Helmsman, on me," Arthur ordered calmly, keeping his eye on the reflected surface, willing his eyes to adjust to the darkness faster.

"Aye, Captain."

Arthur nodded once. "Starboard, carefully. Half ahead."

The helmsman obediently turned the wheel while Dean shifted the EOT into the half ahead position.

"More," Arthur told the helmsman, gesturing with one hand.

The wheel turned further as silence blanketed the bridge.

"There," Arthur said. "There. That's it."

Everyone on the bridge waited, watching as the ship slowly, but cleanly, passed the iceberg.

Arthur nodded slowly, breathing easier. "Very good. Back to port slightly, helmsman. Resume full speed. Look sharp, I feel we're going to be seeing more ice before the night is out."

The helmsman dipped his chin and moved the wheel as indicated. "Aye, sir."

"Ice ahead!" Bisset and the lookouts roared once more.

With almost a snarl, Arthur narrowed his eyes at the sea. "If we get there without damaging ourselves, it will be a damned miracle," he muttered. "Helmsman?"

"Ready, Captain. On your word."

Arthur exhaled slowly. "Now gently to port," he indicated with a flick of his fingers.

Time and time again, Arthur and the helmsman took the ship safely around and between icebergs. Some were immense, others barely visible from the bridge. Bisset and the lookouts called out warning after warning, so many that Arthur lost count, but always in time for the ship to shift as needed. Mountains of ice passed on both starboard and port, and a strange feeling of calm overtook Arthur as his ship continued to move forward.

Somehow, it was as though the bergs moved slowly enough for him to navigate around them cleanly. The danger did not seem so great in the present situation, though Arthur knew full well he could not rest easy or allow himself even the slightest modicum of confidence over them. The moment he did, the very instant he relaxed his focus, disaster would strike *Carpathia* as it had *Titanic*.

He would not allow that to happen.

"Port," he told the helmsman.

"Captain, our speed?" Dean asked in a low voice, careful not to let others hear. "Should we slow?"

Arthur shook his head, keeping his eyes on the sea and its secrets as another iceberg harmlessly passed by them. "Very good, helmsman. And swing back to starboard. Easy . . ."

The helmsman perfectly executed his maneuvers, and Arthur felt as if they were somehow of one mind, as though he might have been at the helm as well as in his present position.

Another flare suddenly lit the sky, closer now than before, though still a good distance off.

He traced its light across its path in the heavens. "Now further starboard, half ahead . . ."

Two more bergs, both minor by stature, passed by, and a sigh of relief seemed to expel from those on the deck and the bridge as the ship came free of the ice.

"Very good, Captain," Dean breathed.

Arthur removed his cap and wiped at his brow, exhaling roughly before replacing it. "Well done, helmsman. Well done, indeed."

The helmsman briefly leaned against the helm, managing a smile. "Thank you, sir."

"We'll have more, I can promise you that." Arthur slid back a step, steadying himself and chuckling. "Don't breathe easy just yet."

"Aye, sir."

Arthur glanced at his pocket watch, his mind already working on the next steps in his mission. "Mr. Dean, it is now three o'clock. Please begin firing rockets, interspersed with Cunard Roman candles every fifteen minutes. Then tell the engine crew to resume full speed ahead."

Dean nodded with a quick bow. "Yes, Captain."

Tucking his pocket watch back inside his jacket, Arthur frowned at the sea. "We must give them some hope."

Moments later, Dean returned to the bridge and took the EOT in hand as rockets began to fire off from the deck. "Full ahead!" he barked as he shifted the handle accordingly.

A faint groaning echoed from deep within the ship, and the speed increased. It wasn't long before the walls began to shake and shudder once more, proving the age of the ship despite her abilities and the demands placed upon her.

It wouldn't matter. Somehow or another, Arthur knew it wouldn't matter.

Carpathia was up to the challenge.

They all were.

He stared out at the sea before him. He could not think about more than the present, could not anticipate what the next few hours might hold for him. The clarity of the night sky was breathtaking. It would have been something to marvel at had the circumstances been different. Each star lit its portion of the sky with a brilliance he'd rarely seen.

"A brilliant night of stars," Arthur murmured to himself as he gazed out at it. He swallowed once. "And ice."

But he could not marvel at anything in this moment, not when he had such demands on him. Speed was what they needed now, and the direction of it. All else was in the hands of others.

He could sense the looks of First Officer Dean and Third Officer Rees, standing nearby. No doubt they sought instruction and action just as he did, but, for the present, he had nothing new to give them.

"Ice ahead!" Bisset called out, the lookouts echoing a half second behind him.

Arthur saw the berg to one side and almost absently gave the order. "Starboard, helmsman. Gently now."

Rees cleared his throat uneasily. "Shall we slow, sir?"

"No," Arthur replied without sparing a look. "Maintain speed."

No one said another word, but the tension on the bridge did not ease until the berg passed without issue.

Arthur nodded as it did, the gesture for no one but himself.

He turned at the sound of footsteps and saw Cottam approaching, looking rather worse for the wear with dark circles beneath his eyes and his hair slightly disheveled. Arthur went to him at once.

"Any word?"

Cottam shook his head. "No, sir. Not a one."

Blast it. It had been well over an hour since they'd spotted the first flares, and much longer than that since the last radio transmission.

"Nothing?"

"Nothing, sir," Cottam confirmed, lifting his chin just enough to meet Arthur's eye. "Except for some chatter from other ships, it's almost completely silent."

That wasn't what he wanted to hear. It wasn't anything close to it, and a nagging feeling tugged at the pit of his stomach.

He nodded at his radio man and turned back to the front of the bridge. He stared out at the sea, confused and frustrated.

"No new messages," Arthur murmured, "and no sight of the ship."

He paused, then looked at Dean and Rees. "Those flares couldn't have come from *Titanic*."

Where, then, had they come from? There were no other ships in the vicinity, as far as any of them were aware.

Dean cleared his throat, glancing at the chart. "Sir, we are approaching the coordinates."

Arthur swallowed tightly. "I know." He clasped his hands behind his back, frowning out at the sea.

"Sir?"

What should he do? What could he do?

What was there to do?

They had been racing toward the coordinates all night, and they had nothing to show for it. But for a field of bergs, there was no sign.

What could he do?

He inhaled deeply, exhaled slowly, then nodded. "Call standby to all engines."

Dean turned to the EOT again. "Standby to all engines."

Arthur heard the sounds of engines shifting, the walls of the ship quivering with the change.

All eyes were on Arthur, and he felt every one of them.

He exhaled again. "All stop," he muttered, knowing the order would be heard.

"All stop!" Dean's voice echoed about the bridge.

The sounds from below increased as the engines, and the ship, ground to a halt.

When they settled, and the engine stopped, there was no sound except for the water slapping against the ship, and even that was barely audible.

Arthur looked out at the darkness before them, seeing but not seeing. Slowly, the officers came forward, joining him, their eyes no longer on him, but on the sea.

If only there was something to see.

He strained to see better, to see more, hoping against hope.

"Bisset?" Arthur called out.

"Nothing, sir," came the reply. "There's nothing."

He knew that already, but hearing the words cut through him.

Those words were the death knell for more than he could say.

They really were too late.

Arthur shook his head and voiced the words currently pounding through his mind: "She's . . . she's gone."

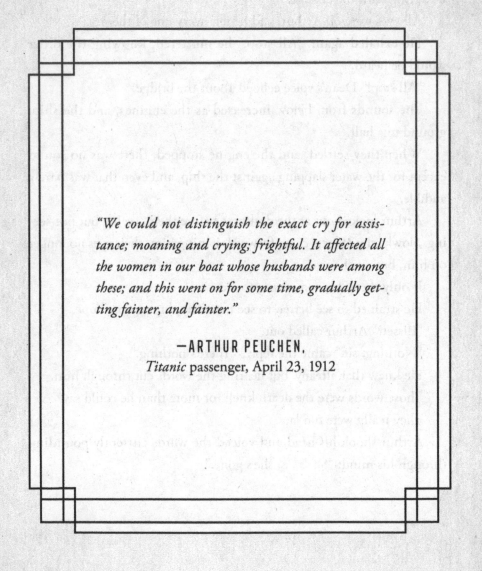

"We could not distinguish the exact cry for assistance; moaning and crying; frightful. It affected all the women in our boat whose husbands were among these; and this went on for some time, gradually getting fainter, and fainter."

—ARTHUR PEUCHEN,
Titanic passenger, April 23, 1912

CHAPTER 12

LIFEBOAT 13 · APRIL 15, 1912 · 3:30 AM

It was colder without Margit in her lap.

It was cold anyway, but giving the child back to her mother made Kate more aware of her numbness as their boat sat upon the waters. Artie whimpered and shivered in the care of Julia and Mary Mac, but Ethel and Margit had drifted off to sleep, as had Margit's little sister.

Only the adults were fully awake, and fully aware of what was happening.

Or not happening, as it were.

The sea was quiet, and the night's chill was heading toward a hard freeze. Kate had been cold for so long, her only clue to the changing temperature was the dense fog her breath created in the air before her. The clouds slipping through her painfully cracked lips were transfixing at times. Almost as though she could hear the ice cracking into existence in the sky.

"I saw a family in boat fifteen," one of the ladies murmured softly to no one in particular. "There were perhaps nine of them, all told. The

119

officer was trying to force one of the daughters into the boat with the rest, but the girl would not go."

"Whyever not?" another asked.

"Her father and brothers could not come in the boat. She refused to be parted from them, though her mother and sisters were going to safety."

"Rather a Solomon's choice, that. I'm not sure I could have lived with either option, were I in her place."

Kate swallowed with some difficulty at the thought. She had spent the last few hours going over events again and again, imagining other scenarios and alternatives, and she had come to only one positive conclusion.

She was fortunate to have been traveling without any loved ones.

She had her friends, of course, but they were here with her.

What if her family had been with her? Had any of her siblings or her parents been aboard, the situation might have changed. She might have had to stay behind for their sake, or go on ahead without them. She might have been parted from them cruelly in the melee of evacuation, and in this endless waiting, not known of their fate.

Or she could have had a husband or sweetheart. What if she had been traveling with a man she loved? Would he have been forced to remain on the ship while she was forced into a lifeboat?

He would have begged her to go, but would she have clung to him? Would she have been like the girl who stayed with her papa and brothers? Would Kate have stared death in the face boldly while clutching love in her hand?

Would her beloved have carried her to the boat himself and sent her away, breaking both their hearts to save her life? Hours upon hours in this lifeboat, knowing he lay somewhere in the depths of the sea . . .

Tears sprang to her eyes at the thought. Though no such man existed for her, he existed for a number of other ladies in lifeboats tonight. How many of them cried now for his loss? For his unknown fate?

How many were beyond tears now?

She thought of Martin and Margaret, sharing a final moment together outside the lifeboats, and her heart clenched.

"The screams have quieted," one of the men said unnecessarily as he and the others at the oars gently rowed together.

A rumble of acknowledgment rippled through the boat.

It was true, and it was unnerving. The sounds of those in the water were barely audible, leaving the stillness of the night to fill the space. The silence was both a relief and a nightmare.

Kate glanced around at the water, her neck stiff, as though it had frozen in the cold. Life belts bobbed at the surface of the water, holding aloft faces and limbs nearly as white as the belts themselves. The forms were still and unmoving, more lifeless than any creature she'd seen or imagined. She squeezed her eyes shut and huddled close to her friends, wishing she hadn't looked at all.

She recalled how lively life on *Titanic* had been, and comparing that to the present silence brought its own numbing chill that had nothing to do with the temperature around them.

Every now and then, the oars splashed into the water and the men would row, though it was more to keep the lifeboat from drifting too far from the site of the wreckage than it was to head in a specific direction. There was nowhere for them to go, after all.

Once the sea had fully swallowed the *Titanic* into its depths, the desperation of the survivors to get away faded into a somber, mechanical action to keep them from freezing.

"Mary Mac," Julia asked through chattering teeth. "Did you bring that bit of Saint Mogue's earth with you?"

"As it happens, I did." Mary Mac reached into the pocket of her gown and showed them the parcel.

Julia grunted softly as she folded her arms more tightly around her. "Well, there's that, at least."

Kate scooted to the edge of her seat and put a hand on the woman they had rescued from drowning. She still lay wrapped in spare clothing. "How are you feeling, my dear? Helmina, was it?"

She barely moved, her skin pale as snow and her lips cracked and thin. "Cold," she whispered.

"Here," Mary-from-Clare murmured, carefully rising. "Let me lay beside you; I'm small enough. It may help."

"Aye, that it may," a man agreed. He rose to help her cross over and offered his coat as another layer. "Take this too, lass."

Mary-from-Clare nodded her thanks and tucked herself against their frigid companion, pulling her close as she might have done a child. She exhaled sharply as she did so, her eyes closing.

"Mary?" Kate prodded.

She shook her head. "It's like cradling a block of ice," she whispered, rubbing her hands quickly over the woman's back.

"Let's all scoot closer," a man across from them suggested. "It may not be much, but perhaps . . ." He shrugged.

The other passengers followed his lead, moving as close together as possible, personal space and questions of propriety erased.

Survival was their aim. Nothing more.

"Sir, you are weary to the bone," a lady near Kate said gently. "Please, let me take the oar."

"No, I can manage. I can—"

"I must insist," she overrode. "You have been at it for hours, and I can row in your place."

"So can I," another lady announced. "You men have earned your stripes, now take a rest."

Kate smiled as the women stepped over to the oars and motioned for the men to move. They barely protested, which testified of their true fatigue and pain more than any words would have done.

The night would make heroes of them all and reveal their true mettle, even to themselves.

"Is anybody out there?" a voice in the distance called, drawing everyone's attention.

Kate frowned, squinting against the night. "What is it?"

"One of the other lifeboats," someone replied. "I heard them an hour ago. Probably looking for survivors."

"Are there any?"

No one answered, and Kate swallowed hard at the implication.

No cries had come from the sea in some time, no splashing sounds from someone attempting to swim or keep warm, no moans or groans of suffering.

Even the magnificent stars had begun to fade in the sky, which meant the water had grown more opaque. They were surrounded by such a deep darkness that even the other lifeboats were hidden from them.

Were they surrounded by icebergs like the one *Titanic* had struck? Or was the sea a vast, open emptiness as bleak as the darkness they presently endured? Were they in danger from more than the paralyzing cold?

"Do you think the wireless got a message out before the ship went down?" a man asked through chattering teeth.

"I don't know," another grunted. "Some ships don't have a radio man on all night. Mr. Phillips and Mr. Bride mentioned that the other day when I stopped by."

"Do you think either of them got away?" the first man asked in a low voice, though it carried in the still air.

A young woman near them broke into the conversation. "We are going to be rescued, aren't we?"

The question hung in the air, silencing all other words.

"The officers will have flares," their steersman eventually replied with would-be confidence, smiling weakly at them all. "I have no doubt they'll fire them off when it's appropriate."

"Are the officers alive?" another asked.

No one dared to answer or offer a guess.

"Do we have anything we might burn for a signal of sorts?" one of the men asked. "In case there are ships in the area, or coming for us. I've got matches, if we do."

"As it happens," an older woman remarked with some shuffling about, "I have."

"Is it worth attempting a signal now?" another member of the boat grumbled dubiously.

Kate glanced over to see the woman pulling a sheet of paper from her handbag. She handed it to the man without reservation.

He frowned at it, then looked up at her. "Are you sure, ma'am? This is—"

"A letter to my daughter," the lady replied. "Yes. I have several sheets, as I have several daughters. I hardly think the letters need sending now, do you?" With a weary sigh, she handed over a second sheet.

The man lit the first sheet and held it high over his head, waving it through the air gently.

More than one person, Kate included, began to scan the horizon as if the signal would summon their saviors to them at once.

Nothing and no one appeared.

The dark water rocked beneath them in a lullaby of sorts, splashing ominously against the wood of the boat. It seemed to be the only sound for miles.

No voices, no bells, no lights.

No help.

No hope.

Someone in the lifeboat began to recite the rosary, and a few others immediately joined in, without any attempt at unison, without any sort of order. They prayed for their own peace and comfort as page after page of hurriedly written letters were slowly and methodically set aflame and turned into a signal.

A cry for help.

A plea.

Kate closed her eyes, letting herself rock with the motions of the boat, her fingers and toes frozen beyond feeling, her cheeks quickly following suit. The muffled voices of her boatmates soothed her as much as her mother's voice might have done.

She could not say she was comfortable, and yet her distress began to fade. Her body relaxed, and she sagged in her seat as the toll of the events of the night made itself known.

She was so tired. So tired . . .

With a sigh of release, Kate leaned against Julia beside her and felt Julia lean toward her in response. If they could hold each other up, they could perhaps rest enough to regain their spirits and their hope. Could rest until this nightmare was over. Until they were rescued.

If they were rescued.

She would rest for just a little while, now that she was so numb.

Rest . . .

How long she dozed, she couldn't say. Time had little meaning, and though someone in their boat likely had a pocket watch, there was little point in checking.

A hushed intonation woke her: "Lord have mercy—"

Kate's eyes opened with a jolt, the effect of those words the same as a shout, and she blinked at the change of their surroundings.

Dawn was approaching, the sky beginning to lighten to a pale blue on one side, though true sunrise would be some hours away. The addition of even the slightest bit of light on the horizon provided more of the view to the eyes of all who had spent such dark hours on the sea.

All about them were towering figures, barely discernible, almost resembling sails of schooners or fisher boats.

"Are they ships?" someone asked in a hushed tone, echoing Kate's suspicions.

But the approaching dawn cast a pinkish hue on the items, and silenced such speculation before it could spread.

Ice was all about them, floating in bergs of all sizes. It was still too dark to tell how far the ice extended, or how many lifeboats there were of survivors. Thankfully, it was also too dark to make an account of the bodies that might also be about them.

The ice, however, was plentiful, and it was somehow majestic in its terrifying spectacle. It was scattered everywhere, surrounding its victims on all sides.

Somewhere ahead of them, green flares shot into the air, and Kate and her fellow passengers looked about them for rescue. But they saw nothing.

Only ice.

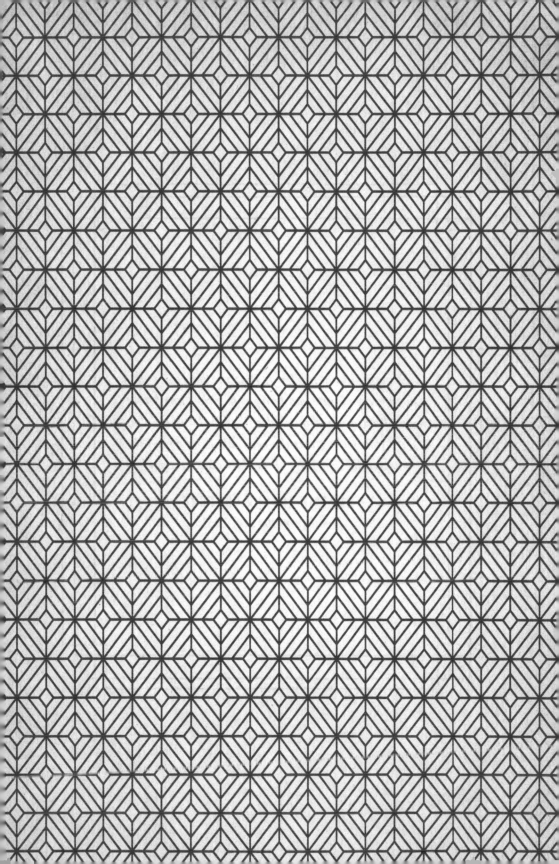

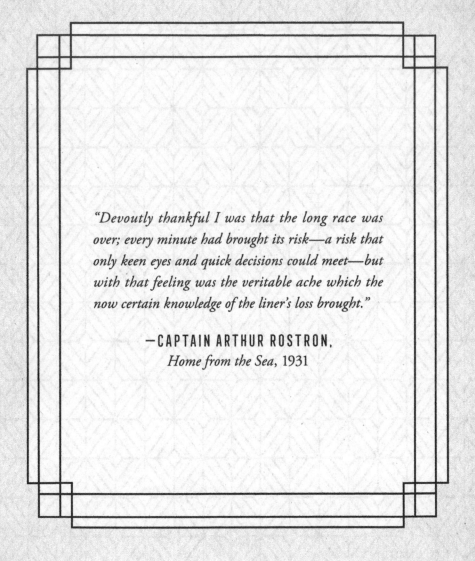

"*Devoutly thankful I was that the long race was over; every minute had brought its risk—a risk that only keen eyes and quick decisions could meet—but with that feeling was the veritable ache which the now certain knowledge of the liner's loss brought.*"

—CAPTAIN ARTHUR ROSTRON,
Home from the Sea, 1931

CHAPTER 13

RMS *CARPATHIA* • APRIL 15, 1912 • 4:00 AM

"There! Survivors! Slow ahead!"

Arthur and his fellow officers stared at the green flare as it arced across the sky. He did not dare smile, given the horrendous possibilities ahead, but the relief that even one person might still be alive coursed through him with enough power to weaken his knees.

"Survivors. Thank God." He swallowed the sudden lump in his throat. "Prepare to swing the ship starboard, helmsman, so we can pick up the lifeboat."

"Aye sir."

"Ice ahead!" Bisset and the lookouts bellowed in chorus.

The impulse to smile vanished, and Arthur scowled. "Of course, there is. Where?"

"Starboard!" Bisset's voice was frantic, sending a jolt of adrenaline through Arthur's body.

Suddenly the mountain of ice was visible, dark and looming.

"Hard to port!" Arthur called, clenching his hands together painfully.

"Hard to port!" Dean echoed with more volume.

The helmsman turned the wheel as far as it would go, swinging the ship over to avoid the iceberg.

Arthur held his breath, imagining that the entire bridge and deck did the same.

The dark iceberg floated harmlessly past them.

Arthur and his crew stared at it, then at each other.

This wasn't going to be easy, but nothing so far this night had been.

Arthur moved to look out at the sea again. "Right. Where's the lifeboat now, Mr. Bisset?"

Bisset appeared, clearly startled by the unexpected mountain of ice they had dodged. "Windward side, sir. And the water is getting choppier."

Arthur nodded, then took a megaphone and headed out to the starboard bridge wing.

A voice called up to them from the darkness of the sea. "We have only one seaman in the boat, and the rest of them can't work it very well!"

"All right!" Arthur called down to him. He looked over at the helmsman. "Gently now."

The helmsman nodded and began the careful maneuvering.

Turning to his officers, Arthur already had a new list of tasks in his mind. "Bisset, go down to the starboard gangway with two quartermasters and guide their lifeboat as it comes along. Watch her so she doesn't bump, and be careful she doesn't capsize."

"Yes, Captain." He left the bridge and signaled to two quartermasters nearby, who followed at once.

"Stop your engines!" a panicked voice from the water called up.

Arthur turned back to peer over the edge and saw the lifeboat floating toward the gangway. "Reverse engines!" he bellowed to the bridge.

"Reverse engines!" Dean echoed.

Arthur moved out to the deck to meet Hankinson, eyeing the bobbing lifeboat.

It was barely half full.

Arthur blinked, his thoughts vanishing as he tried in vain to comprehend what that meant.

Hankinson leaned closer, his eyes wide. "Why isn't it full, sir?"

"That is another conversation for another time," Arthur told him—and himself. He looked over at the crew awaiting his command. "Ready, men—drop the lines!"

The men dropped their lines, and the silent, wide-eyed passengers in the small boat gripped them, bringing the boat nearly flush with the *Carpathia* and securing it to her side to be brought up later. Another line was tossed out, and a rope ladder was dropped down to them.

An officer in the lifeboat secured the line around the arms of a young woman and helped her to the rope ladder. Slowly, awkwardly, she began to climb, visibly shivering. Each step seemed a hundred times more difficult for her than it ought to have been.

Arthur turned to Hankinson, who watched the process in almost horror.

"I'm returning to the bridge to survey our position in relation to the next boat," Arthur told him, forcing himself to take control of the tumultuous emotions rising within him. "Please send that officer to me when he's aboard."

"Of course, Captain," Hankinson replied absently, still staring at the too-empty boat.

"Immediately," Arthur insisted, injecting a firmer note in his voice.

His chief officer blinked and looked at him. "Yes, Captain."

Arthur left for the bridge, but he paused as the first *Titanic* passenger was pulled aboard.

Purser Brown lifted the woman from the rope ladder. "Up here, miss. There you are." He released her but kept a hand on her arm, as she did not appear steady. "What happened to the *Titanic*?" he asked, a handful of other crew members gathering around to hear the answer.

The woman stared at him, shocked and lost.

"Miss?" the purser prodded gently.

She wet her lips and managed, "She . . . she sunk."

There was silence on the deck for a long, sobering moment, the weight of those two words hitting each of them.

Arthur turned for the bridge, throat tightening, chest burning, and he forced his emotions to the side. His initial elation at retrieving a boat had changed to dismay at seeing the space available in the lifeboat and then to horror at hearing the fate of the *Titanic* from one of her own passengers.

He could not afford to feel anything at the moment. He had a task to do—several of them—and he must see to his duty.

Officers Barnish and Rees reported to the bridge, giving Arthur updates on the status of other parts of the ship, as well as the activity on the deck. More footsteps caught their attention, and a young White Star officer entered, his expression drawn yet somehow full of energy in spite of the toll of the night.

The *Titanic*'s officer offered a quick, faltering bow when he reached Arthur. "Fourth Officer Boxhall, Captain."

Arthur nodded, eyeing the young man carefully. "Welcome aboard, Fourth Officer. Was it you who gave us *Titanic*'s position?"

"It was, sir, yes." He swallowed once. "I had been working our navigation all evening, and when it . . . Captain Smith asked me to relay our position, and—"

"Excellent calculation," Arthur said, seeing the weariness in the young seaman's demeanor. "Very impressive."

"Thank you, sir."

When he said nothing else, Arthur exhaled slowly, continuing to study Boxhall. "The *Titanic* has truly gone down?"

"Yes." His voice broke, his hands shook, but his composure remained intact. "She went down about two thirty."

Arthur glanced at the clock, running the calculations in his head. The survivors had been on the water for at least two hours, likely more. The flares they'd seen hours ago must have been released from one of the lifeboats just after *Titanic* went under.

There was no telling what state the other survivors would be in.

He returned his focus to Boxhall as Dean joined them. "Were many people left on board when she sank?"

Boxhall's composure began to crack, his jaw quivering. "Hundreds and hundreds. Perhaps a thousand! Perhaps more!"

His face crumpled completely, and he put a hand to his forehead, turning away as his grief set in. He gripped the nearest rail for support.

"They've gone down with her, sir!" he cried, his voice breaking, choked with emotion. "They couldn't live in the cold water. We had room for maybe a dozen more people in my boat, but it was so dark after the ship . . . We didn't pick up any swimmers, but I could . . . I should have—" He shook his head, releasing a shuddering breath. "I think . . . I think people were drawn down by the suction created by the sinking. After a while, I fired the flares."

He took a moment, recovering himself.

The bridge remained utterly silent.

What an unspeakable sight. What horrors had this poor man endured? What had all of them endured?

It was so much worse than what Arthur had anticipated.

Boxhall steadied himself, turning back and trying to appear like the perfect officer.

He almost succeeded.

The path of his tears was still visible, the pain in his eyes raw. The young man appeared both years beyond his age and too youthful to even be at sea.

"The other boats are somewhere near," he said. "None of them would have got far."

Arthur was not immune to what he had heard. Could not be. Not in the least. He allowed his emotions a moment to surface, sorrow and compassion filling him, as he drew in a deep breath. It took him a moment to find the words to reply with, let alone actually manage to speak.

"Thank you, Boxhall," he told the man gently. Though he wanted to rest his hand on the officer's shoulder to offer his strength, he knew any show of kindness might break through his carefully rebuilt composure. "Take yourself to the First Class dining saloon and get some refreshment and rest. That's an order."

Boxhall nodded, relief flashing across his features. "Yes, Captain. Thank you, sir."

Arthur nodded and watched as Boxhall left.

For a moment, Arthur's emotions were unbearable. He closed his eyes, lowering his head as the scenes Boxhall had described flashed across his mind. His chest squeezed his lungs until he was nearly gasping for air, his own composure weakening on behalf of all for whom the pain of this night would never end. He focused on breathing in and out for a long moment, deeply moved and praying silently for the strength to attend to his duties and to not add to the profoundly sad burden his new passengers would bear.

"Bless us, heavens . . ." he heard Dean murmur.

Arthur opened his eyes at the words, looking out at the sea. Light had appeared on the horizon, though sunrise was still some time away.

More light meant more boats had become visible.

And with them, more ice.

Arthur stared at the ice, his emotions fading fast as determination set in. He turned from the bridge, and, as he headed for the deck, he saw more than one of his officers wipe a tear from his eyes.

"Come," he called to his men on the deck. "There are more survivors, and we must see to them all!"

The men shifted and worked with more speed and efficiency, hauling the lines and ladders back in, resetting the gangways, and preparing for the next lifeboat.

Arthur turned to his nearest officer. "Count the bergs and growlers, Barnish. Give me a number as soon as you have it."

"Yes, sir."

Arthur watched as the ship moved toward another lifeboat, his eyes occasionally flicking to the deck where some of the *Carpathia* passengers were gathering. Most stared in horror as stewards and crew gathered children and women in blankets. Others looked out at the field of ice before them. One couple even went so far as to take a photo of the scene with a camera.

The next boatload of survivors began to come aboard *Carpathia*, starting with a terrified, shivering girl of perhaps twelve years. She said nothing as her life belt was cut off of her.

"I count twenty-five bergs ranging from two hundred to two hundred fifty feet high, sir," Barnish told Arthur, keeping his voice low. "And a dozen more from one hundred to one hundred fifty."

Arthur blinked at the magnitude of the icebergs, then nodded to his officer. "Thank you, Barnish." He turned to the helmsman. "Once this lifeboat is unloaded and affixed, we'll go starboard. There's another pair of boats a mile or so out, and three bergs in our path."

The helmsman nodded, though a bit warily. "Aye, sir."

Raising a brow, Arthur smiled slightly. "I'll get you around them."

He received a smile in return. "I know, sir."

"Good man." Arthur nodded, then turned back and sighed. "Rees."

The man stepped forward. "Captain?"

Arthur lifted his chin toward the deck. "Go out and help Hankinson and Bisset, would you? There's going to be quite a lot to do very shortly."

"Yes, sir."

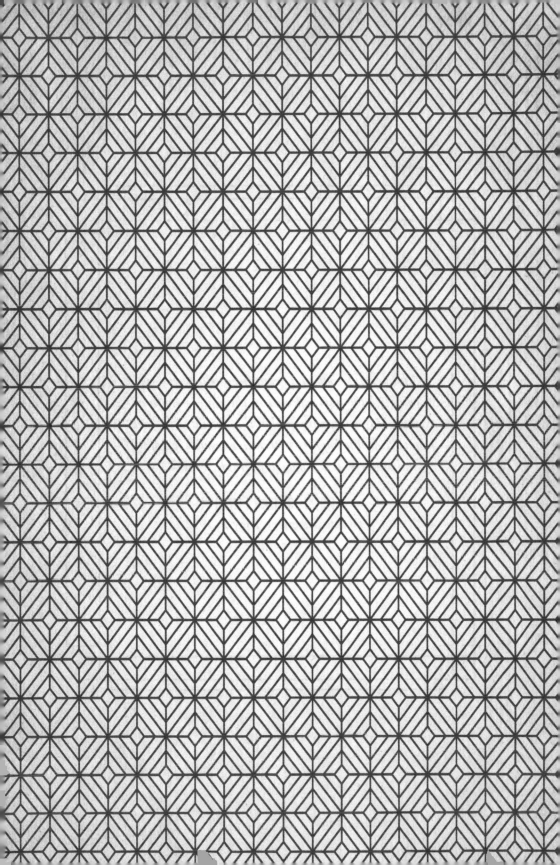

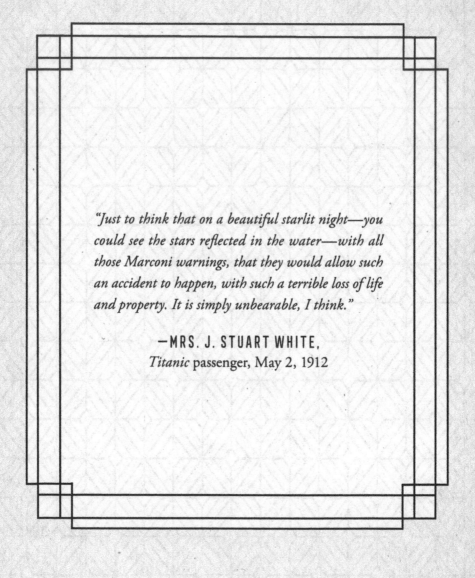

"*Just to think that on a beautiful starlit night—you could see the stars reflected in the water—with all those Marconi warnings, that they would allow such an accident to happen, with such a terrible loss of life and property. It is simply unbearable, I think.*"

—MRS. J. STUART WHITE,
Titanic passenger, May 2, 1912

CHAPTER 14

"Look! Everyone, look! We're saved!"

Kate turned in her seat, scanning the horizon, and gasped in abject relief at the sight of lights and portholes of an approaching ship.

Tears sprang to her eyes, blurring the glorious sight farther in the dim light of approaching morning. She dropped her head, letting her tears fall freely.

Julia took her hand, squeezing hard. "It's a ship. Glory be, it's a ship."

Kate could only squeeze her hand back. She had no words in this moment, no ability to vocalize anything at all. It was too much to take in after too much to bear, and no single emotion could encapsulate all she was feeling.

Her only thought was this:

We will be saved.

It would still be some time before their rescuers reached them, given the surrounding ice and the other boats in closer proximity, but Kate was willing to wait.

There was a ship, and she was picking up all the lifeboats.

Kate raised her head and gazed at the ship, watching it work.

"Do we row toward it?" one of the women asked on a hitching cry.

"Not yet," a crewman said. "Soon. We need to see where she heads next, get a feel for her pattern."

"Can you see who it is yet?" another crewman asked him. "Looks like a Cunard."

Kate ignored the conversation around her, fixated on the ship.

It was strange how hope and joy could exist within her at all after what had happened, but she felt a great deal of both. She would not die on the sea or drown within it, and that was miraculous.

What was also strange was how the joy she felt wasn't enough to change her facial expression or make her laugh or warm her.

She could only cry.

The sensation was unsettling. Her cheeks were the coldest they had ever been, and there was a weight to her tears. She could feel them pressing against her icy skin, and each one had its own individual path, it seemed. Had she not felt the warmth and weight of those tears, she would not believe they were hers.

Yet the emotions were real, and they were hers. As full dawn approached, she knew her hope would continue to grow. Hope that her troubles were over. Hope that she would never know this feeling again. Hope that more people had been saved than had been lost.

Hope that one day the pain would fade.

"I hope they have coffee," someone muttered through chattering teeth, his tone devoid of emotion.

There was a general pause in the rocking of their small boat, and then, almost reluctantly, a few people began to laugh in low tones.

"I'd rather have a brandy myself," an older man said with a chuckle.

They all looked at the ship again, watching as it approached the first lifeboat.

"Well, that's that, then," one of the crewmen announced, his voice rasping. "We should have placed a bet on lucky number thirteen, eh?"

"Turn your money over, boys," the steersman said with a bright grin, bits of ice clinging to the edges of his mustache. "That is, if you have any with you."

Good-natured chuckling rippled across the boat.

"Ah, the curse of thirteen must be broken, mustn't it?" a man said.

The steersman nodded fervently. "I shall never again say that thirteen is an unlucky number. Boat thirteen has been the best friend we ever had."

Kate sat back at that. She'd never considered such a thing, but it was true. Any superstition she might have held around the number thirteen would certainly be gone for herself and her companions after being so safely cared for in the lifeboat bearing that number.

Blessed thirteen forevermore.

"The ship looks small," one of the women commented. "Do you think they'll have room for us all?"

"It's not that small," the steersman said. "It is only not the size of *Titanic*."

The mention of the ship sobered the passengers again.

Yet all one had to do was look at the approaching ship, and the despair became less consuming. Less chilling.

Kate kept her focus there, on the ship. She needed that connection to hope, that break from her reality, the reminder that the end to her misery was at hand.

"What is *that*?" a woman asked.

"I think it's another ship. A steamer," a crewman answered.

Kate shifted her attention to the curious item in the distance. Its size was evident even so far removed, and its shape far different from the icebergs they'd seen earlier, but what was less clear was the direction of the ship's trajectory. More than that, they could not make out any details of her.

Would they come to aid the closer one? Would they offer their own assistance? Could they save some of the people in the water?

Or was it too late to hope for that?

"Are they coming for us as well?" a lady asked, hope in her voice.

"Hard to say," the crewman answered. "But they'll be far behind this one, so it may be irrelevant."

Kate blinked at the possible second ship in the distance, then looked at the one she knew was coming for them, the one she could count on, nearly touch. She could almost see the people already on board.

Just a little longer and she would be among them.

Just a little longer.

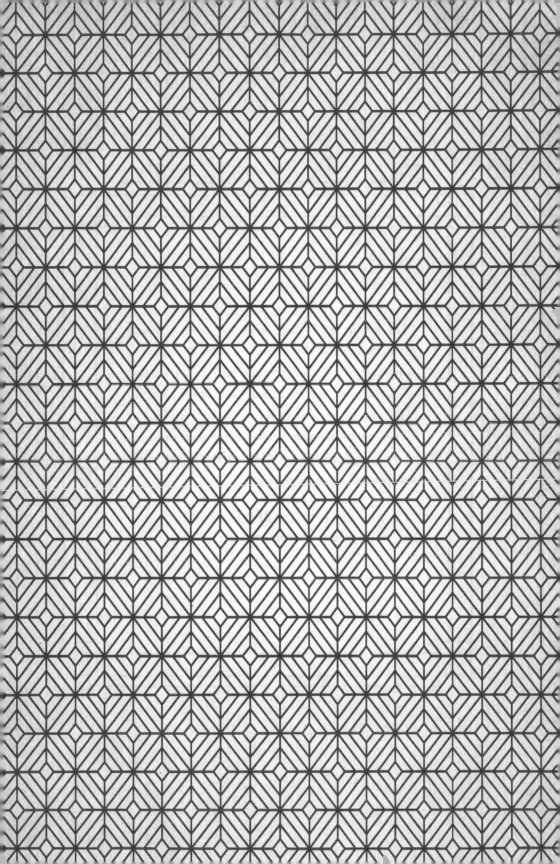

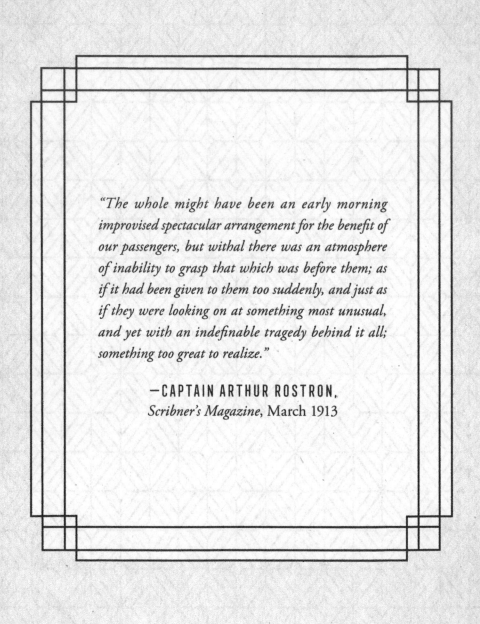

"*The whole might have been an early morning improvised spectacular arrangement for the benefit of our passengers, but withal there was an atmosphere of inability to grasp that which was before them; as if it had been given to them too suddenly, and just as if they were looking on at something most unusual, and yet with an indefinable tragedy behind it all; something too great to realize.*"

—CAPTAIN ARTHUR ROSTRON,
Scribner's Magazine, March 1913

CHAPTER 15

"A ship, sir. We all saw it."

"What?" Arthur did not dare ask his first officer to repeat the statement, but it was an inopportune time to be distracted from the work at hand.

Dean nodded his certainty, clasping his hands behind his back. "A steamer, I'd think. Large one, it seems."

Arthur stared for a long moment at his first officer. "Do we know of any ships in the vicinity?"

"No, sir. Not a one."

The notion was a strange one. Any ship in the vicinity must have heard of the disaster and certainly would have made contact with *Carpathia* if she had any intention of assisting her in the rescue.

And yet . . .

"Pay it little mind," he instructed. "We have other matters to see to. If she's near enough, Cottam will communicate with her."

"Yes, Captain."

Arthur turned toward the bridge, then stopped, glancing back at Dean. "Make note of her appearance and bearing, though."

Dean nodded. "Aye, sir."

After Dean had gone back to work, Arthur slowly retraced his steps closer to the deck. He needed to see for himself how their situation was developing as well as the state of his new passengers. He wondered how much he should hope and where his expectations ought to lie. He kept himself as hidden as he could from his position just inside the bridge, his responsibilities there needing his presence of body, if not mind.

But what he wouldn't give to be pulling those poor souls from the boats himself.

Watching the deck was almost overwhelming. Passengers sat on tables, having their wounds tended. Children with tearstains on their cheeks were being comforted by stewardesses; a few of the youngest ones began to smile. Two confused, wide-eyed boys in particular stood alone, unwilling to approach the kind stewardess who tried to speak with them.

Other passengers laid on the deck itself, covered with blankets. Some were shaking wildly, others eerily still. Stewardesses hurried up and down the rows of them, feeding soup to passengers too weak to eat on their own. Other sturdier passengers had their hands cupped around steaming mugs.

On one of the gangways, the body of an oarsman was lifted onto the deck. His skin was the color of the growlers and bergs they had steamed past, his eyes closed as if in sleep, the utter lifelessness of his frame haunting to witness. The sounds on the deck faded the moment he was set down, and then were silenced completely when another lifeless body was slowly brought up and put beside him.

Many eyes were fixed on the two bodies, and Arthur saw the light of hope beginning to fade in several of those watching eyes, even as the work resumed to bring aboard more of the living.

His own hope was in turmoil.

Arthur's attention was caught by a man standing by the gangways, his fingers drumming on the ship's rail, his damp hair streaked with ice. He brushed off any attempt by the stewards or stewardesses to take nourishment or move into the medical quarters. He only watched as the ship neared the next lifeboat, his eyes fixed on each passenger who would shortly come aboard.

Then suddenly, the man gripped the side of the ship, his knees buckling. "Margaret!" he called out, waving madly. "Margaret! It's me—it's Billy!"

The woman was not yet visible, but there was no mistaking the emotional response that lit the air, soon followed by a much younger voice calling back in reply.

"Clara!" the man exclaimed, his hoarse voice breaking with joy. "Hello, my Clara girl!"

He moved aside slightly as a few seamen came to the gangway ready to throw lines and begin bringing the boat aboard.

Yet the man became more frantic, still searching for something. Or someone. "Where's my boy?" he finally asked, his voice lower.

Clear as the night sky, a voice brightly chimed in, "Here I am, Father!"

Arthur could barely breathe as the man he was watching grinned, then he leaned heavily against the ship, lowering his head, shoulders quietly shaking.

A pained whimper drew Arthur's attention away from the joyous reunion. A woman was scanning the faces of those around her, eyes wide and unfocused. Her hair was loosely bound and would soon lose its hold completely. The babe in her arms screamed, inconsolable despite her weak attempts at bouncing and soothing her. Two other children clung to her skirts, their faces streaked with tears, swaying with fatigue where they stood. The woman bit her lip, looking around anxiously.

"Have you seen Edith? Or Robbie? Sarah?" she asked of no one in particular, her voice trembling.

Seeing her rising distress, a nearby stewardess came to her with a warm smile. "Who are you looking for, ma'am? Perhaps I can help."

The woman looked at her, blinking slowly. "I only have three of my children here."

The stewardess instantly pressed her hand to the woman's back and rubbed slowly, up and down. "How many are missing, ma'am?"

For a moment, the woman only stared at the stewardess. Then her face crumpled, and she swayed into her, a wracking sob escaping her frame. "Seven. I'm missing seven of my babies."

Eyes wide, the stewardess slipped her arm completely about the woman, her face tight in an attempt to not react further. She led the woman and her children from the main area of the deck.

Arthur knew it was unlikely they were going to find those seven children.

He turned back to the bridge, tension rising in his chest, constricting his throat, dampening his eyes as thoughts of Ethel and the children raced through his mind.

"How many more boats?" he asked the helmsman.

"A fair few, sir."

He nodded. "Keep her steady. I'll just . . . I'm . . . I'll return shortly."

Without another word, he left the bridge, moving toward the chart room, swallowing repeatedly. He shouldn't have watched the deck, shouldn't have let his curiosity cloud his judgment.

He leaned against the door and gasped a choked, dry sob, though the dampness in his eyes had somehow vanished. So many people had suffered that night, had witnessed suffering, yet some were finding their families. Others were not, and there was neither rhyme nor reason to any of it.

How could a woman with ten children have only three by her side? Were the other children somewhere in the frigid waters around them? Or had one or two been fortunate enough to be stowed in the medical wing or perhaps still in one of the remaining four or five lifeboats?

What of the two boys he had seen standing alone, hands holding tight to each other, no adult nearby to care for them? Had they lost both parents? One parent? A sister, aunt, or nanny?

How many of his new passengers had traveled alone, and thus were whole yet forever changed? How many were now alone when only hours ago they had been surrounded by loved ones?

He shouldn't have viewed the deck. He should not have allowed the situation to become one of emotions rather than numbers. There were more lives to save, and he would soon have to make difficult decisions that weighed the safety and welfare of others above his own feelings. Yet his own feelings were in chaos, and until the boats were up, he would have no new tasks to occupy his mind.

Shaking his head, he strode out of the chart room and down toward the Marconi room.

Harold Cottam sat at his table, headset in place, listening carefully. "Cottam."

Looking up, the lad slid his headset off. "Captain. I've no new information for you. I'm picking up bits from other ships on their way to us, but so far, none have—"

"Some of the men believe they saw a ship on the horizon," Arthur told him brusquely. "Heard anything?"

Cottam's brow furrowed as he stared at him. "No, sir. Are they certain?"

Arthur nodded once. "I believe a few passengers are also convinced they saw one."

Cottam looked at his radio, frowning in confusion. He shook his head, his expression clearing. "If there is a ship that close, sir, she isn't making herself known. And she isn't responding to my calls."

Silence filled the space between them, and Arthur looked toward the position of the rumored vessel, as though he could see through the walls of his ship. He knew well the sea could play tricks on a man, and water in early light could do the same, but for so many to have seen the same thing?

It was uncanny, and now was not a time for such things.

"Keep me apprised, Cottam," Arthur said quietly, nodding in approval.

"Aye, sir." Cottam replaced his headset and leaned forward, listening closely once more.

Arthur turned with a heavy sigh and made his way back to the bridge, steeling his emotions for both his own sanity and the morale of his crew.

"Captain!"

He glanced over his shoulder, fighting a frown at the sight of the man almost chasing him. The tall, lanky frame, the round, dark eyes, and the speculative look brought the name to mind shortly. "Hurd, isn't it?"

"Yes, sir, Carlos Hurd." The man jogged up to him, full of focused energy. "Sir, the *Titanic* is sunk?"

Arthur stopped and stared at the man. "So it would seem."

"And all aboard her were lost?" he asked immediately.

"Not if the souls being brought aboard represent anything," Arthur grunted.

"Why do you think such a disaster has happened?" Mr. Hurd asked him. "Was Captain Smith a fool for taking on such a ship? Was the route too dangerous with the ice? Would you have chosen differently?"

Arthur barely restrained a growl and stepped closer to the man. "Mr. Hurd, my task at present is to save the souls who can be saved and ensure they are tended to and cared for. When that is completed, my officers and I will decide the best course of action to take as our next step. At no point in time will any of us be speculating on reasons, assigning blame, or maligning anyone or anything associated with *Titanic* and those who were lost aboard her.

"And if I hear of you doing anything that jeopardizes the comfort, safety, and well-being of any of my passengers, I will see that you are personally escorted by the master-at-arms at all times for the remainder of this voyage. Do I make myself clear?"

Mr. Hurd glowered, clearly unused to being told what to do, and he nodded once, his jaw tight.

"Good." Arthur took a step, then looked at Hurd again. "And you might consider adopting a more somber demeanor while you scurry about for your story. Opportunity for you has come by way of a nightmarish catastrophe for them. Kindly remember that." He dipped his chin and moved toward the bridge, not particularly caring if the newspaperman followed.

His task was quite clear to him now, and he had never been more determined to accomplish it.

"Ah, Captain," Rees greeted as he returned to the bridge. "All well?"

Arthur inclined his head as he took up his position near the helmsman. "Yes, Rees. As well as can be expected. Let us see to these remaining boats."

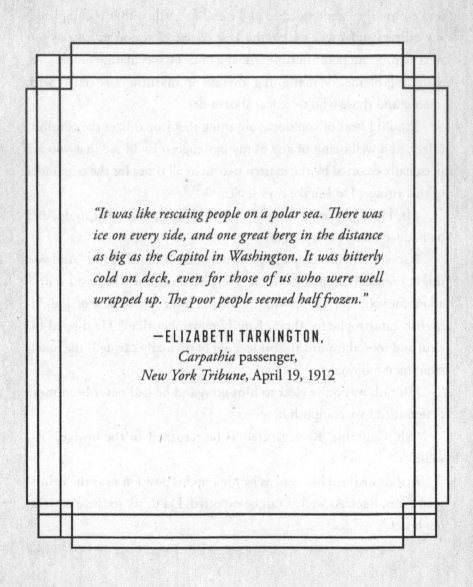

"It was like rescuing people on a polar sea. There was ice on every side, and one great berg in the distance as big as the Capitol in Washington. It was bitterly cold on deck, even for those of us who were well wrapped up. The poor people seemed half frozen."

—ELIZABETH TARKINGTON,
Carpathia passenger,
New York Tribune, April 19, 1912

CHAPTER 16

LIFEBOAT 13 · APRIL 15, 1912 · 7:00 AM

"Don't cry now—you've still got to climb up."

Kate managed a laugh at Julia's words, but the statement was remarkably true. Her legs ached something fierce, and she hadn't even started to climb yet. Soon it would be her turn to climb the ladder to board the ship using limbs that somehow felt both pain and numbness at the same time. She had watched as a few of the other ladies had been lifted up in some sort of pulley system, and she thought, for a moment, that the same would need to be done for her.

But she had no desire to have such a fuss be made for her.

She only wanted to be safely aboard the ship, wrapped in a blanket, and given a bowl of broth. She wanted to find the people she had met aboard *Titanic*. The other Kate Connolly, and the two Katies she had been with. Both of the Martins, who had facilitated her getting to a lifeboat. She wanted to see the woman she'd encouraged to wear a life belt and her children.

Beyond that, she would not hope for anything.

It was unfathomable that she had ever known anything other than this cold. There was a gaping hollowness at her core that she dared not consider too closely.

She was not prone to overwhelming despair, but spending hours freezing on the water while others died all around her had hollowed her, possibly for good.

"All right, lads," someone from the ship called. "Hold her steady. Which boat is this?"

"Thirteen," one of the men in the lifeboat answered.

A smiling face peered over the edge at them. "Welcome to *Carpathia*! Who's first?"

A young Swedish girl started toward the ladder, and she struggled her way up, several seamen reaching for her hands, steadying the ladder, and seeing to her safety.

Others from the boat began to make their way up, and Kate watched it all as if from a very great and safe distance.

Margit was swung up in a mail sack and easily caught by a strong crewman; he took a brief moment to hold the child close before handing her off to a stewardess. The woman they had pulled from the water was carefully hauled up to the *Carpathia*'s deck in a canvas sling. An older woman was raised up in the same manner and half crumpled as she reached the deck. Two crewmen took her arms and helped her away. Another woman was swung up to the deck.

"Careful, fellows," a crewman called out. "She's a lightweight!"

Lighthearted laughter broke out, but the sound grated against the silence that seemed to emanate from everything and everyone else. So out of place after that night, so foreign to Kate's ears.

Yet were the men of the ship not rescuing them all? Seeing to their care? Could they not also see to the brightening of their souls and lightening of their burdens along the way?

"Kate, let's go," Mary Mac urged, prodding her fingers into Kate's back.

Kate nodded and moved to the ladder, forcing her fingers to open enough to grab the rough, damp ropes, then tighten around them. She pulled herself onto the first rung. The ladder felt unsteady, though it was anchored by the men at the top and the kind crewmen from boat thirteen at the base. Still, it was the only way forward unless she wished to be hauled up in a canvas sling, and the thought of that mortified her.

She pulled herself up, forcing her breathing to calm as she slowly ascended. She found the attempt was smoother if she struggled less and instead focused on breathing calmly, on moving one hand at a time, at raising one leg, then the other. But oh, how her arms and fingers ached!

Each turn at gripping the rope made her want to cry out in pain, and the action of pulling herself up burned all the way into her body. Her legs had little enough strength in them and were stiff from hours of sitting without moving. The ladder of rope seemed endless to her, extending far beyond what she was capable of, and her weary body protested with each subsequent motion she made.

"There you are, miss," a seaman above her called, reaching out a hand. "Come on, a bit farther."

His voice was encouraging, yet the distance he wanted Kate to cross seemed impossible.

Exhaling, Kate pulled herself up one more rung, then another, until she could reach up and put her hand in his. The warmth of his skin stole her breath, the strength in his grip the most comforting thing she'd known in an age. This was safety, and the sensation brought tears to her eyes.

Another set of hands took her opposite arm, and she was pulled aboard with more ease than a feather carried on the wind. Her feet settled on the deck, and the firmness of it ricocheted up her legs until her entire frame shook with relief.

"This way, miss," a kindly, fair-haired stewardess said, smiling and wrapping a warm blanket around her. "Come see the purser first, and we'll get you settled. You'll have to remain on deck a little while, but we are preparing beds for all."

She steered Kate past other blanket-shrouded figures being tended to by other stewardesses and stewards, the crew of the ship calling to each other as they worked with the ropes to lower their own lifeboats to assist others, and a young, dark-haired, finely dressed woman who stared at nothing and waved off all attention.

"Who's that?" Kate asked her stewardess quietly.

The woman spoke softly. "Mrs. Astor. She and Mr. Astor are some of the wealthiest passengers. But he hasn't come aboard yet, and she's expecting."

Kate swallowed hard at the implication and looked away. They continued toward a tall, thin man with an equally trim mustache.

The purser looked at her expectantly, paper in hand, his smile gentle. "Your name, miss?"

Kate shivered without warning. "Catherine Connolly."

"And your class on *Titanic*?"

"Third."

He jotted it down, smiling at her again. "Thank you, miss. Welcome aboard the *Carpathia*."

It was a strange thing to say, well-meant as it was. To be greeted as warmly as though she had chosen to sail on the *Carpathia*, as though she had paid for a ticket on her, sailing on her route to some far-off destination rather than being pulled from the sea by her.

Welcome to *Carpathia*, indeed.

The stewardess shepherded her off to a part of the deck where other survivors sat wrapped in blankets and coats. Every face wore the same blank expression, devoid of emotion, sensation, or thought.

Kate was situated near the rest, and soon her friends were wrapped in blankets and settled beside her. None of them said a word, but they huddled close, warmth and comfort a necessity now more than ever.

Time ceased to have meaning while they sat there.

More and more survivors came aboard and found themselves immediately in the care of a steward or crewman. A few were taken for medical treatment, some sat along the deck as Kate and her friends did, while others paced, waiting for other passengers in other lifeboats to be picked up, frantic for any news of family members or friends. Hope was still alive on the *Carpathia*, but only for some.

A brief commotion started as a wealthy, well-dressed man came aboard, sighing deeply. He carried a small dog in his arms and looked as though he might have been boarding the ship in broad daylight from any port in the world for a pleasure cruise for all the distress he showed. He was followed by a stuffy woman in ostentatious finery—no doubt his wife—and a dragoman behind them both. Nothing about the couple seemed perturbed, distressed, or particularly bothered.

The man smiled as if nothing were amiss and brightened further at seeing a familiar face. He strode toward one of *Carpathia*'s passengers who was tending to their new companions.

"Ah, Louis!" he greeted jovially. "How do you keep yourself looking so young?"

His friend looked at him in silent astonishment.

Those around the pair had the same expression.

A steward approached them. "Mr. Harper, please, will you come to the dining saloon?"

Mr. Harper nodded, clearly finding it a capital idea. "Ah, yes, yes . . . I could use a good brandy." He collected his wife and dragoman, and the entourage moved on, leaving disbelieving looks in their wake.

"No! No! Oh, no, no, no . . ."

Kate looked across the deck to see a young woman crumple into a heap, sobbing uncontrollably.

"Noooo!" another cried, the sound haunting. "No, no!" An older woman cried beside her, bending low to soothe her. A pair of stewards helped the first sobbing woman to her feet, her cries carrying through the still night as if they'd been ripped from her soul. Suddenly she swooned, fainting into the arms of one of the stewards. She was quickly carried away, but the effect of her display left its mark across the faces of the others on the deck.

"Kate," Mary-from-Clare whispered, lifting her head from her shoulder. "Look!"

Two young boys stood side by side in pajamas, blankets around them, dazed but not seemingly upset by what was happening around them. They were nearly the same size, and neither could have been even five years of age.

A stewardess crouched in front of them. "Hello, lads. Who are you looking for?"

The taller of the two boys said something in French, his voice young and high.

The stewardess frowned. "Sorry, love, do you speak English?"

The boy looked back at her, clinging to his blanket.

The stewardess bit her lip, glancing around the deck. "Does anybody speak French?"

A neatly dressed young woman, shivering despite being wrapped tightly in a blanket, came forward. "I do. Margaret Hays." She turned to the boys and smiled. "Bonjour, je m'appelle Margaret. Qui cherches-tu?"

The tall boy peered up at her, clearly relieved at hearing his native tongue. "Notre papa. Nous étions sur le navire avec lui, et il nous a mis dans les petits bateaux."

Miss Hays's face tightened, and Kate saw her swallow. "Et ta maman?"

"Elle n'est pas venue avec nous. Papa nous emmène en Amérique."

The stewardess looked to Miss Hays for a translation.

"They're looking for their father," Miss Hays told her, eyes wide. "He was taking them to America. Their mother did not accompany them."

The stewardess bit her lip again. "The boats are almost all in, miss. If he's not aboard one of the last ones . . ."

The silence was telling, and Kate gripped Mary's hand, suddenly overcome with emotion for the sweet-faced boys who were suddenly fatherless.

Miss Hays turned back to the boys, forcing a cheery smile. "Pourquoi ne restez-vous pas avec moi? Nous allons chercher de la nourriture et essayer de retrouver votre papa dans peu de temps."

The boys nodded in awkward unison, taking her hands and letting her lead them from the deck.

"Kate? Kate Connolly?"

Kate perked up, her heart leaping at the thought of someone, anyone, on this ship looking for her. "Yes?"

"I heard there was a Kate Connolly here!" the voice continued to cry out, breaking a little.

"Here!" Kate called out louder, her voice rough. The attempt increased the scratching pain in her throat.

A woman wrapped in a rough blanket appeared and stared at Kate with wide eyes.

It took a moment, but Kate recognized the woman's fair hair and green eyes. "You're one of the Katies from Tipperary."

Katie nodded, but her eyes filled with tears. "Katie McCarthy. I thought . . . I thought . . ."

Kate's chest tightened, and her throat almost immediately clogged. "You thought I was *your* Kate Connolly."

Katie brushed away the tears sliding down her cheeks. "I cannot find any of my friends. I asked the purser, and he said Catherine Connolly was on board, but—"

Kate struggled to her feet and moved to hug Katie, who pulled her close, crying harder. "I'm sorry," Kate whispered, her tears falling on the rough blanket. "I'm so sorry I'm not your Kate."

Katie sniffled and pulled back. "I am so glad you're alive though." She looked around at the group, smiling through her streaming tears. "All of you. So pleased."

The tightness in Kate's chest squeezed further as a panicked realization settled inside her. "The other Kate . . . her family . . ." She shook her head. "There will be such confusion if they discover I'm alive and their Kate isn't. They'll wish me dead!"

"No one will wish you dead," Katie assured her as she squeezed her hands. "Not a soul."

Kate hiccupped a cry and covered her mouth with a hand. She tried not to think of the family seeing her name on a list of survivors, of the hope they would feel, only to have to face the terrible truth.

"Ach, Kate," Julia whimpered from behind her. "No."

Katie hugged her tight. "There's room in this world for as many Kate Connollys as the Lord sees fit." She shuddered against her, then pulled back again, wiping her eyes. "And I already miss mine terribly. Can I sit with you girls awhile?"

They all nodded and sat down together, adopting Katie McCarthy into their midst and wrapping her in the same comfort and warmth they had been offering each other.

Together they sat and waited, feeling the hope of the entire deck begin to diminish.

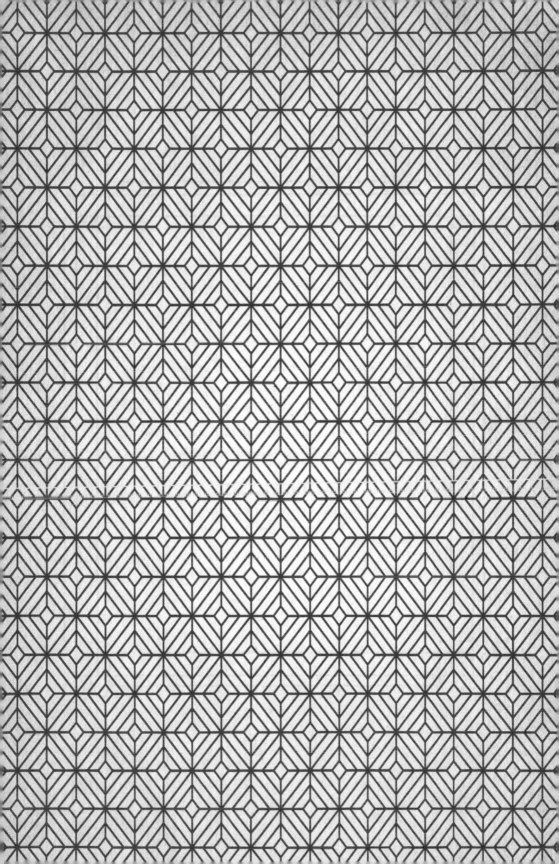

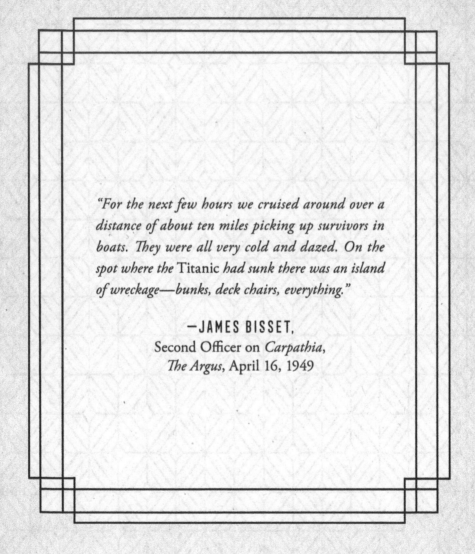

"For the next few hours we cruised around over a distance of about ten miles picking up survivors in boats. They were all very cold and dazed. On the spot where the Titanic *had sunk there was an island of wreckage—bunks, deck chairs, everything."*

—JAMES BISSET,
Second Officer on *Carpathia*,
The Argus, April 16, 1949

CHAPTER 17

Arthur stepped out onto the deck as the last lifeboat was reached, watching as the lines were dropped down.

"Come on, help me fix her," one of the men in the lifeboat called.

He couldn't see who had said it, but a few moments later, a young man appeared from the rope ladder. Then another and another.

"We'll need a lift!" the first man called up, still in the lifeboat.

"Righto, give us a second," one of Arthur's men replied.

Another passenger boarded, and Arthur watched as his first officer peered over the side of the ship with a grin. "Hullo, Lights! What are you doing down there?"

Arthur surmised "Lights" was a nickname for Dean's friend Charles Lightoller, which meant a high-ranking officer from *Titanic* had survived and would shortly be aboard.

Marvelous. Perhaps he might shed some light on the course they should take and how best to care for the rescued passengers.

Provided Officer Lightoller felt well enough to do anything at all.

Another young passenger was helped aboard from the ladder, wide-eyed with shock. Arthur shook his head in disbelief at the condition of the young man's feet. He still wore his boots, but the things were mangled and coated in ice, suctioned to his legs until they no longer resembled feet or footwear at all. It was astounding he had made it up the ladder.

The lad was hardly conscious, nodding off into the arms of his rescuers. He was rushed off the deck, though the sight of him was enough to distress several of the ladies nearby.

Arthur surveyed the passengers and crew on deck, watching the stewards and stewardesses help the last passengers to unload. Some of *Carpathia*'s passengers were helping too, taking blankets from the stewards and wrapping some of the women and many of the children in them. Even Mrs. Ogden was sitting nearby, holding hands with an older woman who was anxiously watching the unloading process.

Officer Lightoller came aboard from the lifeboat and heaved a sigh of relief. He embraced Dean tightly, their brief conversation inaudible to Arthur, then he was escorted from the deck by one of the stewards.

Arthur turned back for the bridge, his heart torn between the relief he felt at having recovered so many survivors and the heavy realization of how many had been lost.

The magnitude of this disaster would be devastating, and the fallout from it possibly worse, but he could not consider it now. Now, he had people to watch over and deliver to safety.

But where was that, exactly?

Dean came to the bridge, standing at attention before Arthur. "All the lifeboats are aboard now, sir. Our lookouts cannot see any more in the area."

Arthur nodded. "And the time?"

"Nine o'clock, sir."

"Very good, First Officer." Arthur swallowed, thinking quickly. "Have Purser Brown see me when he has a final count."

Dean nodded. "Yes, sir," he replied before moving back out onto the deck.

Arthur followed slowly, hovering near the deck as his first officer was swarmed by *Titanic*'s anxious passengers. They'd likely seen the crew drawing in the equipment and *Carpathia*'s lifeboats, and not preparing to swing any of it out again, and, after a morning of constant, urgent activity, that would be suspicious.

"Ladies and gentlemen," Dean intoned solemnly, "it is my duty to inform you that all of the lifeboats have now been brought aboard. There are no others waiting for us, and all known survivors have been retrieved."

A woman near Dean blinked, not comprehending. "Wh-what do you mean, all the boats are in?"

"It can't be true!" another cried out. "My husband—"

"No! No, my sister isn't aboard yet!"

Dean looked around at them all, struggling for words, his expression bordering on the raw. "I'm sorry, ladies. There are no more boats." He bowed his head. "I'm so sorry," he added, his voice breaking, before he shuffled off to see to other details.

The women stared after him in horror, their faces etched with despair.

Arthur continued to watch the people as the murmured message spread across the deck, and then a heartrending cry came up from the back. Grief passed like a wave over the passengers on deck, some sinking to the ground, some leaning against walls, and some simply bursting into tears. Others were shocked into stillness, looking completely unaware of the emotion around them.

More of *Carpathia*'s original passengers, who had mostly been spectators to this point, moved to help and comfort the people around them.

Arthur knew he shouldn't watch this; he needed to maintain a respectful distance if he wished to keep his mind clear and make the necessary decisions. There was the safety and well-being of his newly arrived passengers to consider, along with managing the supplies on the ship that would be used to care for all of his passengers and crew. He was determined to do right by the victims and their families.

And then there would be the enquiries they would receive.

Heavens, they would be utterly bombarded by establishments and the press, begging for details, for names, for anything they could get their hands on.

And he already had one dedicated newspaperman aboard.

Arthur would need to tread carefully in this as well as in everything else.

There was simply too much to be considered. Too many questions and too few answers.

The long, sleepless night was taking its toll, and his head was throbbing.

"Take some refreshment, Helmsman," Arthur gently ordered the young man behind the wheel. "It'll be a bit before we're off again."

"Aye, sir." The lad moved out of the bridge at a brisk clip, driven by hunger, need, or curiosity—or a combination of all three.

Purser Brown entered the bridge and approached Arthur. The man looked as worn out as Arthur felt. His eyes were more lined, his attire less tidy, his mouth set. He nodded his head in a salute.

"I have the final count, Captain," he said, his voice hoarse.

Arthur exhaled and crossed to him, clasping his hands behind his back in expectation. "Excellent, Brown. And?"

"Three men came aboard already dead, sir," Brown told him

simply, little to no emotion displayed on his features. "Another one, I am told, will not be with us much longer."

That was a sobering thought indeed. For a man to be rescued, either by being pulled into a lifeboat or safely lowered in one, only to still die upon the sea—the perspective of such a thing was not lost on him.

Arthur nodded soberly. "And the living?"

Purser Brown did not so much as blink. "Seven hundred and five, sir."

Arthur stared at him as the numbers raced around in his mind. "Seven hundred and five?" he repeated, barely comprehending. "That's it?"

Brown swallowed hard. "Yes, sir."

It could not be. It could *not* be. Surely, they had recovered more than that. They had come to the *Titanic*'s aid as quickly as possible. Surely, they had not been so late as to have lost—

Arthur shook his head. "That means . . . Brown, that's at least fifteen hundred passengers lost."

Brown nodded once. "Yes, sir. *Titanic* reported twenty-four hundred aboard."

Arthur opened his mouth to say something, anything, but words failed him. Thought failed him. Sense and dignity failed him. He brought a hand to his mouth and turned away. He looked out at the sea, now bright with morning light, searching the area as though he would somehow see another collection of lifeboats bearing more souls to save.

But there was nothing.

Seven hundred and five. Such a painfully small number compared to what it should have been. He took a moment to send a short, fervent prayer to the heavens, then faced his head purser again. He curled his hands into fists, ignoring the sharp pain of his fingernails digging into his palm.

"Brown, would you take an inventory of food and linens, please? We need to know where we stand."

"Yes, sir," came the response, the tone matching Arthur's exactly.

For all the miracles that had transpired thus far to get them here, they had saved less than a third of *Titanic*'s passengers.

He could not be unaffected by such a thing.

Once alone on the bridge, Arthur lowered his head and allowed himself to feel the events of the night and the morning in all its crushing awfulness. He reached out, gripping the railing before him, trying to steady himself so his knees would not buckle.

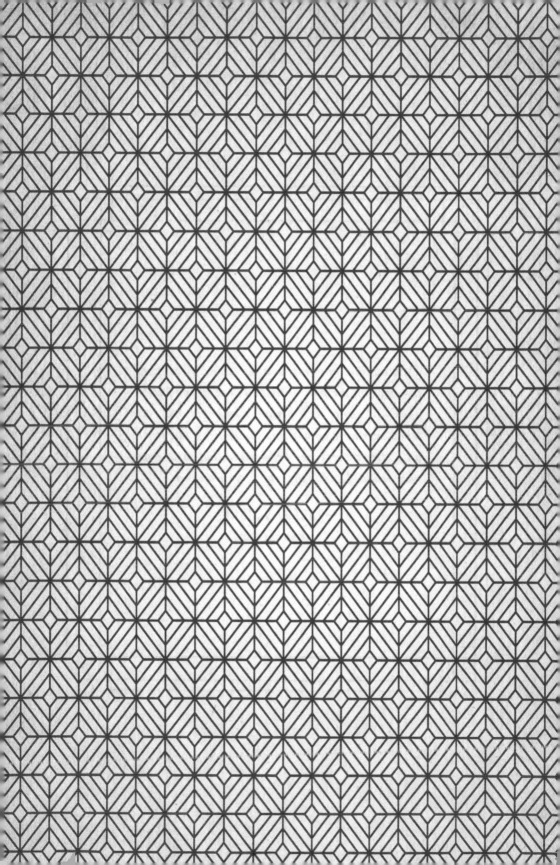

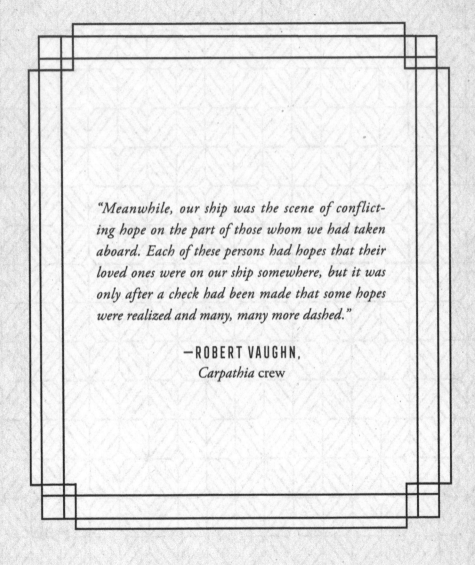

"*Meanwhile, our ship was the scene of conflicting hope on the part of those whom we had taken aboard. Each of these persons had hopes that their loved ones were on our ship somewhere, but it was only after a check had been made that some hopes were realized and many, many more dashed.*"

—ROBERT VAUGHN,
Carpathia crew

CHAPTER 18

"Julia, you do not look well at all."

Julia looked at Mary Mac, blinking her swollen, reddened eyes, wisps of her red hair darting about in the cold wind. "I do not feel well at all."

The girls all looked at each other, used to Julia's witty retorts more than an honest answer. That alone relayed the severity of the situation.

Katie McCarthy put her hand on Julia's brow. "Dear girl, you are burning with fever. Let me take you to the doctor—get you some proper tending."

Julia did not protest and allowed Katie to help her stand. "It might be best." With a little wave to her friends, Julia walked away, secured by Katie's arm about her back.

"I hope she's all right," Mary-from-Clare murmured as she and Mary Mac scooted closer to Kate. Though the sun was warming, the day was brisk, and their bodies seemed to still hold the cold from the night and early morning in a way that any brush of wind lanced through them with an icy cruelty.

Kate wondered if it would be impolite to ask for another blanket.

She watched the people on the deck, the cries and wails having softened into a hum of whimpering and the occasional sniffle of tears.

Her own emotions were worn raw, and she had only recent friends to mourn. They'd not seen the other Kate Connolly, nor the third Katie. No sight of Martin McMahon or Martin Gallagher, though they had seen his sweetheart, Margaret, being carried to medical in a distraught state.

So many new friends and faces, and so many of them gone.

A steward approached a young woman holding a sleeping infant in her arms.

"May I get your name, miss?" he asked.

The woman looked up, confused. "Have you seen the Allisons? Mr. and Mrs. Allison? From Montreal? I'm their nursemaid, and this is their baby . . . I can't . . ."

The steward nodded immediately. "Come with me, miss, and we'll see if they've checked in with any of the pursers."

She followed him, holding the baby closer.

Was that baby now an orphan? Were there other relations to care for it? Would the nursemaid continue to care for it while aboard, or would she leave the child to others now that her employers were gone?

Kate's attention was drawn to an older man sitting nearby, dressed in a military uniform, who simply stared at his battered and blistered hands without a word to anyone. A woman, presumably his wife, was leaning heavily against him.

A stewardess approached them and indicated his hands. "Have you had those looked at, Colonel?"

He shook his head slowly. "No, my dear. Perhaps later."

"Oh, but—"

He raised his hand, palm out, showing the tortured skin to her. "From the oars, you see. I rowed all night." He looked at his hands again, seeming both dazed and transfixed by them. "All night, I rowed . . ."

The stewardess smiled sadly and moved away.

Another stewardess offered a tray of steaming drinks to a pair of ladies nearby. "Something to warm you, dears?"

They both shook their heads and waved her off, taking each other's hands.

"Go away," one of them said weakly. "Please. We've just seen our husbands drown."

The stewardess paused, her expression torn, but then she nodded and moved away, her eyes shining with tears.

"Come, come, lads! We must have a photo of all of us that were in boat one!"

A booming, authoritative voice broke through the general murmur of the deck, and it was impossible to not look in that direction.

An overdressed couple stood on the deck, a little dog in the lady's arms, with both a stoic-faced younger woman and a man of Arabic descent nearby.

The older gentleman waved his arms at some *Titanic* officers. "Come, lads! We must have a picture."

Kate, and several others on deck, stared at the group, shocked and disgusted by the superior attitudes of people who clearly shared none of the heartache and despair so prevalent in the rest of them.

"Who is that?" Mary Mac asked someone nearby, her distaste evident.

"Sir and Lady Duff-Gordon," came the bitter reply. "They had their own lifeboat with their secretary, their translator, and a few officers. Twelve in the lifeboat, and that is all."

Kate swallowed the taste of bile at such an injustice and watched in irritation as Sir Duff-Gordon continued to wave and shout. "Come on, we must commemorate this! Dr. McGhee, will you take the photo, sir?"

The doctor, who had emerged from the medical rooms to check on a few passengers, looked very much as though he would rather not be anywhere near the Duff-Gordons, but he went to the group anyway and took the camera.

"You must get a good picture of my sweet Sophie here," Lady Duff-Gordon crooned, stroking her dog. "And Miss Francatelli must stand here beside me. Poor dear lost a beautiful nightdress in the accident."

Her husband tutted. "Such a pity, my dear."

"Fix your mustache, Cosmo," she instructed briskly.

Dr. McGhee waited for the seven crewmen to gather round, then sighed. Nearly everyone on deck was staring, and he made no secret about his feelings. "Now, smile, everyone!" he muttered dryly as he snapped the picture.

They did so, and the doctor handed the camera back without a word, leaving the group before any other requests could be made.

Kate fervently hoped the picture would be dreadful, blurred, and utterly ruined.

"Marvelous," Sir Duff-Gordon said to their group. "Simply marvelous. Thank you, lads."

Scoffing to herself, Kate looked away, only to see a middle-aged man in an officer's uniform watching the idiotic scene with a dubious expression. All officers seemed the same to her, one uniform identical to another, but he seemed more alert and less frozen than others, so perhaps he was from the *Carpathia* and not the *Titanic*. He cut a fine figure, tall and stately, his hair the color of aged wood.

Something about his attention to the passengers and the workings of the crew fascinated her. He didn't move about in any proud, striding fashion, had little to no airs about him, and yet seemed to see everything happening on this ship. More than that, he seemed to have complete command of the ship.

Could he be their captain?

He moved to an older, balding man in a dark shirt who was crouched, speaking with a mother and child not far from Kate and her friends.

"Reverend Father Anderson?" he said softly.

The reverend looked up, then murmured something to the mother before standing and coming over.

"Captain Rostron, sir," he replied with a smile, his fair eyes bright, a starched white collar at his throat.

Kate looked at the uniformed man again. So, he *was* the captain. How intriguing that he was out and about on the deck at present.

"I wonder, Father, if you might assist me," the captain inquired.

The reverend nodded. "Of course, Captain. In any way that I am able."

Captain Rostron bowed his head for just a moment. "I should like to have a brief religious service, if you are willing. Both a memorial and a thanksgiving for the *Titanic* passengers. And for us from *Carpathia* as well."

Kate's brows rose as she listened. A religious service?

Her heart warmed with hope. It felt right to express gratitude for having been saved and to offer a reverent pause to honor so many lives lost. Kate hoped that a moment to turn their hearts heavenward would be appreciated by all the passengers, no matter their faith.

She took great comfort in the thought that the captain of the *Carpathia* was a religious man.

Reverend Anderson seemed touched but not particularly surprised by the request. "A noble idea, Captain. I would be honored. We'll do so this afternoon in the First Class lounge, if It is available."

The captain nodded. "I will see that it is." He paused then, almost as though he needed to collect his thoughts. "We will also be burying some men at sea this afternoon. One of them was Catholic. Do you know if we have someone able to properly perform such a service for him?"

Unbidden, tears sprang into Kate's eyes. Being Catholic herself, she was touched by the captain's sensitive attention to detail and his desire to honor the faith of a stranger.

While being Catholic in Ireland could render her scorned, or even spat upon in some counties and towns, here it was both acknowledged and respected. Rather than hatred, there was honor. Instead of prejudice, there was tolerance.

She had never felt more privileged to be aboard a ship in her life.

Reverend Anderson, it seemed, was of a similar mind. "I am sure we do, sir. I will see to that as well. All will be performed with the utmost care and respect."

"Thank you, Father." The captain shook his hand, then turned and walked away, presumably back to his position on the bridge.

Kate tightened the blanket around her and closed her eyes on grateful tears.

"Hello, dears."

Kate opened her eyes and looked into the kind face of a stewardess.

"Can I take you ladies somewhere to rest?" she asked of their little group. "All of the available berths are full, but we have set up the library rather well."

Kate smiled up at her apologetic tone. "We'll take anything you can offer. Anything at all."

The stewardess smiled with relief and gestured for them to follow. "I cannot imagine any of you have a change of clothes," she said by way of conversation. "But we will need to have you out of those freezing things unless you've a desire to visit Dr. Lengyel. Some of our passengers have already begun collecting available items as donations, and they will be provided to you shortly."

"Oh, we couldn't possibly—" Mary Mac managed through chattering teeth.

"It does no good to protest, miss," the stewardess interrupted in a bright tone. "I understand the ladies of *Carpathia* are really quite insistent upon helping. I believe one or two have begun sewing some of the linens and blankets into makeshift garments as well. It won't be much, but at least it will be fresh and dry."

Kate nodded absently. She had been fortunate enough to have stayed dry during their escape, so it was of little matter. Mary, on the other hand, had spent a good deal of time trying to warm Helmina in their boat, and she would certainly need dry clothing soon or she might take ill.

Her thoughts turned to Julia, and she sighed as they wound deeper into the ship. It would be too cruel to survive the *Titanic* only to take ill aboard their rescue vessel. Would there be medicine enough to treat her if she was unwell? How many days were they from shore?

Where would they go?

There were so many questions, and she doubted Captain Rostron and his crew had many answers. How could they, when it had been a scant few hours since *Titanic* had disappeared beneath the surface of the water forever?

None of these questions were her responsibility, Kate realized with a slow exhale. She was safe, she was well, and she was whole. There were no decisions to be made at the moment, and no picture of strength to maintain.

She could be as dismal, morose, or weepy as she liked, and not a single person would think less of her for doing so.

Biting her lip, she swallowed a sob, only the faintest squeak of distress escaping her.

Mary Mac immediately put an arm around her waist, her own chin quivering, as they made their way to their new quarters on their new ship.

"The saddest moment of all, after the boat load had been landed on the deck, was to see the poor widows and sons and daughters whose family relations had been broken, standing at the rail, looking into the distance with hands outstretched trying in hope to see their loved ones. There were numerous sick persons on board, but the illness was not so much physical as it was mental agony."

—FRANK BLACKMARR,
Carpathia passenger, April 20, 1912

CHAPTER 19

Questions and answers. Answers and questions.

What was he to do now? The survivors were aboard, they were being cared for, and their identities were being noted. What next? How did Arthur best care for the living, as he could do no more for the dead?

Arthur shook his head as he headed back to the bridge, but paused as he passed Officer Barnish. "Barnish, have the *Titanic*'s boats all brought up and settled aboard, if possible. As many as we can."

His young officer nodded in quick deference. "Yes, Captain."

"Very good. I will be in the chart room."

Barnish frowned in confusion, his brow creasing. "Sir?"

Arthur allowed himself a bland smile. "At this moment, I'm not entirely sure of our destination, Barnish."

Realization dawned, and Barnish nodded. "Of course, sir."

Arthur nodded, clasping his hands behind his back, and continued on.

"Captain," Purser Brown broke in, coming to his side. "I have the numbers of supplies for you, sir."

"Very good," Arthur replied. "Walk with me to the chart room. What do you have?"

He listened intently as the purser began his list, though his mind still spun with the present concerns assailing him. Every item the purser mentioned registered in Arthur's mind, adding to the collection of details he needed to consider.

They entered the chart room, and Arthur began looking over the maps and charts, weighing his options even as he continued listening closely to the purser.

"Apart from what was used for extra bandages," Purser Brown said on an exhale, "Third Class has enough linen for the bunks, but none to spare for additional needs."

Arthur nodded slowly, then turned to look his purser in the eye. "Not enough now that we've doubled our passenger load. We cannot continue our course east. Italy will have to wait." He glanced down at the chart before him. "Make the passengers as comfortable as possible, Brown. I must chart a new course." He offered the purser a resigned smile.

Brown nodded, then left to see to his assignment. He passed a haggard-looking Harold Cottam as he exited, the two men nodding to each other as they passed.

Cottam stepped into the chart room, his steps dragging, his expression drawn, and his eyes red.

"Cottam," Arthur greeted, "what news?"

"The *Mount Temple* is approaching, Captain," Cottam said without emotion. "Anything you would like me to relay to her?"

Arthur lowered his eyes in thought, frowning as his mind sorted through possibilities and needs. "Yes. Please have them continue the search for survivors. We have all the boats, but there's no telling what else may be found."

"Yes, sir." Cottam stepped toward the door, then paused. "We won't see any other ships for some time. Nothing else is in range."

"Thank you, Cottam. Keep me informed, as usual. That will be all."

"Right, sir." He turned back for his office, rubbing at his eyes.

Arthur watched him go, his brow knitting in thought. The lad had not had a wink of sleep since Saturday night, and yet Arthur could not grant him leave to do so. He was the only one on board who could see to the radio, and with all that had happened and all that had changed, Arthur would need to rely on him every moment of the remainder of the journey.

Perhaps Arthur could find an hour or two tonight to grant the lad some rest.

But he had more to consider than his crew's sleep deprivation. He needed to decide on a destination.

He turned back to his charts. "If not east, we go west," he muttered to himself. "So where . . . ?"

His fingers traced over the maps, first along a route to Halifax. He jotted down numbers below the chart, then returned to it, his hands now flying along the route to New York and making similar notes.

He looked between the two cities, stewing over them in thought.

He had hundreds of additional women aboard, many new widows, and, from what he had seen, many were hysterical and in a bad state. He needed to get them the help they needed as soon as possible.

Halifax was the closest course, and he could get the ship there all right, but he needed better numbers as to the physical and mental state of his passengers before choosing that route. How many of the survivors were half dead, how many were injured, or how many were really sick?

Docking at Halifax would also mean a good number of *Titanic*'s passengers would need to make an additional railway journey in order to reach New York, as they had originally planned. It would be a miserable prospect for those poor souls to have more journeying ahead of them once they disembarked. And there was no telling what the weather in Halifax would be or what accommodations would be available to them.

Halifax also brought with it the possibility of coming across more ice, and traveling through more growlers or bergs could be harrowing for those who'd endured too much already. They would still have to face some ice just to continue west, but even a short reprieve from the sight would do them all some good.

There would be a delay choosing New York, but—

"Captain Rostron!"

Arthur looked toward the bridge, alarmed at the tone of his first officer, then moved quickly for the door.

Dean and Bisset pointed their binoculars at something in the distance, and Dean glanced up as Arthur appeared on the bridge. "The ship from before, sir. It's back and coming in."

He took the offered binoculars, frowning. "The *Mount Temple*? Cottom said she's the only ship in range at present."

"I don't think it's the *Mount Temple*, sir," Dean said with a shake of his head. He frowned as he looked out at the horizon.

Arthur paused, then turned to Bisset. "Flag her. See who she is."

Bisset moved out to the deck and exchanged the necessary flag signals. The others waited and watched for a response.

"It's the *Californian*, sir," Bisset said.

The *Californian*? What in the world was she doing in the vicinity, and why hadn't she made herself known before?

Arthur stepped forward, eyes narrowing on the faint view of the ship he had. "Do they have any survivors?"

Bisset relayed flag signals again, then reported her response. "No, sir."

If the ship had been close since earlier that morning, why had they not joined in the rescue efforts?

Arthur grunted in irritation. "Fine. Tell them we're on our way, and ask if they'll take one last look around."

"Yes, sir," Bisset answered, beginning the next series of signals.

"We can't have anyone left behind," Arthur murmured, more to himself than to either of his officers present.

"Sir," Bisset said slowly, once his signals were finished. "There are bodies still—"

Arthur shook his head at the implied suggestion. "These people have been through enough, Bisset. If there are other ships coming, they can recover the dead."

"But, sir, out of respect—"

"My concern, Officer Bisset," Arthur overrode firmly, but gently, "is for the living. I cannot act under any other guidance."

Bisset gave him a morose but knowing look. "People back home will not understand when they hear we've left them."

Arthur met his gaze steadily. "They were not here."

Chief Steward Hughes appeared on the bridge, looking uncertain. "Pardon me, Captain."

Arthur waved him over. "Yes, what is it?"

"It has just been brought to my attention, sir," Hughes said with some hesitation, "and I thought you should know, sir . . . Mr. Ismay is on board."

All of the men on the bridge stopped and looked at Hughes in disbelief.

Arthur stared for a long moment before he could make a reply. "Mr. Ismay? The managing director of the White Star Line?"

Hughes nodded. "Yes, sir."

What in the world was Arthur to do with this information? Captain Smith and more than a thousand others had drowned, but Mr. Ismay had survived and was aboard the *Carpathia*?

"Thank you, Hughes," Arthur eventually said. "Would you ask him to come see me?"

Hughes winced and averted his gaze. "I would, sir, but he refuses to leave the quarters we've given him."

One of the officers, possibly two, muttered under their breath.

Arthur, however, did not. "Then I will go to him. Take me to him, if you will."

Hughes nodded and turned from the bridge while Arthur followed. They wound their way to the staterooms, nodding at various stewards, stewardesses, and passengers hurrying this way and that to provide aid and comfort.

It occurred to Arthur that he could tell the *Titanic*'s passengers from *Carpathia*'s simply by looking in their eyes. Every one of the ill-fated ship's passengers held a lifetime of pain in theirs and would never be the same.

What would Mr. Ismay's eyes hold?

They reached the quarters, and Arthur would have known Ismay's room even without the assistance of the chief steward.

A sign had been posted on the door that read Don't Knock.

Arthur stared at the words for a moment, then, pointedly, knocked on the door before nodding at Hughes.

Hughes returned his nod, then left him to his task.

"Come," a dismal voice within called back.

Arthur pushed into the room.

The dark-haired, mustached Ismay sat on the bed of his cabin, appearing either at the end of a nervous break or on the verge of one. He sat perfectly upright in his posture, yet he seemed small in appearance. He barely acknowledged Arthur when he entered.

"Mr. Ismay, Captain Arthur Rostron. It's a pleasure to meet you."

Ismay nodded, but said nothing. He seemed to shake without actually moving.

Arthur waited for a response.

When it became clear he would not get one, he went on. "I was hoping to confer with you regarding our course of action now that we have all the survivors on board."

Ismay stared at nothing. And said nothing.

Arthur frowned and did his best not to sigh. "I considered Halifax, but there would be more ice possible if we go so far north. I worry about the effect the sight of more ice might have upon the passengers. What are your thoughts, sir?"

"Whatever you want is fine," Ismay replied faintly, not even looking at Arthur.

For a man who had been so determined to save himself from a watery grave, he did not seem to have strong opinions on anything else.

But perhaps spending hours on the water with the rest of the survivors had affected him in ways he had not anticipated.

Still, it was clear to Arthur that he was not going to receive any assistance or input from the now-broken man.

He exhaled roughly. "Well, if there's anything we can do for you . . ."

Ismay made no response.

With a sigh of unexpected pity, Arthur turned to go but stopped when he saw Cottam standing at the door.

"Pardon me, Captain," Cottam said, more alert now than he had been earlier. "First Officer Dean told me you were here."

Arthur was grateful for the distraction and did not mind showing it. "No trouble. What is it?"

"I've just been talking with *Olympic*, sir," Cottam told him. "She's heading this way, and she suggests that, when she arrives, the *Titanic* passengers be transferred to her."

A larger ship taking on his additional passengers would relieve the burden placed upon his ship and his crew, but after a brief moment of consideration, Arthur dismissed the notion with a shake of his head.

"Impossible. *Olympic* is the twin of *Titanic*. What does Captain Haddock think the sight of it will do to these poor passengers?" He looked at Ismay for confirmation or response of any kind. "What do you think, Mr. Ismay?"

Ismay shuddered and bent over, folding his arms around his midsection as though in pain. "I beg you, keep *Olympic* out of sight of the passengers."

If the man were to say only one thing in this bizarre interview between them, Arthur was grateful it was this.

He nodded. "I quite agree." He turned to face Cottam, finally satisfied with the conversation in some respect. "Politely decline Haddock's offer, and tell him our course is set for New York."

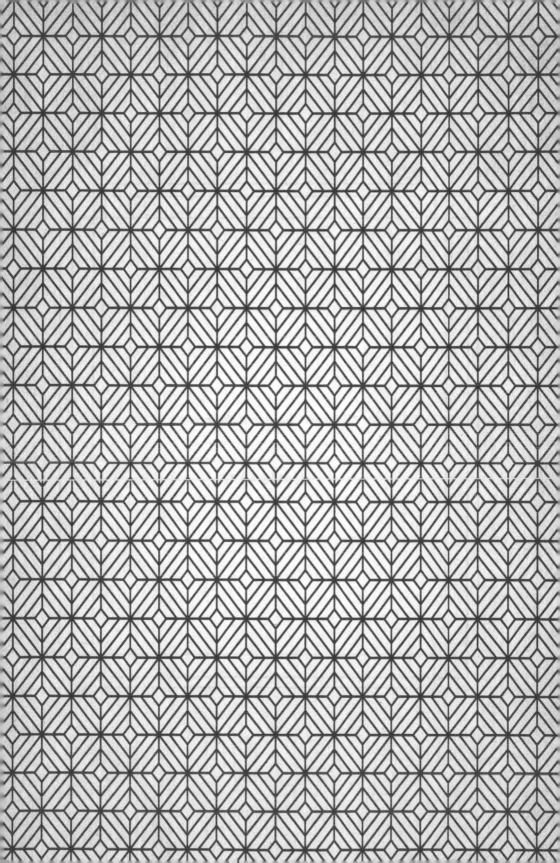

*"Who hath measured the waters
in the hollow of his hand."*

—ISAIAH 40:12

CHAPTER 20

The First Class saloon on the *Carpathia* was the finest room Kate had ever seen aboard a ship in her life. Admittedly, she had never seen the First Class rooms on *Titanic*, but she could not imagine they would have been any grander than this. And in the afternoon light, it was even more majestic.

The room was immense, extending the full width of the ship, and decorated in cream and gold tones. The furniture and seating accommodations were a rich mahogany—a tastefully ornate display of finery in every respect. They had been pushed aside to accommodate the passengers who needed the space.

There were nine ports each on the starboard and port sides, with ten additional ports forward, showering the room with an abundance of natural light. Each port was screened by gold curtains, which only made the room somehow brighter and more luxurious.

More than that, the central dome was glazed with stained glass, bringing a cascade of diamonds in all shades from the sky itself.

Kate suspected the room could have held all of the passengers of *Carpathia*'s First Class comfortably. Yet at present, the room was filled with both the finely dressed and the tattered, with no distinction between high station and low. They had all simply gathered for one unifying reason.

Reverend Anderson entered the room and smiled in a soft, kind manner. "The captain has requested a service of memorial and thanksgiving today, and it is my privilege to help us do so. I should like to begin this service with a hymn, and then the Lord's Prayer. There is a piano, if anyone feels they can play to accompany us. Otherwise, we will simply sing from our hearts."

A woman moved toward the piano before he had finished, clamping down on her lips hard, her tears already falling. "Which song, Father?"

"Do you know 'Abide with Me'?" he asked her.

She nodded and began to play, and soon the voices of those gathered filled the room.

> *Abide with me, fast falls the eventide*
> *The darkness deepens, Lord, with me abide*

Kate could not sing, could not even find the power to speak, so instead, she let the lyrics and the music sink deep into her soul. For all the sorrow and weariness she felt, for all the fear and despair she had known, there were so many others around her who felt the same, and even worse. Yet now they were all lifting their voices to the Lord, turning the cries of their souls heavenward, their religions differing, but their faith united.

It was a powerful, moving moment, and she needed to simply feel it for a time.

When the song concluded, Reverend Anderson stepped forward

and nodded to them all. He bowed his head, and the gathered passengers did the same.

"Our Father, which art in heaven," he began in a slow voice. "Hallowed be thy Name."

"Thy kingdom come," the room recited in near perfect unison, and Kate felt the cry resound in her heart. She began to whisper along.

"Thy will be done in earth, as it is in heaven: Give us this day our daily bread; and forgive us our trespasses, as we forgive them that trespass against us; and lead us not into temptation, but deliver us from evil."

The voices collectively grew stronger, more unified, more pleading, more reverent. And Kate felt every sacred word to the center of her soul. She lifted her chin, raised her voice, and with tears streaming down her face, she finished the prayer with the rest.

"For thine is the kingdom, and the power, and the glory, for ever and ever. Amen."

A few scattered sniffles could be heard among the group as they raised their heads and looked at Reverend Anderson.

He inhaled slowly, then exhaled before saying, "In Isaiah, we read, 'Who hath measured the waters in the hollow of his hand, and meted out heaven with the span, and comprehended the dust of the earth in a measure, and weighed the mountains in scales, and the hills in a balance?'

"The only way I believe any of us will find solace in the events of this tragedy is to recollect that it is the Lord who controls the waves and tides of the sea, who has power to calm the winds and the storms. He alone knows the purpose of all things, and in His strength, we may find healing and peace."

Tears flowed down Kate's cheeks as she nodded, taking Julia's arm beside her. "How are you feeling?" she whispered.

"Not well," Julia replied, though she seemed better than she had that morning. "But I need to be here."

There was no point in arguing, and Kate supposed many others would have felt the same way. She'd managed an hour or two of sleep herself, tucked away as she had been in *Carpathia*'s fine library with her friends. But too much solitude would only bring back painful memories and unpleasant thoughts.

It was better to be here, to be doing something.

Reverend Anderson glanced around at the room, compassion filling his eyes. "I have heard, and so have my brothers of the Catholic orders, that some of you are questioning why you were spared, why you did not perish with so many others, and why the Lord would part families in such a way. I submit to you, my friends, that those are questions that may not have answers in this life. May we remember those we have lost, and take comfort that they are, even now, with the angels above, looking down on us without pain or sorrow."

The sniffles and tears seemed to intensify, as a somber and deep sorrow rolled through the group. Kate bowed her head both in gratitude for being rescued and in reverence for so many others who had been lost.

"O merciful God, and heavenly Father," Reverend Anderson intoned, his voice deepening, filled with fervency, "who hast taught us in thy holy Word that thou dost not willingly afflict or grieve the children of men; Look with pity, we beseech thee, upon the sorrows of thy servants for whom our prayers are offered. Remember them, O Lord, in mercy; endue their souls with patience; comfort them with a sense of thy goodness; lift up thy countenance upon them, and give them peace; through Jesus Christ our Lord. Amen."

Echoing replies of "amen" filled the room, and Kate felt Julia squeeze her hand tightly.

"Almighty God," he continued, his words wavering with emotion, "who art a strong tower of defense unto thy servants against the face of their enemies; We yield thee praise and thanksgiving for our deliverance from those great and apparent dangers wherewith we were compassed. We acknowledge it thy goodness that we were not delivered over as a prey unto them; beseeching thee still to continue such thy mercies towards us, that all the world may know that thou art our Savior and mighty Deliverer; through Jesus Christ our Lord. Amen."

Kate could barely vocalize her own amen through her tears and felt she was not alone in that.

Reverend Anderson cleared his throat, and, through apparent tears, went on. "Most gracious Lord, whose mercy is over all thy works; We praise thy holy Name that thou hast been pleased to conduct in safety, through the perils of the great deep, these thy servants, who now desireth to return thanks unto thee. May they be duly sensible of thy merciful providence towards them, and ever express their thankfulness by a holy trust in thee, and obedience to thy laws; through Jesus Christ our Lord. Amen."

"Amen."

In one profound chorus, the room closed their prayer, as tears were freely shed and shared.

Reverend Anderson spoke with the woman at the piano, who then began to play the haunting, stirring strains of "Amazing Grace."

A chorus of voices sang out through choking sobs and wavering words as the hymn rose in perfect sounds of praise.

> *Amazing grace! (how sweet the sound)*
> *That saved a wretch like me!*
> *I once was lost, but now am found,*
> *Was blind, but now I see.*
>
> *'Twas grace that taught my heart to fear,*
> *And grace my fears relieved;*

How precious did that grace appear
The hour I first believed!

Through many dangers, toils, and snares,
I have already come;
'Tis grace hath brought me safe thus far,
And grace will lead me home.

When we've been there ten thousand years,
Bright shining as the sun,
We've no less days to sing God's praise,
Than when we first begun.

Not a single voice was without tears in it by the end, and Kate turned to embrace her friends, all of them grasping hands as their emotions took over.

"Thank you, ladies and gentlemen," Reverend Anderson said. "We will now bury the four men who were recovered, but who ultimately lost their lives. If any wish to accompany us for the service, we will proceed out to the deck." He moved to the grand stairs that led up toward the bridge deck and the setting for the burial at sea.

Kate was pleased to see every person from the service following Reverend Anderson up the stairs to honor the men they would bury, as though any one of the four strangers could have been a loved one lost the night before.

Had it really been only a matter of hours since *Titanic* was lost? It might have been a lifetime ago for all the grief that weighed down the survivors. Men carried children who belonged to women they'd met only that morning. Women carried babies who would never know their fathers. Children walked among the group without fully comprehending any of it, some of whom were now orphaned and alone.

Scattered throughout their throng were devoted passengers of

Carpathia herself. They had given so much already, including their own clothing and rooms, as well as tending to and caring for their new companions without a second thought.

All of them had been changed; all of them carrying a grief they could not yet explore.

Reaching the deck, Reverend Anderson moved to the four figures wrapped in canvas, weights tied to one end of each of them, as a few crewmen draped a Union Jack flag over each form.

A woman ahead of Kate crumpled at the sight, the women on either side of her taking an arm to steady her, helping her to finish the course before her.

The *Carpathia*'s crew, who had been working on deck, removed their hats and silently waited for them all to arrive.

Reverend Anderson gestured for another man to join him.

"Who is that?" Kate asked her friends.

"Father Hogue," Julia whispered back. "He's a Catholic priest as well as a passenger on the *Carpathia*. I spoke to him while in medical. I asked for a blessing, and he gave it."

Reverend Anderson waited for the gathering to settle on the deck, Father Hogue by his side, and then he spread his hands out. "Let us pray."

As one, the gathering and the crew members bowed their heads.

"O almighty God," Reverend Anderson prayed, "the God of the spirits of all flesh, who by a voice from heaven didst proclaim, Blessed are the dead who die in the Lord: Multiply, we beseech thee, to those who rest in Jesus, the manifold blessings of thy love, that the good work which thou didst begin in them may be perfected unto the day of Jesus Christ. And of thy mercy, O heavenly Father, vouchsafe that we, who now serve thee here on earth, may at the last, together with them, be found meet to be partakers of the inheritance of the saints in light; for the sake of the same thy Son, Jesus Christ, our Lord and Savior. Amen."

"Amen."

Several people crossed themselves, and Reverend Anderson nodded at the nearby crew of the *Carpathia*.

Iron doors at the side of the deck were opened, a platform let down, and the four bodies were moved into position.

The only sound on deck was of fabric rippling lightly in the breeze.

Reverend Anderson moved to the bodies while Father Hogue remained respectfully back. "We commend unto thy hands of mercy, most merciful Father, the soul of this our brother, William."

He paused, swallowing, and stepped to his right, addressing the next body. "Our brother, David."

Again, he stepped to his right. "And our brother, Sidney, departed, and we commit their bodies to the deep; in sure and certain hope of the Resurrection unto eternal life, through our Lord Jesus Christ; at whose coming in glorious majesty to judge the world, the sea shall give up her dead; and the corruptible bodies of those who sleep in him shall be changed, and made like unto his glorious body; according to the mighty working whereby he is able to subdue all things unto himself. Grant this, O merciful Father, for the sake of Jesus Christ, our only Savior, Mediator, and Advocate."

Among sniffles and whimpering cries, a scattered "Amen" came from the crowd.

"I heard a voice from heaven, saying unto me, Write, From henceforth blessed are the dead which die in the Lord: even so saith the Spirit; for they rest from their labours. Now unto the King eternal, immortal, invisible, the only wise God, be honour and glory for ever and ever."

"Amen," the gathering replied.

Reverend Anderson stepped back and gestured for Father Hogue to come forward.

Father Hogue reverently moved to the fourth body on the platform. "Lord God, by the power of thy Word, thou stilled the chaos of the primeval seas, thou made the raging waters of the Flood subside, and calmed the storm on the sea of Galilee. As we commit the body of our brother, William, to the deep, grant him peace and tranquility until that day when he and all who believe in thee will be raised to the glory of new life promised in the waters of Baptism. Through Christ our Lord."

He paused to sprinkle holy water upon the head of the man before him, then bowed his head again. "Into thy hands, O Lord, we commend thy servant, William, our dear brother, as into the hands of a faithful Creator and most merciful Savior, beseeching thee that he may be precious in thy sight. Wash him, we pray to thee, in the blood of that immaculate Lamb that was slain to take away the sins of the world; that, what so ever defilements he may have contracted in the midst of this earthly life being purged and done away, he may be presented pure and without spot before thee; through the merits of Jesus Christ thine only Son our Lord. Amen."

Kate and the other Catholics on board duly replied, "Rest eternal grant unto him, O Lord: and let light perpetual shine upon him. Amen."

Father Hogue swallowed hard, then concluded:

> *Requiem æternam dona ei, Domine*
> *Et lux perpetua luceat ei:*
> *Requiescat in pace.*
> *Amen.*

Father Hogue placed his hand upon the enshrouded head of William for a moment, then stepped back and nodded to Reverend

Anderson, who shook the Father's hand. The two men put their hands on each other's backs as the platform was raised and the flags removed from the bodies.

The entire crew of the *Carpathia* stood at attention, and the bells of the bridge and the crow's nest began to chime alternately. A haunting sound of honor, as though the ship itself mourned these men who would now be commended to the deep. Kate shivered at the sounds, feeling that even her breath was too loud for the occasion.

As the first body began to slide from the platform, a few of the ladies turned away, covering their mouths or their eyes. Grown men had tears silently rolling down their cheeks, unchecked. The seamen on board were somber, heads bowing in respectful anticipation. More than one man wiped away tears, and Kate felt her own heart shatter each time a body hit the water.

Silence reigned on the deck, the cold wind whipping at skirts, at blankets, at cloaks.

A woman among the gathering began to sing softly, her voice stirring and lovely, though not entirely steady. The strains of the song wrapped the gathering in its embrace, filled their souls; and, though the English translation was new to Kate's ears, hearing the familiar verses of home comforted her immensely.

> *Be Thou my Vision, O Lord of my heart;*
> *Naught be all else to me, save that Thou art.*
> *Thou my best Thought, by day or by night,*
> *Waking or sleeping, Thy presence my light.*

> *Be Thou my Wisdom, and Thou my true Word;*
> *I ever with Thee and Thou with me, Lord;*
> *Thou my great Father, I Thy true son;*
> *Thou in me dwelling, and I with Thee one.*

Throughout the burial service, the woman sang, the splashing of each body into the sea the only disruption to her sad tribute. But the words of the song warmed Kate's heart, bringing an unexpected solace. Though her tears did not stop, nor were they likely to, as Kate squeezed Julia's hand tightly, a glimmer of hope stole through her.

> High King of Heaven, my victory won,
> May I reach Heaven's joys, O bright Heav'n's Sun!
> Heart of my own heart, whatever befall,
> Still be my Vision, O Ruler of all.

"Oh, yes, there is a divinity that shapes our ends . . ."

—CAPTAIN ARTHUR ROSTRON,
Home from the Sea, 1931

CHAPTER 21

The spirit on the ship had changed the moment the service began. Arthur had felt it, even though he'd been helping his crew on the deck and was not with the passengers in the First Class saloon. He thought it right that he serve alongside his men, at least while they had no one else on deck and could get things done quickly. Ideally, they would be finished before the burial, as he rather wished for a reverent solitude there.

He'd ordered the lifeboats swung inboard and landed on blocks and secured. Then the davits were swung out and the falls disconnected. The task of getting all of *Titanic*'s lifeboats up had been daunting. He was grateful the passengers had not seen the work. Bringing in the empty vessels had been harrowing enough for those completing the task; he could not imagine the horror and additional pain it would bring to those who had endured the tragedy itself.

They had seven of *Titanic*'s lifeboats up in their davits with six more on the forecastle head with the forward derricks. They'd managed to accomplish all of that before the passengers had returned to the deck to bury the bodies, which had suited Arthur perfectly.

He had returned to the bridge and offered to take over the helm, where he'd been manning the aged wooden wheel ever since. The feeling of each handle in his palms and the sight of open sea was more comforting than anything he'd known yet that day, even with the ice about him.

He had needed some time of near-normalcy after the impossible events of the last few hours. His body was tense from maneuvering around the wreckage and the ever-present ice. His mind was fixed on the body.

He tried to ignore the shiver in his spine as he recollected what he had seen.

One body. Only one body had crossed their path, though he knew there had to have been more out there. Ones who had not been fortunate enough to find a place in a lifeboat. But since they'd adjusted their course on their way to New York, he had seen only the one body.

A man, possibly a member of *Titanic*'s crew, based on the clothing visible beneath the life belt, had been floating in the water, roughly a hundred yards from the ship. The body had been lying on his side, head awash, and Arthur had no doubt the man was dead. He could not have survived for long. Not in that position. Not with the water at that temperature.

Arthur's first instinct was to recover the body, but after thinking on it, he stayed the order.

How could he bring a corpse onto the ship, still in its life belt, and allow his traumatized passengers to see such a thing? How could he bring hope to those still desperate for the return of their loved ones, only to renew their crushing despair when it was not the man they sought?

And what of the rest? What hysteria would set in with such a scene? They had been through enough, and he could not bring any more unnecessary pain to them.

Bringing the man aboard would not bring him back to life, so he had steamed past the body. If any of his officers or crew had seen the body, they had kept silent on the subject. And he'd not heard of any passengers witnessing it either.

But he could not get the image out of his head. He did not regret his decision, but neither could he forget the sight.

Perhaps the events of the night and the morning would leave them all more affected and changed than they thought.

"Captain?"

Arthur blinked and shifted his attention from his reflective thoughts to his first officer, who approached with a helmsman in tow.

Dean inclined his head as he neared. "I've brought you relief, sir."

Shaking his head to clear his thoughts, Arthur stepped away from the helm. "Yes, thank you, First Officer. This ice field . . ." He gestured helplessly to the glistening peaks around their ship, all heights and shapes and sizes, each posing a distinct threat to them. He'd done his own navigation this time, the task being easier by daylight, though still not simple, and he was weary of the sight of them.

"Yes, sir." Dean nodded and considered the ice as well. "It is rather expansive."

"Three hours, has it been?" Arthur inquired, his lack of sleep beginning to wear on him.

"Closer to four, sir."

The note of apology in Dean's voice ought to have embarrassed Arthur, but all he felt was a fog of confusion that made his thinking slow and his actions slower.

He could not afford to be slow now.

He lifted his chin and clasped his hands behind his back as he looked out at the sea. The mountains of ice seemed to be thinning. "I believe we are at the end of it."

"Yes, sir."

It was impossible to tell if his first officer was agreeing with him or humoring him, but he supposed it did not matter. He nodded almost absently. "Once we are free of the ice, continue the course to New York. Full speed."

"Yes, Captain."

Arthur glanced at him. "How are our new passengers faring? Are we accommodating them well enough?"

Dean exhaled and shook his head in amazement. "I've never seen anything like it, Captain. The tables in each dining room have been turned to beds, designated for those requiring medical care. Nearly all of our own passengers have given up their the berths to those from *Titanic*, and men are making up spaces for themselves in the hallways and smoking rooms."

"Are they really?" Arthur nodded in approval. "And you've given up my rooms, yes?"

"Yes, sir. All of the officers have done so as well." Dean smiled. "And you'll be pleased to know that the Marshalls' nieces were both saved from *Titanic* and have been reunited with their uncle and aunt. I trust you do not mind the Marshalls keeping their berth, under the circumstances."

Arthur released a deep sigh of relief at such good news; it had been in short supply compared to all the bad news they had received. "Not at all. And the rest?"

Dean hesitated. "They are rather somber, sir. Some hardly seem to be there when you look at them."

It was not difficult to imagine such a thing, and Arthur nodded, exhaling a sigh. He hadn't spent much time among the passengers today, and there likely wouldn't be a great deal of time to change that on the rest of their voyage, so taking a brief moment now might be worth something.

He nodded again to his first officer, then moved out to the deck.

The sight that greeted him was like nothing he'd ever witnessed. He knew many of the passengers had taken refuge in the rooms that had been prepared for them, but those that remained on deck were wrapped in blankets and coats. Their vacant expressions made them seem somehow more lifeless than the corpses they had only recently buried in the sea.

A well-dressed woman sat among some other women in distinctly poorer clothes, rubbing their backs and squeezing hands. She was not familiar to Arthur, so she must have come from *Titanic*. He did not know all of his passengers, but he knew most of the wealthy ones, given their shared suppers on the ship.

The passengers on *Titanic* likely would not have had opportunity or reason to cross paths on that ship, the disparity in classes being so very distinct, but here, after what they had suffered, the class barriers had vanished, and they were simply aching souls needing comfort. There was something innately noble and humbling in that.

As he walked the deck, he saw passengers he knew from *Carpathia* bringing food, drinks, and blankets to the victims, heard offers to tend children, and noted a few who simply sat beside their fellows and held their hands and listened as they spoke. The Ogdens, in particular, seemed desperate to help someone, and were not entirely particular as to who.

Arthur nodded at a few of his crew who greeted him, then paused at the sight of Carlos Hurd leaning against a wall beside a seated couple from *Titanic*, listening intently. His expression held nothing but interest and compassion, which was a relief, given Arthur's previous encounters with the newspaperman. It was difficult to judge a man on a short acquaintance of such a superficial nature, and Arthur generally tried to give people the benefit of the doubt. He would be pleased to find himself mistaken in his previous negative impressions of Mr. Hurd.

The man beside Hurd shook his head, face pale, eyes wide. "They just . . . stood there. Calmly waiting for their turn, and it never came." He looked at Mr. Hurd, his expression tormented. "God knows, I'm not proud to be here. I got on a boat when they were about to lower it, because there was no woman to take the vacant place."

The woman sitting next to him put a hand over his.

He barely seemed to notice it. "I will live with that for the rest of my life. Be judged for it the rest of my life."

There was no avoiding the emotion such a statement brought, not only for the man saying and feeling the words, but for all who heard them. What a tragedy—to feel shame at being alive, to already feel burdened by the opinions of others who would never understand.

Perhaps Arthur should not have judged Mr. Ismay so harshly.

Arthur moved on and found his gaze settling on a little girl crying into her mother's lap. Her mother, whose hollow expression would have arrested any living soul, absently ran her fingers through the girl's hair in a show of comfort.

"Can I do anything for the child?" a fellow passenger asked, gesturing to the tot.

The mother blinked and looked at her. "She . . . she cries because her teddy bear and two dolls were lost on the ship," she confessed in a hoarse, shaking tone. Her slender throat moved on a swallow. "I cannot bear to tell her that her father . . . That he . . ."

"Oh, my dear," the other woman soothed, sinking beside her and putting an arm around her shoulders.

"He's lost," she whispered as tears began to fall. "And with him, all of the money we received in selling our home in England. We were starting a new life, and now . . ."

Arthur shook his head, his heart aching in the face of such personal tragedies, feeling acutely the intimate pains the loss of *Titanic* had on his new passengers when there were so very many of them. One experience was enough to overwhelm a being, but to experience such a volume of equally agonizing tales . . .

It was devastating to hear.

He nodded to a few people who noticed him, then turned, hoping to find some work that could help him focus his energies. He wanted to do something good, bring about some benefit to those now in his care. Some duty he could find satisfaction in when he looked back on a time filled with so much pain.

"Captain."

Arthur paused as Carlos Hurd approached him, expression set, stride determined. "Mr. Hurd."

The man nodded when he reached him. "Captain, I have a connection with the *New York World*, and it is my duty and intention to send a story to them at the first opportunity and for transmission to the *Post-Dispatch*."

Surely, he could not be serious. He wanted to submit the story of what had happened before they could send official reports, or before any of the families of the victims or survivors had been notified? Before the White Star Line or Cunard Company knew the details? He wanted to put his name on a story about the horrors they had witnessed, the suffering so many had endured, and the journey they still had to make?

He wanted to use all of this for his own career?

And under the guise of *duty*?

It couldn't be so.

"Mr. Cottam has much to relay once we are in range to do so," Arthur said slowly, holding his irritation in reserve, hoping it was misplaced. "As you can imagine, it will take some time."

Hurd stepped forward. "Captain, I *must* relay this story to New

York. I insist it be considered a priority. You yourself have heard some of these stories. There are more to be found. Every person has something to say, and it needs to be shared."

Arthur felt utterly bewildered by what he was hearing. Of course, the stories needed to be heard, deserved to be shared, but why should this man feel it his right to share them when the agony of it all was so fresh?

And none of it was his?

Arthur frowned, but prevented it from darkening enough to become a full glower. He had a reputation to maintain and needed to act with respect and consideration.

Even when it was for an opposing view.

Especially for an opposing view.

But still, he was in command.

"Let me be perfectly clear, Mr. Hurd," Arthur said in a steady tone. "I mean to see to it that the rescued persons in my care are not disturbed by pressmen. You may be able to pick up some incidents, but you may *not* use the wireless. A list of the rescued will be drawn up, and you have my permission to see the purser later about copying it. That is all."

He nodded firmly and pushed past Mr. Hurd, who let him continue on without argument or objection.

Time alone would tell if he would comply with Arthur's orders.

Still, the exchange had given Arthur a destination and a task, and he moved directly to the radio room.

He arrived to find Cottam still at the radio, clearly exhausted, head resting in one hand. He seemed to be breathing deeply, perhaps dozing, and Arthur hated to disturb him. A faint beep permeated the room, but the lad did not seem to hear it.

Arthur cleared his throat softly.

Cottam startled upright, glanced over, then shot to his feet. "Captain. Sir."

Gesturing for his officer to be at ease, he nodded toward the radio. "Anything pressing on the wireless?"

Cottam followed his gaze, relaxing just a touch before returning his focus to his captain. "No, sir. Just the usual traffic."

That was a relief. At least there were no demands upon them, and men like Carlos Hurd were not yet getting their way.

Arthur gave a nod and a faint sigh. "I would ask you to give first priority to communicating news to Cunard and White Star, particularly the names of survivors and any personal messages they might have. They must be allowed to reassure their families."

Cottam nodded firmly. "Yes, sir. Some survivors have already submitted messages for transmission."

"They have priority," Arthur insisted. "*Carpathia* passenger messages will have to wait."

"I understand, sir."

Arthur gave the younger man a severe look. "No answering press inquiries. There are far more important details we need to be transmitting and receiving, and we cannot indulge anyone's demands for the story here."

Again, Cottam nodded, his expression as firm as Arthur's. "Understood, sir."

Pleased by Cottam's determination, Arthur felt himself relax. "Can you manage all the transmissions? With our equipment, I mean."

Cottam shrugged, completely unconcerned. "Well enough, sir. I'll ask *Olympic* to relay messages for us."

"Excellent. The purser will be by momentarily with the lists for you."

"Yes, sir."

Arthur hesitated, then reached out and put a hand on Cottam's shoulder. "If you need anything, Cottam, please do notify me."

Cottam smiled weakly. "Aye, Captain. Apart from some sleep, I don't believe I need anything at the moment."

Arthur chuckled. "We both could use some sleep, I imagine, though we won't have much opportunity, I fear." He nodded again, then left the room to return to the bridge.

He passed Carlos Hurd on his way and nodded to himself as he imagined the man's impending disappointment.

Hardly fitting behavior for a captain, but a captain's orders were obeyed by his loyal crew, and Harold Cottam was certainly among that number.

There was great satisfaction in that.

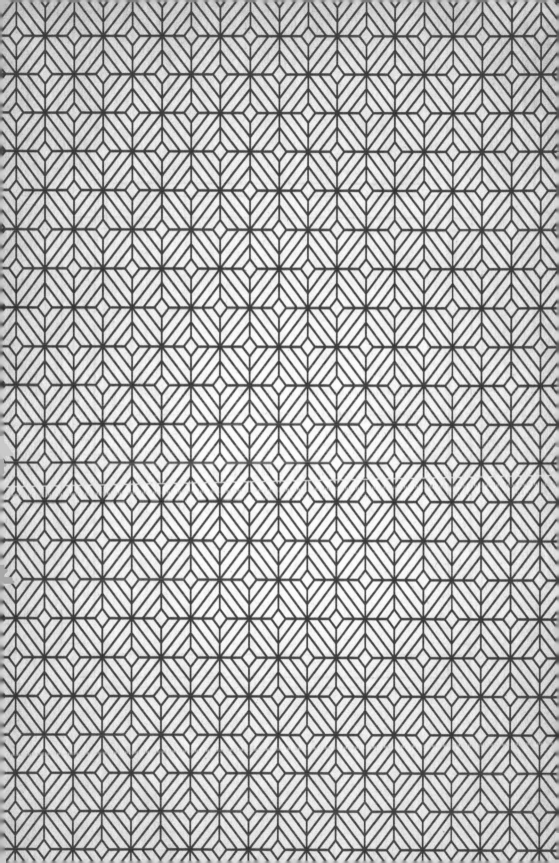

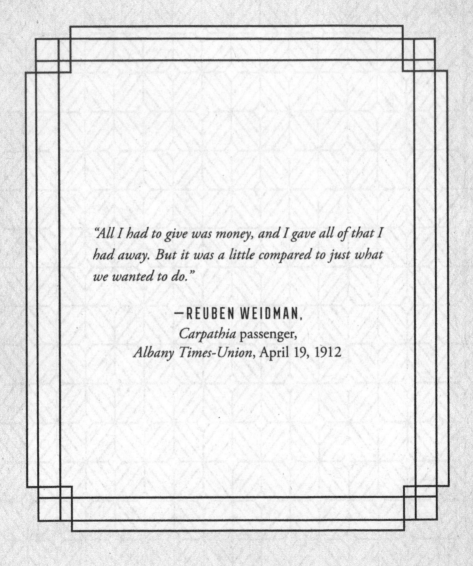

*"All I had to give was money, and I gave all of that I
had away. But it was a little compared to just what
we wanted to do."*

—REUBEN WEIDMAN,
Carpathia passenger,
Albany Times-Union, April 19, 1912

CHAPTER 22

RMS *CARPATHIA* · APRIL 16, 1912

Soft voices were all that could be heard in the library as steward-esses flitted in and out with offers of breakfast. That had been the pattern all morning the day following the burials at sea. Kate had heard that some of the *Carpathia* passengers had come in during the night to offer their beds to a few people in the library, but she hadn't witnessed it herself.

She had been fast asleep, and deeply so, and likely would not have heard a storm, an attack, or an explosion.

She had not slept since the disaster, so having a respite was a blessing. It was still very real, the images and sounds in her mind and the lingering memory of the cold in her legs, but even a slight distance from the event had deadened the emotions enough for her to bear.

Although she mourned the loss of many of her new friends, she had not lost a loved one.

Some of the women around her in the library had lost dear ones, and they lay on their makeshift cots, eyes wide open, unable to do more than breathe in and out.

The library was a grand space. The wall-to-wall bookcases and writing tables had been pushed aside so beds could be made up both under and atop them. The decor and upholstery spoke of comfort, good taste, and finery, nothing ostentatious or imposing. And while certainly finer than what Kate and the rest of the steerage passengers would have been used to on *Titanic*, the library did not hold the same awe for Kate that the dining room had.

The library also contained a grand staircase that led down to the First Class dining saloon where the religious service had been held, and some of the more intrepid children took great delight in darting up and down the stairs until their mothers put an end to it. Kate found the children's resilience charming and hopeful, their energy a much-needed balm. The children likely did not fully comprehend the loss of fathers, siblings, or mothers, in some cases. They might not even know exactly what had happened.

Their remaining family members would have to find the strength to relay the awful truth to them at some point, and there were many among the group who were not ready to give up hope that somehow, someone they loved might still be saved.

She'd overheard some widows consoling each other, saying that their husbands would be picked up by other ships seeking survivors, and that they would be reunited with them in New York in a few days.

Kate wished they might be right, but everything within her told her that there was no chance of such a thing. There had been no more lifeboats on the waters, and given the number of lookouts on the crew, as well as self-proclaimed passenger lookouts, someone would certainly have told the captain if any more survivors had been seen. She wouldn't dash the women's hopes of such a reunion; it could very well be the only thing keeping them from falling completely to pieces.

Who was she to ruin that hope?

She thought again of the woman she had met who had found only three of her ten children aboard. The memory of the agony in the mother's eyes still took Kate's breath away. She would hope until her dying day that more of the missing children would yet be found.

"Oh, Kate, whatever is the matter?" Mary Mac inquired softly as she sat on the straw mattress beside her. Her blue eyes were full of concern, though there lingered in them the same exhaustion Kate felt. Her friend was pale, but at least she was no longer frozen. Her hands were warm as she took Kate's in her own. "Are you all right?"

Kate hadn't realized she'd been crying. She sniffed and offered a sad smile. "Yes. I'm only thinking of the woman missing her children."

Mary sobered and rubbed Kate's back soothingly. "Poor lamb. Let's find her today and see if there's aught we can do for her or the children. I'd offer to help entertain them, but she may wish to keep them close to her for now."

The discussion was not helping Kate's emotional state, and she wiped away another tear. "What have you found in your exploring, then? Anything interesting?"

"The smoking rooms don't look anything like what I expected a smoking room to look like," Mary told her, wrinkling her nose. "It's rather like another library, minus all the books. The lavatories are en suite, which seems marvelous, and bars as well, though having a pub aboard a ship makes little sense to me. Still, the room is paneled in what I think is walnut, of all things. A very masculine room to be sure."

"So I should expect," Kate said with some amusement. "Anything else?"

"The cabins, Kate." Mary shook her head, eyes wide with amazement. "I got a look at one of them when a pair of fine ladies emerged.

Two beds—actual beds, mind you—a sofa, a wardrobe . . . I would wager they each have their own lavatory, too. Such a large room!"

Kate smiled at the descriptions and leaned against the wall behind her cot. "Are you envious, Mary? Wishing we had better accommodations?"

Mary rolled her eyes and scooted closer beside her. "Of course not. But one day, if I can save enough to do so, I think I may travel higher than steerage."

"And where will you go?" Kate asked, finding it unfathomable that Mary would even think of taking another voyage now.

"Perhaps back home. I haven't thought about it yet."

Kate sobered at the thought. "There might not be much of a life at home, Mary. We all agreed on that when we left. That's why you're going to New York, isn't it? Patrick found you a position?"

Mary shrugged. "Something of the sort. Even if I have found my place in America, a visit to Ireland someday would be lovely, don't you think?"

Thoughts of Ireland and her family pulled at Kate's heart, but she quickly shoved them aside. Her sister, Nellie, was waiting for her in New York, as well as an opportunity for herself. That had to be enough.

"Would you ladies care for some oatmeal porridge?" a stewardess asked, carting a tray of bowls around. "It's not much, but it's warm. I also have bread with butter, jam, or marmalade. We're not being particular about dining rooms at the present." She smiled, dimples appearing in her cheeks.

Kate nodded and got to her feet. "Yes, please. Can I help?"

"No, you may not," the stewardess answered brightly, turning the tray toward Kate. "You deserve a good rest today, and it is my duty and pleasure to wait upon *you*. Now, when I'm done with this tray, I'll be back with tea and coffee. What would you like?"

They quickly gave their orders, and the stewardess was off to see to the others in the room, leaving Mary and Kate cradling their bowls of porridge and slices of bread.

"This is heaven," Mary gushed around a mouthful of food. She shivered and looked at Kate. "How are your new clothes?"

Kate looked down at herself ruefully. "Warm and clean, so I won't complain." She smiled at her friend. "Though it would fit better if taken in a touch, I suspect. It was so kind for the ladies to give them to us. You?"

"Rather perfect, as it happens." She folded her borrowed shawl around her more tightly. "There is a great, thick fog out on the deck, you know. And it is most chilly, but hardly anything like . . ."

There was no need to finish the thought.

Nothing would ever feel as cold as that night among the ice.

"I heard talk this morning," Mary murmured, still focused on her oatmeal. "It would seem there is a clean bill of health for all of us from *Titanic*."

Kate stared at Mary, waiting for her to amend the statement.

When she did not, Kate shook her head slowly. "How is that possible? Those hours on the water . . . Some of the people were actually *in* the water . . ."

"I don't know," Mary replied as she took a quick bite of her bread. "But that is what was said. Even Julia is feeling better, though she is weak."

"And Mary-from-Clare?" Kate pressed. "I haven't seen her this morning."

Mary Mac smiled. "She's out on the deck. Lord only knows if she is flirting with the crew, holding a baby, or enjoying the fog, but she seems quite content. And Katie McCarthy is still in the medical berth. I believe she is offering her assistance there."

"Likely she needs to keep busy," Kate murmured, curling closer to her porridge, grateful for its warmth. "Did she tell you what happened?"

"No," Mary said slowly, eyes going wide. "What?"

Kate shook her head, a lump forming in her throat. "The lad they were seeking that day we met them—Roger Tobin? He was the other Katie's sweetheart. He came to their cabin and said they must get up, get dressed. He told them to get their life belts, then head up to the deck. He said there was no danger."

"Oh, no," Mary whimpered. "But so many people said that in the beginning, do you recall?"

Nodding, Kate went on. "Katie said she begged her friends to come with her, but Kate and Katie Peters didn't see a need to hurry if there was no danger. So Katie McCarthy came up alone, got into a lifeboat, and until yesterday, did not know the others hadn't . . . That they weren't . . ."

Mary leaned against Kate, her silence speaking far more than Kate's words could have.

"I'm so glad we were all saved together," Mary murmured in a low tone. "I couldn't imagine losing any of you girls."

"I know." Kate swallowed and looked over at some of the other women in the library. "We are the lucky ones, aren't we?"

Mary nodded against her, and the two of them finished their breakfast in the hushed quiet of the room.

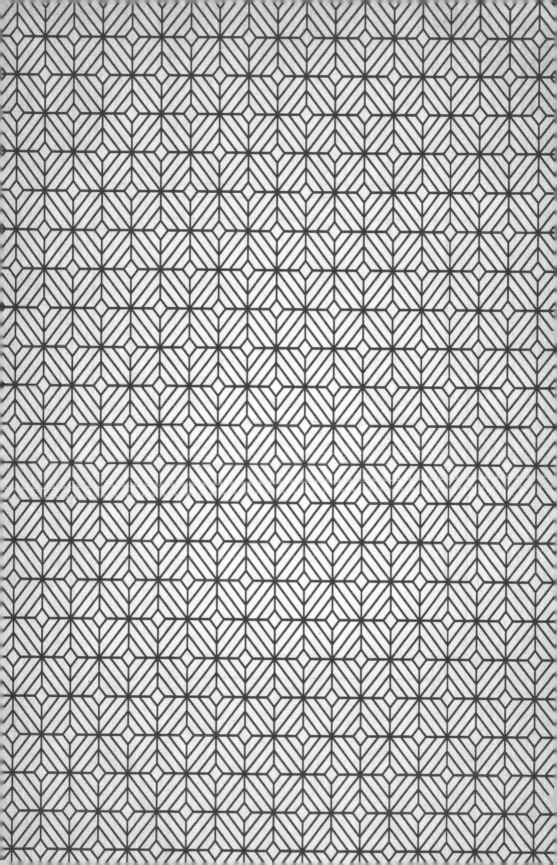

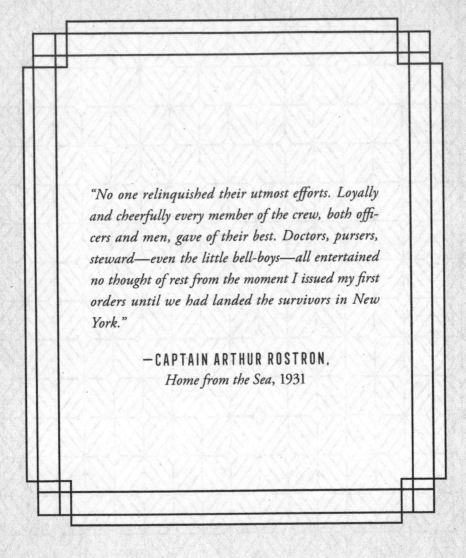

"No one relinquished their utmost efforts. Loyally and cheerfully every member of the crew, both officers and men, gave of their best. Doctors, pursers, steward—even the little bell-boys—all entertained no thought of rest from the moment I issued my first orders until we had landed the survivors in New York."

—CAPTAIN ARTHUR ROSTRON,
Home from the Sea, 1931

CHAPTER 23

"Dean, what is our status?"

Arthur had gone over almost the entire ship to check in personally with every department now that he had the luxury of doing so.

First Officer Dean turned to face Arthur as he approached. "Steady, Captain," he replied easily. "Cottam says he's getting hammered by requests."

Arthur heaved a sigh, the few hours of sleep the night before clearly not enough for dealing with the details of the day. "I know, I've just spoken with him. I told him yesterday that we were not answering press requests, and he has stood by that, despite Mr. Hurd's offer of money."

"Good man," Dean grunted.

"I cannot condone sending the story to the papers when the families deserve first word," Arthur went on, acknowledging Dean's response with a nod. "The White Star and Cunard both have been informed, and if they wish to tell the story, that is their business, but I

221

will not allow it to come from this ship until we know that all has been done for the passengers."

Dean gave him a severe look. "That will likely get you criticism, sir. Some might claim censorship."

Arthur remained unruffled by the suggestion. "So there is. Ordered by Arthur Rostron, Captain." He smiled at his first officer, then sobered. "I know it will not be popular, but that is how it will be."

"People will say you are a company man, sir," Dean cautioned. "That you are toeing the line."

"They can say what they like. God and I know my heart and my intentions, and that is enough for me."

Dean watched a moment, then nodded slowly, smiling at last. "And for me, sir."

Arthur nodded. "Thank you, Dean." He sighed as he looked out to sea, seeing nothing but the water below and the dense fog above. "A pity the day is not finer. I think a good many of our new passengers would benefit from it."

"A good many of our new passengers have made themselves at home in the First Class dining saloon," Dean told him with a laugh. "A woman named Mrs. Brown was quite insistent on having a meeting place, so I suggested the dining saloon."

"Good heavens, what are they meeting about?" Arthur asked with some amusement.

"I haven't the faintest idea." Dean shook his head, clasping his hands behind his back. "They seem to be in better spirits today, all things considered."

Arthur nodded. He'd had the same impression earlier today. "They have been a most impressive bunch, I think. Rather plucky, wouldn't you say?"

"I would."

A stretch of silence passed between the two men, and Arthur's thoughts drifted back over the actions of the past few days.

The miracles. The horrors. The dangers.

It was not over yet, but surely the worst had passed.

"Sir," Dean began slowly, "I know you are a religious man . . ."

Arthur turned to his first officer, patiently nodding in expectation. "I am."

Dean's brow creased for a moment. "How do you explain what happened the other night? How we were able to come across the distress signal—how Cottam even heard it—and how this rickety ship made it there so quickly?"

Dean's questions did not surprise Arthur; on the contrary, they had been his near-constant companions since the moment the *Titanic* passengers had been brought aboard. They were simple enough questions and likely would be asked by every person who heard the story for years to come.

The answers, however, were much less simple.

"The whole thing was absolutely providential," Arthur told Dean, his voice dipping low. "I have no other explanation for it. I've spoken with Cottam on the subject. He was in his cabin, not on official business at all, but just simply listening as he was undressing. He was unlacing his boots at the time. He had the apparatus on his ear, and the message came. That was it. Ten minutes later, Cottam would have been in bed, and we would not have heard the messages."

"It boggles the mind," Dean murmured, his tone almost reverent. "And then we ran safely under a full head of steam—through an ice field, no less."

"How could we do otherwise? Had I known the amount of ice we would face, perhaps I would have thought twice, but in that moment, I knew it was the right course."

"None of us doubted it," Dean assured him. "Not a one. If you ask those in the engine rooms, they'll tell you they pushed the ship beyond any of their expectations, and they'd have done it again. They came straight from their beds, Captain, and worked her for all they could get."

"The entire crew is to be praised, and I mean to do so." Arthur felt pride and contentment swell in his chest, and he smiled faintly. "We were not prompted by testing our mettle or our might, Dean. We were prompted by our humanity. We risked our ship, our passengers, and ourselves to save the lives of others."

"And still we were too late," Dean murmured sadly.

Arthur gave him a sharp look and gestured out to the deck where many of their new passengers padded about despite the fog and rain. "Not for them, Dean. Not for them."

Dean looked at the people for a long moment. When he turned back to Arthur, he had a smile on his face. "Aye, sir." He wet his lips, then shook his head again. "How did we do it, sir?"

The whole experience boggled the mind, to be sure, and all rational thought rebelled. Knowing all he did, knowing what had happened, there was only one explanation that would satisfy him.

"I can only conclude," Arthur said simply, "that there was another hand at the helm than mine."

"Providential, you say," Dean mused. He nodded slowly. "I may have to agree. Though I do think your experience and skill had something to do with it."

Arthur laughed softly, giving his companion a rueful smile. "Captain Smith had experience and skill, Dean. The ice still won, and we could have as easily met the same fate."

Dean exhaled in faux exasperation. "Sir, if you continue to downplay all of this, history will forget the part we played here."

"I have no doubt they *will* forget," Arthur told him, his tone serious. "The magnitude of the tragedy will overshadow everything else—as it should. The losses will outweigh the gains; that is simply human nature. Our providential moment in the sea will fade against the tales of each life lost, each lifeboat launched, and each member of the crew who sacrificed himself or herself to the sea.

"We don't matter, Dean. Not in this. When we land in New York, when we've unloaded these poor souls and the lifeboats they came in, when we've answered all of the questions that will come, and we finally get to lay our heads down on our pillows without thoughts of *Titanic*, we will know that we did everything we could to help and save as many as possible.

"The comfort such a thought will bring cannot compare with any of the fame and glory that the world might think to bestow upon us. We have not done anything heroic, Dean. We have only done what was right."

Arthur swallowed against his rising emotion, the deep passion of his thoughts filling him with warmth from the inside out, and, for a moment, he was embarrassed at having revealed so much to one of his officers. Such thoughts ought to have stayed on the pages of his journal, or in discussions with Ethel. His professionalism ought to have remained intact.

Dean continued to stare out at the sea, then, with a sigh, looked at Arthur with steady, clear eyes. "I must disagree with you, Captain. We *have* done something heroic. We've done something *miraculous*. There is too much providence in it to be anything less. We have done what was right, I concede your point there, but that does not mean there was not something glorious in it. Even if it falls by the wayside on the pages of history." He smiled slightly. "I hope I will not be marked as being insubordinate."

Arthur laughed with true humor and shook his head. "Not this time, Dean, though I wouldn't recommend disagreeing with me often."

"Yes, sir."

The two shared a companionable smile, then returned their attention to the sea and the fog and the rain.

"Cottam will not have the range he needs to transmit in this," Arthur muttered, the warmth of their exchange already fading as their duty returned to the forefront.

"No, sir," Dean confirmed. "Which means when we get in proper range . . ."

"He will be hard-pressed to keep up with anything, let alone have the ability to get much out." Arthur half-growled as he exhaled. "What I wouldn't give for another man to relieve him for a time. He'll need rest. He hasn't had proper sleep in days."

Dean nodded. "I don't think he's eaten much either. Hasn't really left his room. I've had one of the stewards bring him something on occasion and check on him every few hours."

"Excellent decision. Mr. Bride from the *Titanic*'s radio room is still recovering, so we cannot ask him for help just yet. We've got a clean bill of health for our entire ship at the present, and I'd very much like to keep it that way."

"Yes, sir," Dean agreed.

Arthur kept his focus on the sea.

They had faced an ice field right out of the wreckage, and now had fog and rain to impede them, and, if he was right, they would have a storm to contend with later. It would seem that getting the *Titanic*'s passengers to New York would be nearly as eventful as getting to them had been.

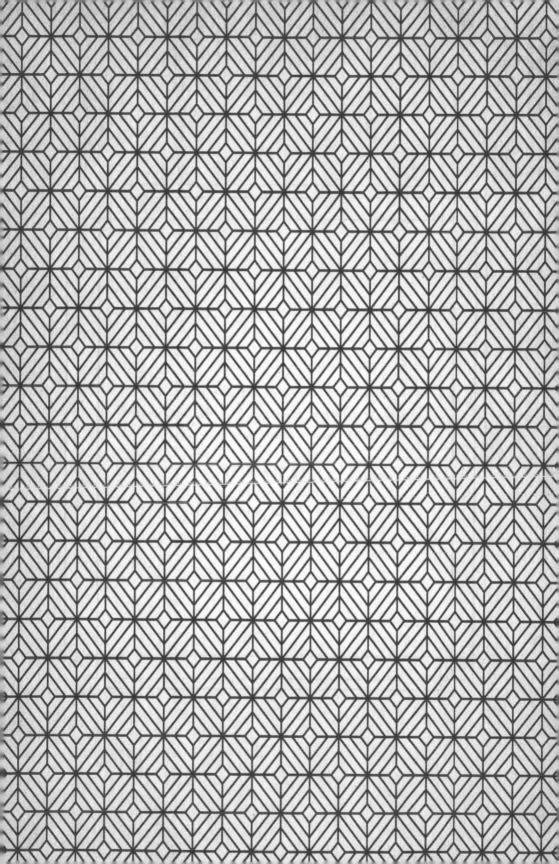

"*The spectacle on board the* Carpathia *on the return trip to New York at times was heartrending, while at other times those on board were quite cheerful.*"

—FRED BEACHLER,
Carpathia passenger,
New York Herald, April 19, 1912

CHAPTER 24

RMS *CARPATHIA* · APRIL 17, 1912

It was raining again, and the fog was as dense as it had been the day before. It made for a rather morose crossing, especially when the *Carpathia* was holding more than the capacity she was meant for and space was limited.

Kate would never complain about it aloud. She knew how fortunate she was to have been on the ship at all instead of meeting her death in the depths of the sea, but she still longed for days of sunshine.

At least the crossing had been smooth thus far, despite the weather. It would have been unbearable to endure a tumultuous sea, though she suspected the passengers would not be able to feel the water's fury too much in a boat this size.

But something about the sedate, gloomy air that pervaded the ship still made Kate uncomfortable. She could not take the rest of the journey to New York sitting among the others who were full of their rightful grief and mourning when she had only a cursory version of the same. Her experience on the water in the lifeboats might have echoed theirs, but she had not lost a parent or a sibling, a child or a husband. She had heard the voices crying out in the water, but she hadn't feared that any of them were her loved ones.

She could not sit among them and feel herself their equal.

She needed to do something, or her thoughts would have the better of her.

Thankfully, the chief steward welcomed her help, and Kate had never been more pleased to don an apron and speak to strangers in her entire life.

"Mr. Bride, please don't get up," a stewardess pleaded from the other side of the medical quarters.

Kate glanced over to see a young man with dark hair swing his bandaged feet off the table and his makeshift bed, determination in his dark eyes.

"Mr. Bride!"

He glared at the stewardess in exasperation. "Miss, you have one radio man on this ship, and he likely has not slept since Saturday. His traffic has doubled, and the messages he must send have possibly increased five times what they should be. I am lying in this bed with nothing to do but heal from frostbite, and I do not require my feet to help at the radio. Please, let me offer him some help."

The stewardess stared at Mr. Bride for a long moment, and it seemed that everyone in the room held their breath.

With a weary nod and a resigned sigh, the stewardess turned slightly. "Henry, James—could you take Mr. Bride down to the radio room? I don't believe the doctor will be pleased if he walks."

The two stewards came over, and Mr. Bride was quick to loop his arms around their necks as they lifted him from the table. There wasn't another word spoken as he was carried out of the room, and Kate smiled to herself as she focused on folding the freshly washed linens before her.

It seemed Mr. Bride needed an occupation as well.

She prayed he would find it in the radio room.

"Miss Connolly?" a young stewardess asked as she came over to her. "Might I borrow you to help with distributing soup to the passengers? I'm afraid there are quite a few bowls."

"Of course!" Kate finished folding the linen in her hand, then brushed her hands off to accompany the stewardess.

They made their way to fetch the food, and soon enough, Kate had a tray laden with bowls of warm soup.

"I'm terribly sorry, miss," the stewardess said, glancing over her shoulder. "I know you're a guest on the ship, but we have ever so many more people to serve on board now, and we always seem to be a little behind in our work."

"Not at all," Kate assured her. "I am happy to help. I think it's a better occupation than simply sitting around the ship. I'd go quite mad."

The stewardess gave her a wry look. "With all you've been through, miss? I'd think a bit of rest would be well-earned and deserved."

Kate shook her head. "Not for me. For others, yes, but not for me."

"You'll not convince me of that, miss. Not a jot." She turned her attention forward, and Kate followed her out into the corridor, heading toward the deck to start with the passengers there.

The passengers were in better spirits than they had been yesterday, but they were hardly jovial. Many of the ladies still clung together, and the children not seated near their mothers played in subdued tones. Many people met her eyes as she offered them soup, thanked her for doing so, and took from her tray.

Others barely acknowledged her, refusing the soup without much thought. They simply existed, and Kate could not imagine feeling so numb as to turn away food, but when one has lost all, perhaps even breathing would take considerable effort.

"Pardon me, are you one of the *Titanic* passengers?" a well-dressed woman with a kind smile, dark hair, and an American accent asked Kate.

"I am," Kate replied, setting her tray at her hip to tuck a lock of hair behind her ear. "Would you care for some soup, ma'am?"

The stately woman rose to her feet and beamed as though Kate had complimented her. "Bless you, no thank you. I'll dine later. What are you doing acting the stewardess? So many of us are sitting about."

There was no accusation or disapproval in her tone, and there was something in her direct manner that Kate instantly liked. She could easily see how other First Class ladies might not feel the same, but this woman's friendliness would be very much welcome in steerage. Or, indeed, in many parts of Ireland.

"I'm not particularly good at sitting about, ma'am," Kate admitted. "I felt at odds yesterday, and I don't feel entitled to being waited upon, given I haven't lost any family members. I had to do something, and the chief steward was kind enough to give me a task."

"Good for you!" the woman boomed, her accent more pronounced. "I am of exactly the same mind myself. Even if we were still on *Titanic*, I'd have been bored without something to do. As it is, there is no end of work to be done here and now. And then there is the Countess of Rothes." She indicated a well-dressed woman without hat or bonnet, her skirts tied back, an apron covering her finery as she fed soup to a weak, elderly woman.

"Countess?" Kate repeated, astonished.

"Oh, Noël is a pillar of goodness," her companion assured her with a warm smile. "I heard she gave away her entire wardrobe, though if you want my opinion, I don't think she had her whole wardrobe with her. Not much room in the lifeboats." She winked, chuckling softly. "But I have no doubt the rumor is true. I'm just trying to keep up with her good example. So I've been seeing to people here, checking on the mothers missing their children, the widows mourning their husbands, and making sure that nobody wants for something we can offer."

Kate was touched by the woman's statement, though she sensed the woman had no expectation of praise or to impress. She was simply another woman finding something to do when there was so much to be done.

It was amazing how compassion could bridge the divide of classes when little else could.

"That is a fine thing, ma'am," Kate murmured. "Is there a very great need?"

She met Kate's eyes with a newfound softness. "Oh, yes. Not that we are not well tended and cared for here. The *Carpathia* and her passengers have been wonderful, not a single complaint. Some of these poor lambs have lost everything and will have nothing when they get to New York. We've made sure there is enough clothing and food and blankets until we get there, but I'm very distressed at the thought of leaving some of these women alone in New York." Her eyes widened. "Are you in dire straits, dear? How will you fare in New York?"

Kate smiled with what she hoped was encouragement. "I am well enough, ma'am."

"Call me Mrs. Brown, dear," the woman insisted. "I should have introduced myself, but better late than never."

"Kate Connolly, Mrs. Brown. From County Cavan."

Mrs. Brown tilted her head. "Why the distinction? Isn't your name enough?"

Kate felt a lump rise in her throat. "There was another Kate Connolly on board *Titanic*, Mrs. Brown. She . . . That is . . ." She swallowed hard. "She is not on *Carpathia*. I don't want to give anyone false hope when they hear my name."

Mrs. Brown reached out and softly touched Kate's cheek. "Poor dear. You must live for the both of you now. Honor both of your names."

"Yes, ma'am."

"Now, kindly answer the question," Mrs. Brown said firmly, dropping her hand. "How will *you* fare in New York?"

Kate sniffled back the hint of tears that had started. "My sister is to meet me, so I have lodgings. I will find work there, so I shall earn money soon enough."

Mrs. Brown eyed her speculatively. "You're a determined Irish lass, aren't you, Kate Connolly?"

"I'm afraid I am." Kate shrugged.

"Well, the first meeting of the *Titanic* Survivor Committee took place yesterday," Mrs. Brown told her, "and we are raising funds for the survivors. If you'll give me your sister's address, I'll be sure to send you some relief."

"Oh, Mrs. Brown!" Kate protested at once with a shake of her head. "That is not necessary. Please, there are so many others—"

"There can be many others without negating your own loss, Kate," Mrs. Brown overrode Kate's words with a hard look. "You have lost belongings and funds, and we of the committee are in a position to help. And help we will. Besides, I like you, so you will simply have to cope with what doting I decide to bestow upon you. I assume the purser has your destination address, so I will speak to him presently." She nodded once and moved away before Kate could refuse again.

What an extraordinary woman, Kate thought as she watched Mrs. Brown stride down the deck. What must it be like to have the desire to act and the ability to make such a difference for so many in need?

"Do you think they are really sending out our messages?" a disgruntled male voice nearby muttered. "I walked by the radio room and heard the man myself. He told the other chap that the message was to send prominent names, and something about the USS *Chester* wanting passenger names and position. You think they aren't taking all the press inquiries they can?"

"Captain Rostron doesn't seem the sort," another man replied reluctantly. "He's a respectful man."

The first man snorted in derision. "He'll want his own name to be touted as the hero of the *Titanic* disaster, mark my words. Our families will be reading our names in a survivor list rather than getting the messages we sent."

"Are you impugning the captain of this ship?" a burly, dark-eyed crewman demanded, his expression livid.

The man straightened up. "And if I am?"

"Then I'll toss you overboard to join the fishes, and pray God might forgive me for not bringing aboard someone more deserving of life," the man snarled, stepping forward with clenched fists.

Kate rushed between them before she could stop herself. "That's enough, I think." She turned to the first man. "Sir, you are entitled to your opinion, but it is monstrously ungrateful to think so poorly of the captain who saved us. If this member of his crew feels such loyalty to him, surely we can have more faith and trust in the captain until we reach New York."

The man stared at Kate, then turned away, grumbling and slinking off of the deck.

Kate exhaled slowly, her legs quaking from the confrontation.

"Thank you, miss."

She turned to the crewman with a smile. "Not at all. The captain is a good man; I have seen it myself. I have no doubt he continues to do the best for all of us."

"He does," the crewman affirmed with a nod. "But unfortunately, now I have to report to the officer of the watch what is being said about the captain. I pray he will not take offense. God knows, he doesn't deserve that slander."

"When we established communication with the various coast stations, all of which had heavy traffic for us, in some cases running into hundreds of messages, we told them we would only accept service and urgent messages, as we knew the remainder would be press and messages inquiring after someone on the Titanic.

"It is easy to see we might have spent hours receiving messages inquiring after some survivor, while we had messages waiting from that survivor for transmission.

"News was not withheld by Mr. Cottam or myself with the idea of making money, but because, as far as I know, the captain of the *Carpathia* was advising Mr. Cottam to get off the survivors' traffic first."

—HAROLD BRIDE,
Titanic junior Marconi man, April 27, 1912

CHAPTER 25

RMS *CARPATHIA* • APRIL 17, 1912

Arthur ground his teeth as he marched to the deck, his carefully worded and clearly written note in one hand.

It was unfathomable. All that he had given and done, all that he had seen fit to accomplish, and he was being accused of this? It was more than his conscience could bear. If the complaints had been limited strictly to passengers, he could have dealt with it. Passengers did not know everything, and their ignorance could be forgiven.

But when the White Star Line began accusing him . . .

Enough was enough.

He would not take this.

He slammed the paper up onto the notice board on deck, alongside the other announcements, and stared at it for a moment, seething.

Notice to passengers:

It has come to my knowledge that several passengers and other entities are under the impression that the delay in dispatching passengers' private messages is due to the radio instruments being used for press news.

I hereby declare that no press messages have been Marconied from this ship (with the exception of a short one of about twenty words to the Associated Press, sent immediately after the passengers had been picked up) and that passengers' messages have been dispatched with all possible speed.

Signed

A. H. Rostron, Commander

He nodded once at it, then started away.

"Captain?"

Arthur stopped, forcing his expression into a calm, cool politeness. "Father Hogue."

The Catholic priest was smiling, but it faded with one look at Arthur's expression. "Is something amiss, Captain?"

"It could be." Arthur pressed his tongue to the front of his teeth, eying the man as his thoughts spun. "Would you be willing to do me a very great favor, Father?"

"Of course," the man said, spreading his hands out.

"Would you gather the nearest dozen or so men and follow me? I have a pressing matter to inquire about."

Father Hogue nodded quickly and without a word headed for a nearby group of men, a mixture of *Titanic* passengers and some of their own. The Father spoke to them quickly, then the entire group followed Arthur to a secluded part of the deck.

He took a moment before speaking, then lifted his chin. "Gentlemen, this morning, I received a Marconigram from the White Star Line that accuses me of giving early information about the *Titanic* disaster to the newspapers of New York."

"What?" at least two of the men cried.

Arthur ignored them. "Since the collision," he went on, "I have sent only one telegram, and that was to the Cunard Line officials. In view of what we've done for the survivors of the *Titanic*, a White Star Line steamer, I think I am a victim of some rather rank injustice. How do you gentlemen feel about the subject?"

Father Hogue gaped openly. "Captain, no person could have done more than what you have done for any person in distress."

"Hear, hear," another man chimed in. "Any accusations from White Star officials are entirely unjust."

Nods and glowers rippled through the group, and Arthur immediately felt himself justified and consoled by their reactions. He was not mistaken in his reaction, and he would not have his reputation tarnished in this.

There was a great deal of comfort in that.

"Huzzah for Captain Rostron!" one of them called.

As one, the entire group took up the cheer, removing their hats and roaring, "Huzzah! Huzzah! Huzzah!"

Arthur was surprised by the tide of emotion their rousing cheers brought on. He didn't need the accolades, but their support was bolstering, and he wouldn't deny it.

"Thank you, gentlemen." He nodded at the men, then walked away, head held high.

The cheering continued, the men growing hoarse with the volume and fervency of their cries.

For the sake of being thorough, Arthur moved to the radio room to check on the two men who might also be at the center of the slanderous rumors.

Both Cottam and Bride were hard at work; Bride's feet were still wrapped in bandages. Incessant beeps and buzzing filled the air, but neither man seemed to mind.

"All well here, gentlemen?" Arthur inquired as he stepped in.

The lads straightened hastily, and Cottam leaped to his feet. "Captain."

He waved him back down. "Easy, lads. Have either of you slept?"

"Yes, sir," Cottam replied as he resumed his seat. "Mr. Bride relieved me for a few hours so I could do so."

Arthur turned to the young *Titanic* operator. "Your assistance is much appreciated, Mr. Bride. All things considered, it is very noble of you."

Bride gave him a fleeting smile. "It's my duty, Captain. I couldn't feel I had honored the memory of Jack Phillips if I didn't step in." He swallowed with difficulty, then turned back to the radio.

Cottam stared at Bride, then looked at Arthur again. "The stewards have brought us food as well, Captain."

"Excellent." Arthur nudged his head toward the radio. "How go the messages?"

"We are inundated, sir," Cottam said bluntly. "For every two passenger messages we send out, there are five press inquiries coming in. We're ignoring them, as you ordered, but they bog down the lines and delay our sending."

Arthur grunted in disapproval. "And they say we aren't sending things fast enough. There is a rather ironic note there. Anyone being particularly pressing?"

Bride glanced up. "The USS *Chester* isn't leaving us alone. I don't know who their man is, but he's using American Morse, and we can barely tell what he's saying. Keeps asking about a 'Major someone or other.' It gets rather irritating, but at least they aren't the papers. And we did send them the list of Third Class survivors, as you requested."

Cottam nodded. "There are some other ships we are in communication with as well as land stations, when we can get through."

"If they benefit us, stay in contact with them. Otherwise, keep as you are." Arthur shook his head in irritation. "No press."

The two men nodded in obedient acknowledgement, and Cottam and Bride resumed their work.

Arthur watched for a moment, impressed by their speed and competency at the Marconi radio. Where would any of them be now if not for such an invention?

Assured that all was in hand with the radio and messages, Arthur stepped back out into the corridor and headed for the bridge, satisfied that he had done right by his passengers, his ship, and his conscience.

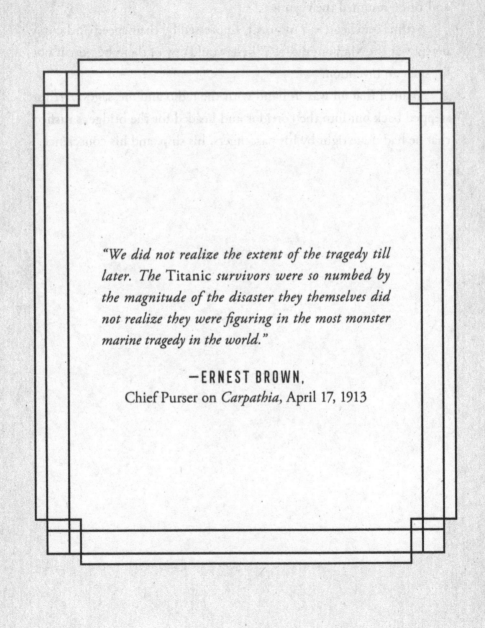

"We did not realize the extent of the tragedy till later. The Titanic *survivors were so numbed by the magnitude of the disaster they themselves did not realize they were figuring in the most monster marine tragedy in the world."*

—ERNEST BROWN,
Chief Purser on *Carpathia*, April 17, 1913

CHAPTER 26

New York was approaching; the sight of land had given Arthur a poignant burst of warmth when it had first been spotted.

The trouble was that when they'd spotted New York, New York had spotted them.

Or, more particularly, the press had spotted them.

The rain was torrential, an onslaught of pelting drops that mercilessly attacked each body not under shelter. And, as *Carpathia* was on her way to docking, there were a great many bodies not sheltered at the present.

Arthur couldn't blame the passengers for lining the deck. After their experience at sea, land would be a glorious sight.

Lightning lit the sky, and thunder crashed, several passengers jerking in surprise at the noise. Poor souls—their nerves and emotions were at the ends of their extremes; and now, to return to America amidst this tumultuousness?

Arthur scowled at the sight before him: a flotilla of boats in the middle of a storm.

That was to be their greeting in New York. A fleet of the press, hungry to make money off their arrival and desperate to take the first photographs of the survivors, bellowing at them all with the decency of hyenas. It was truly a despicable display.

"No press aboard, Mr. Dean," Arthur instructed coldly as he surveyed the scene. "Not a one. Just the pilot to take us into port."

"Right, sir." Dean related the message to the other officers, as well as positions for the protection of the passengers.

Arthur continued to stare at the mass of ships, then at the piers beyond.

They were covered with people, though identities and actual figures were indistinguishable. Each dock was full to the brim with crowds waiting to see the survivors of *Titanic*.

Were they family? Were they press? Were they the general public, curious about the whole affair?

There was no way to tell, but Arthur felt obliged to still care for his passengers and their well-being.

He frowned again at the sight of the approaching small boats. "What do you think about the numbers on the dock, Dean?"

"I don't know, sir," Dean admitted honestly. "There has never been something like this before. But I imagine we'll have eager families *and* the press waiting for our passengers."

"True." He exhaled roughly. "Pray God the pressmen have sense enough to let the families go first."

They watched as the pilot boat approached, trying to make its way through the rest of the boats. Had Arthur a pilot on board his ship to take them in, this whole nuisance would be unnecessary. But as they did not have one, the boat bearing the pilot must come to them.

And the press wanted to take advantage.

"What would you say to us disappointing them, Dean?" Arthur asked as an amusing idea struck him.

"Sir?"

Arthur glanced at him with a quick grin. "Would you ask the *Carpathia* passengers to line the railings and disembark first?"

Dean returned the grin with one of his own. "Of course, sir." He moved quickly to the deck to issue the orders.

Arthur turned to the other officers nearby. "Third Officer Rees, would you man the boarding ladder for when the pilot needs to come aboard? I don't trust the boats and reporters to not take advantage."

"Yes, sir." Rees moved off to take up his position.

The *Carpathia* slowed as the pilot boat drew nearer, the rain pounding harder, joined by more thunder and lightning.

Arthur moved out to the deck, watching as one of the boats carrying reporters and pressmen came alongside the pilot boat.

Five men stood together on the press boat, their attention not on *Carpathia* but on the pilot boat.

Arthur watched as, one by one, each of the men climbed over the railing of their own boat and jumped to the deck of the pilot boat.

The pilot himself, a man nearing his middle age, stared at them in horror and shock, but, as a small boat with one purpose, there was no way he could enforce proper behavior.

The pressmen, not one of them above thirty, moved to the edge of their new boat, their entire attention now focused on the *Carpathia*.

Or, more specifically, on the people upon the *Carpathia*.

The boarding ladder was lowered, and Rees stood at the foot of it, eyeing the pressmen. The reporters began shouting questions up at the passengers and officers on the ship.

"How many passengers died aboard the ship?" one reporter in a heavy coat bellowed above the driving rain.

"Why were more first class passengers saved than the rest?" came another. It was a wonder he could see anything through his rain-spattered glasses.

A third pushed to the railing in front of the rest, tipping his drenched hat back. "Did you see the wreckage?"

"Where are the Astors? Show us the Astors!" a fourth called, booming more than his wiry frame suggested he could.

The fifth man's voice held more anger than the others. "Why all the secrets? What are you hiding?"

Officer Rees only smiled at the group in bemused fascination as the boat drew nearer, the shouting continuing with more fervency. The other crew members scowled at them, clearly protective and possessive of everyone currently on their ship.

It made Arthur excessively proud to see.

The passengers, however, looked on in near terror at the questions, at the cameras' flashes, at all of it.

The pilot boat lined up with the boarding ladder, and the pilot was preparing to board when he was shoved aside by one of the reporters, who rushed toward the boarding ladder himself.

Arthur glowered at the impudent wretch, but Rees moved at once, leaping down to the pilot boat and delivering a swift punch to the reporter's mouth, sending him flying back to the deck. Rees took the pilot by the arm and pushed him up the boarding ladder.

"Pilot only!" he roared to the rest, shoving the pilot ahead of him.

One of the other reporters stepped forward, his face twisting with emotion. "Please! Please, I beg you! My sister . . . My sister was on the *Titanic*. I have to see her! I have to see her, sir, please! She's my sister!"

Arthur shook his head, prepared to forbid Rees from letting the man through.

But Rees was a smart man, and he stared at the reporter without any sympathy. "Why don't I believe you, I wonder?"

The reporter's face shifted to scheming. "Look, I will pay you two hundred dollars to let me on board. Just let me have access to the passengers—"

Rees shook his head in irritation and turned back up the boarding ladder with the pilot. "Bring up the ladder!" he called to the crew.

The ladder was drawn up, and the *Carpathia* continued toward the docks without any additional interruption.

Arthur nodded in satisfaction and turned to the officers near him. "Bisset, would you and Barnish take care of organizing the crew? There is something we need to tend to before we unload a single passenger."

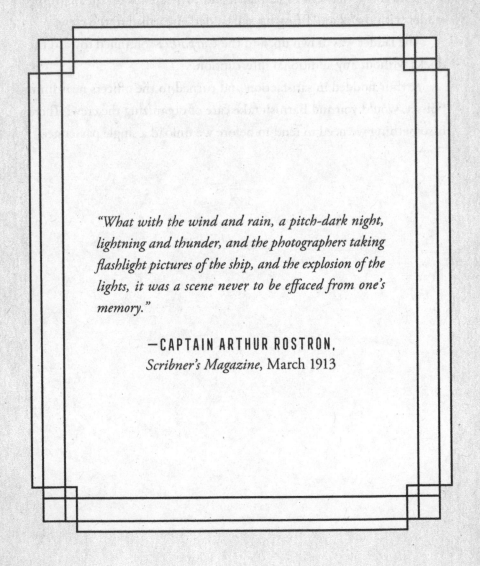

"What with the wind and rain, a pitch-dark night, lightning and thunder, and the photographers taking flashlight pictures of the ship, and the explosion of the lights, it was a scene never to be effaced from one's memory."

—CAPTAIN ARTHUR ROSTRON,
Scribner's Magazine, March 1913

CHAPTER 27

"What is the captain doing?"

Kate's thoughts echoed the same question the man behind her had asked, though she wouldn't have vocalized it. Standing on the deck in a torrential storm was strange enough, but to now be shifting from the course they had expected?

The *Carpathia* should have been heading for the Cunard Line piers, which were teeming with people, but instead, it was headed to a pier where no one stood.

Had the captain decided they should unload away from the crowd? Was that even possible?

"Perhaps they intend to unload the *Titanic* passengers at the White Star piers as a matter of protocol," another man suggested.

"I highly doubt even White Star would be so fussy about such a thing. How can they expect a ship to dock twice?" the first man replied.

That, too, was a valid point.

All Kate knew was that it was cold, it was storming, and it was late in the evening, and she wanted to touch land more fiercely than she ever imagined possible. She wanted to run into her sister's arms and cry for all she had seen and heard. She wanted to put the entire experience behind her and move forward with the hope she'd had before ever boarding the *Titanic*.

So long as she was able to set foot on a pier this evening, she supposed it did not matter what the captain decided to do.

She looked at Julia, who was wrapped in blankets, her face pale. She had developed a fever again yesterday and would be taken directly to a hospital when they arrived. Most of the *Titanic*'s passengers would do the same, given the amount of exposure to cold and icy waters they had experienced. Though they had received a clean bill of physical health from the doctors on *Carpathia*, there could undoubtedly be longer lasting effects not yet known to them.

Kate was due to go herself, though she felt hale enough under the circumstances. She suspected if the doctors could confirm the health of the passengers, it would benefit the businesses of Cunard and White Star.

Rumors were already floating around the ship that an inquiry would be made on both sides of the Atlantic to determine the causes of *Titanic*'s demise, and any perception of wrongdoing would require explanation.

Was that why the passengers would receive dedicated care? So that any hint of illness could be thoroughly examined?

Would steerage passengers receive care in proportion to their class, or would such divisions be set aside for the sake of humanity?

While there had certainly been divisions of class on *Carpathia*, it had not seemed so distinct as on *Titanic*. The separations here had been more for the ease of maintaining care, tracking identities, and ensuring safety for them all.

"Oh, heavens," Katie breathed, her eyes widening. "Look what the crew is doing."

Silence reigned over the deck as Kate and several other passengers watched the crewmen load the *Titanic* lifeboats up and prepare to swing them out.

Kate realized in an instant what the captain was doing.

Carpathia was, indeed, going to the White Star Line pier instead of her designated Cunard one.

They were going to dock where *Titanic* would have.

Slowly and carefully, the ship continued to approach, and the crew of the *Carpathia* continued to prepare the lifeboats.

"No," a man near them murmured in awe. "Are they really . . . ?"

An air of reverence rippled through the crowd like a wave as the *Carpathia* gradually slowed, then eventually stopped its progress directly at the White Star pier, the crew ready at the lines of each lifeboat.

"Lower away," a lone voice ordered from somewhere on the deck.

The pulleys squeaked as each lifeboat began its journey back down to the water. Sniffles and sobs could be heard from multiple passengers, and even the rush of noise from the Cunard pier had ceased.

Kate had no words for this. Each lifeboat seemed to represent the lives not saved, those who had been left behind in the frigid waters and those for whom any rescue was too late to matter. Those who could not get away, those who chose not to, those who had sacrificed themselves for the lives of others.

It was a solemn, sobering moment to watch each boat descend, so very different now than when they had done so from *Titanic*.

Kate could still hear echoes of the screams that had filled those boats, the cries of wives and children leaving husbands and fathers behind. She could hear the panic raging on the deck as each boat hastened down to the sea and pulled away from the sinking ship.

She could even hear the creaking and groaning and snapping sounds of distress from *Titanic* herself as she fought to stay afloat for her passengers.

Even the music Mary claimed to have heard playing on the deck came back to Kate, a haunting accompaniment to all else she could see and hear. All fainter now, dim in her memory, but just as poignant and stinging as the reality had been.

A dampness touched her lips beneath the brim of her borrowed hat dripping with rain. The storm continued to rage, thunder still cracking the sky. The sudden moisture on her face pulled Kate from her memories, and she felt tears streaming down her cheeks. She swiped at them, sniffling softly. Her heart was breaking all over again as she thought of the faces she had seen.

Artur, left in their charge by his father. Ruth, separated from her mother and siblings in the lifeboats. Margit and her mother, the little sister in her arms, fearfully joining them. Martin McMahon, who had not been seen since he helped them back to the cabin. Martin Gallagher, who had gotten them up to the deck and to the boats.

Kate Connolly from County Tipperary.

Her jaw quivered with sharp pains as the face of the woman whose name she shared flashed across her mind. How could losing a near-stranger feel as though she had lost a part of herself?

Kate watched as the crew secured the ropes, one by one. A few of the surviving crew members of the *Titanic* would take up a place in the lifeboat before it was lowered to the water beside the White Star pier. The ladder would be sent down to them, they would loose the boat from her falls, then climb back up into *Carpathia*.

The process continued until each lifeboat belonging to the *Titanic* had been removed from the deck and slipped into the water, the only part of the once-unsinkable ship to reach New York.

Kate could not spot boat thirteen out of the group, but she took a moment to silently thank the blessed vessel for being the means of her escape.

The *Carpathia* groaned as it began to move again, and the ghostly reflection of *Titanic* faded.

It was time to move forward.

As the ship now glided toward the Cunard pier, the silence was broken by a flurry of camera flashbulbs popping like stars in the dark of night and by pressmen shouting questions. A few shouted words of criticism for the *Carpathia* captain and crew.

"Have we entered hell?" Mary Mac whimpered as she crossed herself. She tightened her coat more securely around her.

"It certainly feels so," Kate murmured, squinting at the flashing lights of the cameras.

The *Carpathia* shuddered to a stop at the pier, and the boarding ladder lowered.

"Remember," an officer nearby murmured to them all, "*Carpathia* passengers first. Remain patient—this may help us."

Kate and Mary and Julia glanced over to see Officer Pitman from *Titanic* relaying the message. He was just a few paces away, and he smiled at them with his usual warmth.

"Thank you for everything, Officer," Kate said, her voice raw, her emotions rising to her throat.

Officer Pitman swallowed, betraying the emotion he felt, and touched the brim of his hat. "My pleasure, ladies." He nodded and moved ahead to remind the other *Titanic* passengers of what was to come.

"I may follow him off the ship instead of going to hospital," Julia remarked weakly, trying for a smile.

Her friend's show of spirit despite her illness was cheering, and Kate found herself smiling.

Carpathia passengers began to descend, and they were immediately bombarded with questions from the pressmen and flashes from the cameras. After about ten passengers had disembarked, those on the pier realized the situation, and an irritated rumbling rose from them.

"Serves them right," Mary-from-Clare muttered with a sniff.

Julia and Kate nodded their agreement.

Then, at length, the first *Titanic* passenger began the descent.

Kate didn't recognize the woman, but anyone looking could tell from which ship she hailed. Her dark hair had no hat to protect it from the downpour, her clothes were clearly borrowed, and her eyes were wide and terrified as she journeyed down.

Cameras raised again and flashed at her; questions rained down upon her without waiting for an answer. She reached the bottom of the ladder, her legs visibly unsteady.

A customs official caught her as she swayed, and he held no evidence of sympathy in his expression. "A survivor?" he questioned.

She nodded.

"Your name," he demanded.

She inhaled weakly. "Sarah Roth."

He gave a brief nod and led her toward a particular section of the pier, helping her off the gangplank. He handed her off to one of the nurses standing by.

Sarah staggered in her steps, and her shoulders seemed to bend under the weight of the questions being shouted at her.

What had the press expected from the poor woman—or from any of the survivors—after all they had endured?

The nurse helped stabilize Sarah, supporting her as they walked forward, when a low, groaning wail rose from the crowd of loved ones who waited beyond a fence.

"Sarah! Sarah!" a man cried out. He broke through the double line of customs officials as easily as one might have plowed through a pile of leaves and raced toward her.

Sarah opened her mouth without sound, and she raised her arms, reaching for him, though the effort nearly pitched her forward. Only the support of the nurse kept her upright.

The man barely stopped before hauling Sarah into his arms and embracing her tightly, her brown hair falling to one side as he did so. Without another word, with tears streaming down his face, he turned and carried her away, through the crowd of onlookers, themselves eager for such reunions.

One by one, the *Titanic* passengers made the same arduous journey down to the pier, answering the customs officials, and finding their way to the crowd waiting for them.

As Kate began her own descent, she caught sight of a small man in a suit eyeing them speculatively. He had two uniformed officers flanking him, and he held a stack of papers in one hand. A few of the people in front of her received a paper from him, though he barely spoke a word in either greeting or explanation.

When Kate reached the bottom of the gangway, she glanced toward the man in the suit, but his focus remained on the ship, apparently completely uninterested in her for his means.

Whoever he was, she did not care about being ignored by him. She just wanted to find her sister.

"Can I get your name, please, miss?" the plump customs man asked in a sympathetic voice. "Just need to check you off."

Kate turned her attention to him, clearing her throat. "Catherine Connolly."

The customs man scanned down his list, turning the top page over. "Ah, yes, here you are. From County Tipperary."

A flash of numbness enveloped Kate's body. She had the disconcerting feeling that the pier had vanished from beneath her feet. Her lungs seized, and her knees trembled.

"No," she whispered, her eyes going wide. "No, I'm . . . I'm from County Cavan."

The customs man snapped his head up to look at her with confusion. "I beg your pardon?"

Kate struggled to swallow and couldn't manage it. "There were two of us on board. Catherine Connolly, I mean. I'm the one . . . I'm . . ."

His mouth worked silently in dismay, and he glanced down at his papers again. "Miss Connolly, I am so sorry, but it seems . . . That is . . . We had Miss Connolly from Tipperary down as surviving."

Feeling as though she might snap in half, Kate gripped the man's arm to steady herself. "Sir, was her family notified instead of mine?"

"I fear so, miss."

She could barely see through the sudden tears that blurred her vision. Her breath faltered, hitching in her chest on a pained sob.

Her family thought she had perished.

While the other Kate Connolly's family believed their daughter was alive.

Gasping in anguish, Kate staggered away, one of the nurses catching her elbow and helping her away from the ship.

The Tipperary Connolly family would be devastated. They'd experienced a week of blessed relief and exuberance after hearing their sister and daughter was alive, that she was one of the fortunate few. Now that would come crashing down about their heads, their world crumbling into a devastation worse than the initial despair they must have felt at the news of *Titanic*'s sinking.

Their Kate was gone, and a different Kate remained.

Her own family's experience would be entirely the opposite. For them, their clouds of grief would dissipate as new joy broke through like dawn after a dark night. She would be returned to them, though they had thought her gone forever. Her mother's tears would come to an end.

But the other Kate . . .

What if *her* family had come to greet her?

Her vision suddenly clearing, Kate anxiously scanned the faces of the waiting people, not sure how she would know them but terrified someone had heard her conversation with the customs official. That somehow the family would know.

That they would hate her on sight.

But no one looked at Kate directly.

No one seemed to hear.

"Are you all right, miss?" the nurse holding her asked gently. "Father Grogan or I can take you to the hospital now, or you can look for your family first and make your way there later."

Kate managed to swallow, nodding rapidly. "I'd like to look first, please. Thank you."

"Of course, miss," she replied kindly as she released Kate's arm. "Father Grogan from St. Vincent's Hospital is just there to direct you, when you're ready. Welcome to New York."

What welcome? All she'd known so far was horror and a crushing, overwhelming guilt.

Kate steadied herself on her feet and carefully walked toward the crowd.

Would Nellie or John have come to the docks anyway? Would they have held onto their hope and looked for her, fearing it would be in vain?

A weak flicker of her own hope sparked alight within her as she scanned the people for any sign of Nellie or John. She moved through the crowd, straining to hear any call of her name or voice she might know.

But there was nothing.

Not a thing.

She reached the back of the crowd and turned around, looking quickly through them, but again, she was of no interest to any there.

No one was waiting for her.

Biting down on her lip hard, Kate slowly made her way toward the street and the minister waiting there.

"Are you from the *Titanic*, miss?" he asked with compassion. "This cab will take you to St. Vincent's at no charge."

Swallowing more tears, Kate nodded. "Thank you, Father. If you do not object, I should like to wait for my friends, please. I would rather not go alone."

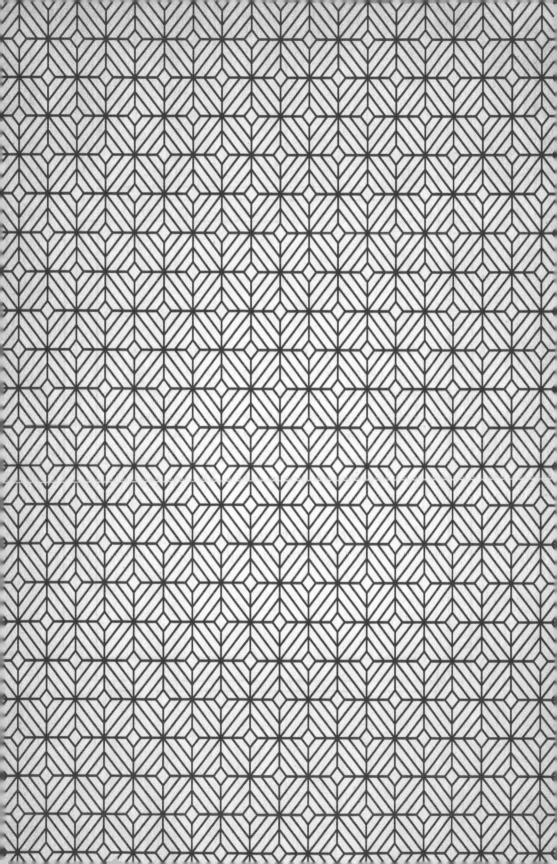

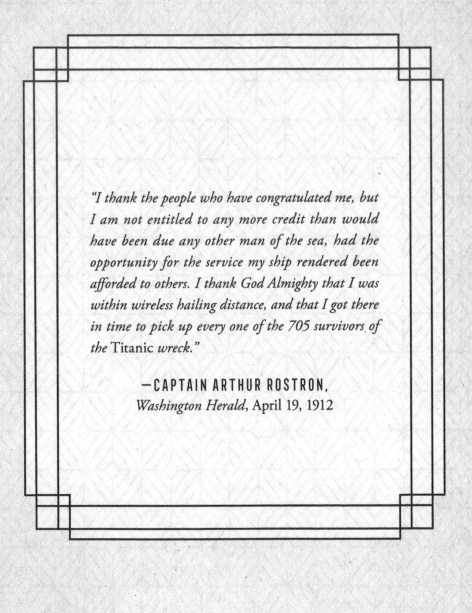

"I thank the people who have congratulated me, but I am not entitled to any more credit than would have been due any other man of the sea, had the opportunity for the service my ship rendered been afforded to others. I thank God Almighty that I was within wireless hailing distance, and that I got there in time to pick up every one of the 705 survivors of the Titanic *wreck."*

—CAPTAIN ARTHUR ROSTRON,
Washington Herald, April 19, 1912

CHAPTER 28

Arthur tugged on his jacket with some finality, checking his reflection in the looking glass once more. His uniform was crisp and clean, the black fabric stark against the shining gold buttons and the gold braids at his shoulders. A full night of sleep had helped reduce the haggard appearance he had worn of late, but he could still see the strain reflected in his eyes.

The senators promised they needed only one day, and then he could be off with his crew and their passengers again.

One.

He doubted they would keep their word, given that the more interviews they held the more questions they would undoubtedly want to ask. He knew they needed to undertake this inquiry, and that the outcome would have great significance to the future of steamship travel, but the timing was inconvenient.

Necessary, given the proximity to the events themselves, but inconvenient.

He had called Ethel the day before, and, though he'd kept his comments on the subject brief, his wife had seen through his reserve. The full conversation regarding his experience would need to be saved for when they were together, perhaps sitting before the fire in their home, when he could draw strength from his hand in hers. But simply hearing her voice and speaking with her had done him a world of good.

Her advice on the inquiry had been simple: "Tell the truth. Speak with honor."

He intended to do just that.

How many witnesses would be called, he could not say, and how many would be from his own ship was also unknown. He could only hope that the number of *Titanic* passengers called upon to testify of their experience would be limited to those absolutely essential to the proceedings. Asking too many to speak would result in heartbreak and despair.

The remaining crew of *Titanic*, on the other hand, were professional, seafaring men, and they should be able to separate the events themselves from the pain of them for the sake of inquiry.

Senator Smith and his enthusiastic dispersing of subpoenas the day before had left a great deal to be desired, but Arthur would not fault the man for doing the task assigned to him.

But Arthur wouldn't have all that much to say, all things considered. He could bear witness of his own experiences of the events and of his professional experience on the sea, but beyond that, any statement he might make regarding the *Titanic* would be hearsay and speculation. If the inquiry would be based on that, he would prefer to have none of it touch him.

Lifting his chin, he left his hotel room at the Waldorf-Astoria and strode down the hall. His thoughts were awhirl as he silently made his way down to the rooms designated for the inquiry. He passed several men in various uniforms—some he knew, others he did not. Yet each man offered a nod of respect, which he returned.

A strange unity had been built between them, the seafaring men and this inquiry. And the disaster, really. Whatever was decided, nothing would be the same for any of them.

Arriving at the designated rooms, he sat on a bench outside of the doors, waiting for his name to be called.

"Captain."

He glanced up to see Harold Cottam approaching, looking much more like the lad he had been when *Carpathia* had left New York the week before.

"Cottam," he replied, rising to shake the man's hand. "You look much better, son."

Cottam smiled, though it did not reach his eyes. "Thank you, sir."

Arthur gestured to the bench beside him. "Will you sit?"

"I will, thank you."

For a moment, they sat in silence, then Arthur glanced at the younger man. "I take it you are giving testimony today as well?"

Cottam nodded. "Yes. I've been told, Captain, that I may not be able to resume our passage with you today. I believe they may need my testimony more than once."

Arthur waved off the note of apology in Cottam's voice. "Don't worry about that. You must do your full duty here. Take the opportunity to rest and recover yourself. I daresay you've done enough in the last few days to last a lifetime."

A soft, emotionless grunt was all the answer Cottam gave.

"Did you have many messages after we docked?" Arthur asked.

"I did," Cottam admitted, looking down at his hands. "But when Mr. Marconi boarded, he said they were hardly worth sending now." He shrugged.

Arthur found himself nodding. "Well, he was right on that point."

He cleared his throat. "Mr. Cottam, should I never have the opportunity to say so again, I must thank you most heartily for all you have done in the last few days. At the expense of your own health, and I venture, some of your sanity, you worked tirelessly to accomplish everything I asked of you and more. I am indebted to you for that."

Color raced into Cottam's cheeks, and his attention on his hands became more pronounced. "It was my job, sir, and my duty. I'd do it again all the same."

"I know you would," Arthur assured him. "And that you even heard the distress call from Mr. Phillips that night . . . I believe you are the hero of this whole affair, Mr. Cottam. I truly do."

"No, sir." Cottam shook his head firmly and met Arthur's eyes with surprising strength. "No, sir, I only received the message. You were the one who acted on it. I can only claim opportunity."

Arthur smiled at the young man, impressed by his modesty and touched by his praise. "You did a great deal more in my eyes, Mr. Cottam. A great deal."

A man in a somber gray suit stepped out of the room and inclined his head. "Captain Rostron, they are ready for you."

"Right." Arthur nodded and pushed to his feet. He turned to shake Cottam's hand again. "All the best, Mr. Cottam. And thank you again."

"It was my pleasure, Captain," came the reply, his handshake just as firm.

Arthur followed the man into the conference room that had been converted for the hearings. He walked down the aisle that had been created in the seating, his eyes scanning the table at the head of the room where seven senators who had been chosen to investigate the disaster sat. There wasn't a seafaring man among them. How could any of them hope to understand? He then caught sight of the esteemed Mr.

Uhler, the steamship inspector general, who was a fair-minded man, though gruff in appearance, and he revised his opinions.

Arthur sat in the chair before the panel, exhaling slowly in anticipation.

Senator Smith was a thin, balding man with hooded eyes, but his face seemed free from the hardness that might have accompanied someone in the position to judge so many. The senator cleared his throat and leaned forward behind the table.

"For the record, first. Please give your full name and address."

"Arthur Henry Rostron, Woodville, Victoria Road, Crosby, Liverpool."

Senator Smith nodded. "What is your business, Captain?"

Arthur flicked a small smile. "Seaman."

"How long have you been engaged in this business?" the senator asked, no trace of humor or irony in his tone.

"Twenty-seven years."

Senator Smith barely acknowledged his answer. "What positions have you filled?"

"Every rank in the merchant service, including captain," Arthur replied simply. He saw no need to spell out each position for the committee. If they were interested in such details, he would oblige, but not of his own volition.

A few of the senators on the panel chuckled, though Senator Smith merely gave Arthur a serious look before clearing his throat. "You are now captain of the *Carpathia*?"

Arthur inclined his head. "I am now captain of the *Carpathia*, Cunard Line."

"And how long have you been captain?"

"Since January eighteenth of this year." Arthur folded his hands in his lap, watching the senator carefully, wondering what thread the committee would explore first. This was an unprecedented affair, and there was no telling what to expect for any who had been called upon to testify.

Other than speaking of the disaster, of course.

But any other avenues . . .

"What day did you sail from New York?" the senator inquired, brisk and businesslike. "And what was your destination?"

"We departed the eleventh of April," Arthur said. "And we were bound for Liverpool, Genoa, Naples, Trieste, and Fiume."

The panel of senators nodded, making notes of his statement. Mr. Uhler watched Arthur with a carefully blank expression.

Senator Smith looked up and down the line of his fellow investigators, then at Arthur once more. "Please tell the committee what occurred after you left New York, as nearly as you can, up to the present time."

Arthur straightened, nodding in acknowledgment. "We backed out from the dock at noon on Thursday. We proceeded down the river, the weather being fine and clear. We left the pilot at the pilot boat and passed the Ambrose Channel Lightship. I cannot give you the exact time, now, because I have not had the time to review the details regarding date or time."

Senator Smith gestured impatiently. "I mean approximately. I don't need the specifics, Captain."

Didn't he? It seemed to Arthur that the specifics might have been rather significant in this inquiry, though he could concede that he was not entirely certain which specifics the senators might have been looking for.

"Very well, then." Arthur cleared his throat and thought back. "Up until Sunday at midnight we had fine, clear weather, and everything was proceeding without any trouble of any kind."

Arthur paused as everything prior to receiving the *Titanic*'s distress call raced across his mind. It felt as if it had happened years ago. He shook his head.

"At 12:35, Monday morning, I was informed of the urgent distress signal from the *Titanic*. That would be 10:45 PM Sunday night, New York time."

"Who informed you of the signal?" Senator Smith inquired without emotion.

What would the panel make of the *Carpathia*'s role in this whole affair? It was certainly nothing compared to the disaster and tragedy of *Titanic*, but Arthur could never forget the efforts of his crew, the wholehearted sacrifice of his engineering team, how the literal walls of *Carpathia* trembled during their race to rescue. He would never think of the events of that voyage as anything less than miraculous.

"Our wireless operator, sir," Arthur informed him clearly. "And my first officer, Horace Dean."

The questions continued along the same vein, usually from Senator Smith, though the others would chime in on occasion if they required clarification.

They asked for details about receiving the signal, what the signal was, how he came to his decision, what he had ordered done.

He recounted everything for them, step by step, until they reached the wreckage. Then he spoke of how they picked up each lifeboat and the conditions under which they had done so.

It was all there in Arthur's mind, clear as the morning sun had been upon the lingering icebergs and the lifeboats drifting in the middle of the frigid Atlantic. It might have been only that morning for how clearly he remembered the events, but in his heart, he felt as if he had aged an entire decade overnight.

The questions that followed were intriguing ones. They asked about the body he had chosen to leave floating, the condition of each lifeboat, and the state of his passengers. They demanded explanation for his choice of New York over Halifax, inquired if the *Titanic* passengers wore life belts, and of the messages they received from other ships and stations in the area.

It did not take long for Arthur to realize that, in spite of everything, the inquiry needed to lay blame somewhere. Yes, they wished to hear the story, to piece together all of the facts, but it became apparent that nothing would be truly settled until someone—be it man, company, or crew—would be found to be at fault.

And that did not sit right with Arthur in the least.

After an endless stream of questions regarding wireless communications after the disaster, Senator Smith narrowed his eyes at Arthur. "Did you know personally of the attempt of the president of the United States to communicate directly with your ship?"

Arthur blinked at the question, and the implication behind it. "Absolutely not. I know nothing whatsoever of that."

The senator raised his brow. "I guess there was no intention whatsoever of either ignoring his message—"

"My word, I hope not, sir," Arthur interjected without hesitation.

"Or neglecting it?" Senator Smith continued as though Arthur had not spoken. "I believe the president's messages were sent via the USS *Chester*, and that he was inquiring about his military aide, Major Archibald Butt."

Arthur resisted the urge to close his eyes with the sinking realization of what had happened in the confusion and flurry of messages at the time. How Bride and Cottam had barely been able to make heads or tails of the difference in communication methods. How inquiries about specific individuals had been passed off as press inquiries instead of being noted as something more. How, in the interest of doing exactly as he had directed, they had all missed a message from one of the most important men in the world.

He forced as much earnestness into his face and voice as possible.

"Absolutely no intention of any such thing, sir," he vowed. "It never entered into the minds of anyone."

That seemed to satisfy the senator, though Arthur felt little relief from it.

"And no one attempted in any way to put a censorship over the wireless service on your ship?"

"Absolutely no censorship whatever," Arthur insisted. "I controlled the whole thing, through my orders. I placed official messages first. After they had gone, along with the first press message, then the names of the passengers and crew were sent. My orders were to send all private messages from the *Titanic*'s passengers first in the order in which they were given to the purser. No preference was given to any message."

The panel of senators nodded among themselves, some leaning nearer to each other to discuss something Arthur had said, while Senator Smith merely checked his notes on the subject.

Arthur drummed his fingers against his knee, the rapid pace of his pulse finally slowing. How could the *Chester* not have told Cottam the reason behind their frequent and incessant questioning? Arthur would never have failed to reply had he'd known the president was the one demanding the information.

He would write to the president personally when this inquiry was over to apologize and to assure him that the slight was unintentional.

The senator looked up from his notes. "You have said that your gross tonnage is thirteen thousand six hundred."

"Yes, sir," Arthur replied.

"What is it as to passengers?" the senator demanded, his tone turning particularly firm.

Arthur heaved a sigh he hoped would not reveal his exasperation, though he was certainly beginning to feel it. "I cannot tell you. I have not come here with any data. I have not looked up anything and am absolutely unprepared for any questions. I have been too busy."

Senator Smith frowned, then glanced at Mr. Uhler. "What was the capacity of *Titanic*? The tonnage, I mean."

Mr. Uhler checked his notes. "Forty-five thousand six hundred twenty-nine tons," he grunted.

Senator Smith nodded. "And the *Carpathia* has, what, twenty lifeboats?"

"Yes, sir," Arthur replied. "That is the regulation of the British Board of Trade, I believe."

"It is," the senator confirmed without looking at his notes. "The fact that, under these regulations, you are obliged to carry twenty lifeboats and the *Titanic* was only obliged to carry twenty, despite her additional tonnage, indicates either that these regulations were prescribed long ago—"

Sensing another fault-finding attempt, Arthur shook his head immediately. "No, sir," he interrupted with as much firm politeness as he could muster. "It has nothing to do with that. Nothing at all."

The panel was silent for a moment, apparently intent on what he had to say.

Which meant he would have to say it very carefully.

He took a moment, then went on. "It has to do with the ship itself. Each ship is supposed to be a lifeboat in itself. The additional boats are there as a standby. The ships are supposed to be built to be unsinkable, and the naval architects say they are—under certain conditions."

He paused again, wanting that to register in their minds. "What those conditions are, I do not know, as to whether it is with alternate compartments full, or what it may be. The reason why we carry more lifeboats on our ship is simply that we are built differently from the *Titanic*—differently constructed."

Mr. Uhler flicked a glance of approval at Arthur, which he took to be a good sign. A faint smile was barely visible beneath the bushy mustache, but it was there.

He waited while the senators spoke quietly to each other.

Senator Smith looked down at Arthur again. "Would you regard the course taken by the *Titanic* in this trip as appropriate and safe and wise at this time of the year?"

"Quite so."

Clearly, the senator had anticipated that response. "What would be a safe, reasonable speed for a vessel of that size traveling on such a course and in such close proximity of icebergs?"

Arthur frowned. "I do not know the ship," he reminded the panel as a whole. "I know absolutely nothing about her."

"How would you have felt yourself about it?" the senator pressed, not entirely pleased with Arthur's evasive response. "Suppose you had been taking that course with your ship. How fast would you have felt it prudent to go in such a situation?"

Arthur recoiled at the idea that the senator was asking him to impugn Captain Smith's actions regarding his own vessel, particularly when Arthur had no details of the *Titanic*'s voyage to verify anything one way or the other. He would never speak ill of a dead man who could not defend himself.

He shook his head. "I can only tell you this, gentlemen, I knew there was ice about."

"How did you know that?" Senator Smith demanded.

Arthur gave him a cool look. "From the *Titanic*."

"From the *Titanic*'s message?"

"Precisely." Arthur nodded, then shrugged a shoulder. "The message reported that the ship had struck ice."

A deep furrow appeared in Senator Smith's brow. "Did you know it any other way?"

With another shake of his head, Arthur replied, "No, sir."

"You did not know it until you saw the ice yourself?"

Arthur sighed at the repetitive direction of this inquiry, uncertain what the senator and his colleagues wanted to hear. "I knew the *Titanic* had struck ice. Therefore, I was prepared to be in the vicinity of ice when I was getting near her, because if she had struck a berg and I was going to the same position, I knew very well that there must be ice about. I went full speed, all we could—"

"You went full speed?" Senator Smith interrupted in shocked disbelief.

"I did," Arthur confirmed. "And I doubled my lookouts and took extra precautions and exerted extra vigilance. Every possible care was taken."

The senator blinked at the response. "Would you have done so in the nighttime?"

Arthur quirked a brow. "It *was* in the nighttime."

Stifled laughter came from a few of the senators, while Senator Smith sat back in his chair, looking dumbfounded. His composure held none of his usual cool complacency and professionalism, and the glimpse of his humanity loosened Arthur's tongue.

"If I had known at the time there was so much ice about—" Arthur frowned, shaking his head. "Although I was running a risk with my own ship and my own passengers, I also had to consider what I was going for. I had to consider the lives of others."

Senator Smith's expression turned thoughtful. "You were prompted by your interest in humanity?"

Arthur nodded. "Absolutely."

"And you took the chance?" the senator asked.

"It was hardly a chance," Arthur replied with more sympathy and consideration than he'd employed yet. He hesitated, then shook his head, needing to correct himself already. "Of course, it *was* a chance, but at the same time I knew what I was doing. I considered that I was perfectly free, and that I was doing perfectly right in what I did."

"I suppose no criticism has been passed upon you for it?" the senator asked with a slight tilt to his head.

Arthur shook his head. "No."

Senator Smith sat forward. "In fact, if I may speak for myself and my associates, I may say that your conduct deserves the highest praise."

"I thank you, sir." Arthur smiled slightly, dipping his chin to acknowledge the compliment. He still felt as if he had not done anything extraordinary; certainly, he had done what any other man of sense and experience would have, given the situation. But he would accept, graciously, the appreciation of others for what had been accomplished.

And the senator, after all, was doing his designated duty as well, much as it may have irked the others who were being asked questions just as Arthur was.

Senator Smith returned his smile. "And we are very grateful to you, Captain, for coming here. I understand it is your purpose to leave this afternoon?"

"Yes." Arthur shifted in his seat, eager to conclude this business. "We sail at four o'clock."

Returning to the business at hand, the senator sobered. "If we should require additional communication, what are your plans for the future? Are you headed for the south of Europe?"

"We go to Gibraltar." Arthur looked down the line of senators. "I am traveling the same old route as before—Gibraltar, Genoa, Naples, Trieste, Fiume—"

Mr. Uhler cleared his throat. "Fifty days back to New York?"

"A little less than that," Arthur allowed as he met the man's eyes. "About forty-three days back. We sail about every seven weeks."

Mr. Uhler nodded, and Senator Smith straightened the pages before him. "We are very much obliged to you, Captain Rostron."

"You are quite welcome, sir. If there is anything further I can do,

I'm happy to assist." Arthur rose, nodded firmly, and strode from the room, praying he had done his duty without overstepping in any direction.

But now, he could put this aside for a time, as well as any lingering thoughts on *Titanic*. He would see his passengers to their destination safely before he was due to England for the second inquiry, and he intended to make the most of the time he had been given.

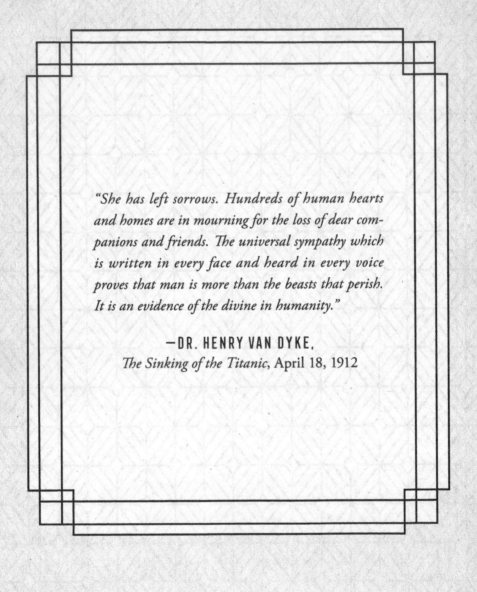

"She has left sorrows. Hundreds of human hearts and homes are in mourning for the loss of dear companions and friends. The universal sympathy which is written in every face and heard in every voice proves that man is more than the beasts that perish. It is an evidence of the divine in humanity."

—DR. HENRY VAN DYKE,
The Sinking of the Titanic, April 18, 1912

CHAPTER 29

There was no need for her to remain in the hospital any longer. Several members of the staff had told her so, and yet Kate remained.

She could have taken a taxi to her sister's address, she supposed, but something about showing up unannounced when she was presumed dead was too macabre to consider. What might such a surprise do to Nellie?

No, the hospital was the best place for her until she determined what her next step would be. Here, at least she had Julia. The Marys and Katie had met their families and returned to their lives, but Julia's illness had taken a turn, which required her to stay for further care.

Kate hadn't been permitted to stay near her friend, but she had visited her several times to keep her company. The words "scarlet fever" had been floating around, but as far as Kate knew, it had not been confirmed. She wasn't overly concerned for her friend; Julia was as hardy and hale as any Irishwoman, and while it might take some time to recover, she surely would.

Kate leaned forward in her chair, her bed having been given up to someone in greater need, and rubbed her hands over her face. She had no clothing, no money, and no family aware of her being alive. It would all be made right, of course, and likely sooner rather than later, but there was no denying the discouragement that seeped into her with each inhale.

She wanted to send a message to the Tipperary Connolly family, apologize for any confusion, and let them know how much she had admired their Kate, though their association had been brief. But such a message would likely pour salt into an already gaping, festering wound, so she knew she could not. At least, not for several years.

In the meantime, what could she do but wait?

Wait for resolution, wait for the next step, wait for any direction, wait for her family to be informed that she was alive.

Waiting was not comfortable, but it was all she could do.

The hospital had been bustling the day before as most of the other passengers from *Titanic* had arrived. Though many appeared to have stayed with family, the passengers most in need of care had come directly to the hospital.

She'd seen Mr. Bride and had had a brief conversation with him, but she had not heard if there had been any firm answers regarding his poor feet.

She recognized other passengers, having seen them but never learning their names, yet still more were strangers to her.

Such had been the vast number of survivors, and such had been the space they had been afforded on the *Carpathia*.

Mrs. Brown had come by the hospital yesterday, and Kate was flattered when the other woman remembered her. Mrs. Brown had gone from bed to bed as though she were a patroness of the hospital rather than one of the "poor survivors," as Kate heard themselves called. But

Mrs. Brown had assured every one of them that they would have the resources of her Survivors' Committee as soon as possible.

Kate tugged at the sleeve of her borrowed dress, now nearly as worn as her frozen one had been. There had not been additional new clothes, and she would not complain of it, as what she had been given had been generously donated, but what she would not give for clothing of her own that was hers in truth, even if it had her own mending to it.

"I'm looking for Catherine Connolly," an emotional Irish voice said from somewhere nearby. "She was on the *Titanic*, and I was told she was here."

"Is she a patient, ma'am?" came the sympathetic reply.

Kate slowly lowered her hands, heart pounding with a painful edge.

An orderly stood in the doorway to Kate's room, blocking her view of the person inquiring about her.

"I'm not sure. All I was told . . ."

Kate swallowed as the orderly shifted, and a voice she had not heard in more than two years faded as the sisters' eyes met across the room.

Nellie clutched a hand to her chest, her fingers curling into the fabric of her dress, her familiar gray eyes widening as they began to swim with tears.

Slowly, Kate rose from her chair, her throat closing on emotion she hadn't anticipated after the disappointment of the day before.

Nellie hadn't moved so much as an inch, her brown hair tucked into a tight, neat chignon, blinking her eyes owlishly. "Kate?" she breathed.

A wobbling smile crossed Kate's lips. "Aye."

Her sister inhaled, then rushed at Kate as a sob erupted from her.

Kate ran to her in response, and soon the sisters were in each other's arms, tears streaming from them both.

"Oh, Kate," Nellie gasped, burying her face against Kate's shoulder. "I thought I'd never see you again!"

"I'm sorry," Kate hiccupped as she tightened her arms around her older sister.

Nellie pulled back and held Kate's face in her hands, touching her face and her hair. "You weren't on the list of survivors, and we thought . . . Oh, bless heavens, I can't believe it's really you!"

Kate took hold of Nellie's wrists, finding laughter amid her tears. "Sometimes I can't believe it's me either."

Her sister did not seem to hear her, so engrossed was she in apparently memorizing Kate's features. "We've been so anxious for any news. John spent hours outside of the White Star offices with a crowd of others, waiting for the names. The reports changed constantly; it was utterly maddening. We heard hundreds had died, but there were no details."

"I'm so sorry," Kate whimpered, her thumbs absently stroking her sister's wrists, more to comfort herself than Nellie. "I should have sent a message. We were able to do so, but I didn't . . . It didn't . . ."

She broke off, dissolving into more tears as the reality of what had happened, what her family had endured, what could have been crashed down upon her with a harshness that nearly buckled her knees.

Nellie gathered her close, holding almost painfully tight, and ran her hands through Kate's hair, just as she had done when they were children. "Hush now, Katie-girl. It's all right. There's no blame on you, and nothing to be sorry for. You're here, you're alive, and we're together. You're grand, aye?"

Kate burrowed against her sister's shoulder, sob after sob wracking her frame. After all the horror and despair, the tears and screams, the fear and uncertainty, she was safe and whole now. She was in her sister's arms, and she could see her family again, if she chose. She had known that truth while on board *Carpathia*, but the reality of it had not struck her until this moment.

Until she had seen her sister.

"Oh, darling girl," Nellie soothed. "Come have a seat, gather yourself." She led Kate back to the chair and sat beside her, rubbing her back in wide circles while holding Kate's hand tightly.

Kate could barely breathe, her cries becoming more and more harried, less controlled, more panicked. "Those families, Nellie . . . *Her* family. I can't bear it."

"Whose family, Kate?" her sister asked with a squeeze to her hand. "What are you talking about?"

"The Connollys." Kate wiped at the tears on her cheeks, forcing her breathing to slow so her panic would not overtake her completely. "From Tipperary. They believe their Kate survived the disaster and will be waiting for her to meet them, only to discover that there has been some horrible mistake and she was lost after all. Oh, Nellie, what will that do to them?"

She buried her face in her hands again, guilt and shame filling her in equal measure as she considered the joy and relief she felt in her own reunion.

There would be no reunion for the Tipperary Kate, no tears of joy at seeing her again or holding her close. Her siblings, if she had any, would never smile or laugh with her, nor would her mother take her hand in a show of comfort. There would be nothing of her for them from this time forward, yet they believed there was all the time in the world.

"Kate, listen to me," Nellie insisted, taking Kate's arms in hand. "John was in the crowd outside of the offices, waiting for word and the names of survivors. He said there was nothing of competition in it, no victory or selfishness. Those who suffered a loss had arms to embrace them, though they belonged to strangers. There was no bitterness for those who retained their hope of a loved one's return, no anger or desire for vengeance.

"He said it was one of the most solemn, hallowed experiences he had seen when those names were released. From chaos came silence, and from anger came sorrow, but all that were there felt the same." She squeezed Kate's arms gently and waited for her to meet her gaze.

Kate swallowed as she tried for a smile.

Nellie smiled back. "The loss of any life was a loss for all, Kate, and there was no time or desire for harboring anything else."

It was a sobering thought: the image of family and friends waiting outside of White Star in anticipation of any word of the disaster beyond the sinking, the desperation to know the severity, the longing for news of safety, the fear of what the scant details meant. That crowd would have been unified in their emotions, regardless of what specifics eventually emerged.

Hadn't the life of any survivor of the *Titanic* been the same from the moment they'd left her deck? Hadn't she felt the pain of the loss, though she had lost no one? Hadn't she been crushed by the magnitude of the catastrophe, though she had been safe from the worst of it? Hadn't tears flowed from her eyes without shame that night while strangers around her froze to their deaths?

She'd held children for their mothers, comforted widows too young to be alone, tended the weak and wounded who had no one else to care for them. She had felt their pain and losses as her own, knew the sounds that haunted them, shared the fears they had all felt. The burial service on the deck had broken them all, though she doubted more than a handful of passengers had actually known those they were burying.

It had not mattered.

A loss for one was a loss for all.

And never had Kate been shamed for not having lost someone in the tragedy.

Why should life off the *Carpathia* be different?

She sniffled back her tears, folding her arms against her chest, and managed a more genuine smile for her sister. "I'm sorry John had a long wait for news. I cannot imagine that was easy."

Nellie shook her head. "No, it was not. There was some very severe criticism of the rescue vessel for not sharing much information. Even John was irritable, and you know he is normally easygoing."

"Don't judge them too harshly," Kate pleaded softly. "It was not so easy, nor so simple. The press would not leave us alone, and the poor radio man had been up for three nights without rest . . ."

"Sure look it, 'tis a wonder any name was correct at all," Nellie murmured with a shake of her head, eyes wide. "Poor lad."

"And the captain . . ." Kate sighed, swallowing. "He was as fine a man as any could have hoped. Risked his life and ship to save any of us, and now they blame him for not jabbering on about the thing while he cared for the lot of us. It's not right; they don't understand."

Nellie nodded and took Kate's hand once more. "I know. It doesn't matter now. You're alive, and you're here in New York. I'll take you home, see you rested and fed, and then we can start your new life in America, aye?"

Kate inhaled and exhaled slowly. Her new life in America.

She'd almost forgotten that lay ahead.

"And one day," Nellie went on, "all of this will be but a faint memory."

Kate shook her head at the kindly meant words. "No, Nellie. These memories will never be faint, and they will never be forgotten." She sighed and got to her feet. "But we must go on. I'll be living for two Kate Connollys now. Best I start on a sure foot."

Her sister rose and took her arm, drawing her close. "It's grand to have you here, Katie-girl. Let's go home."

Home.

Such a lovely, comforting thought. It seemed so foreign now, after all that had happened with *Titanic*, after what Kate and the rest had seen and endured. *Home* had sustained her throughout the ordeal, though it had been less of a location in her mind. It had been a feeling, a gathering, a familiar warmth that had sustained her in good times and in bad.

Now that warmth was in this place, growing breath by breath as her sister's arm rested in hers. Soon Kate would find her own way. A permanent home built on the strength born of a night on icy waters, buoyed by a new appreciation of life and health, and a determination to live for those who could not do so themselves.

For all those lost in the sea with *Titanic*, and all those who were changed because of it.

Kate Connolly was home now, and home to stay.

"His conduct of the rescue shows that he is not only an efficient seaman, but one of nature's noblemen."

—SENATOR WILLIAM ALDEN SMITH,
The Sinking of the Titanic, 1912

CHAPTER 30

Arthur breathed in the sea air deeply, the crisp freshness expanding his lungs with an ease he had not known in days and a lightness he thought he'd forgotten. There was something peaceful and breathtaking about the open expanse of sea, particularly when the water was as calm as it was now. Gazing out across it, at the light reflected from her glossy surface, brought him clarity. He felt a complete and profound proximity to the heavens that Arthur struggled to find anywhere on land.

He was as close to God here in moments like this as he ever was elsewhere.

Ethel, Lord love her, understood that was the way of things for him, and, much as he adored her, he would not give the sea up until he could no longer serve her.

But when next he was home in Liverpool, he would hold her closer than he ever had before. He would take his children into his arms as a whole, then put each on his knee, one by one, and make sure they knew of his pride and his love for them.

New York had faded into the distance the night before, and he had never been so grateful to see it go.

With it had fallen the weight of everything he had carried from *Titanic.*

Not the horror, not the loss, not the poignant memories or the profound experience itself, but the responsibilities and the doubts, the pressures and the problems.

Now he was simply Arthur Rostron, captain of the *Carpathia,* once more.

He would never forget all that had happened, nor the miracles that had transpired to make it so. His own voyages on the sea would have more care and consideration, more security and certainty, after the loss of so many lives in a disaster of such unprecedented scale. The results from the inquiries alone would impact every ship, captain, and crewman of the sea when all was said and done.

But this day, in this moment, he was back in familiar waters with familiar duties and in a familiar setting.

Only he was changed.

Likely forever so.

The hubbub of the day before had been a whirlwind. Photos were taken with his crew, and gifts were given, including money collected by the Survivors' Committee, a silver cup with an inscription for them, medals of gold and silver for himself and his officers, and even a bas-relief of *Carpathia.*

Mrs. Margaret Brown had been the most insistent of any of the committee, as was her nature, and she refused to let Arthur pass the praise off to anyone else or decline all such accolades.

Arthur fully believed what he had said to Dean not so long ago. They would be forgotten when history looked back on the *Titanic* and her tragedy. The *Carpathia* might be recollected as the vessel who picked up the survivors, but the details of her journey there, the people involved in the rescue, and all that had transpired would fade when set against the more pressing, terrible facts and stories of that night.

That was as it should be. Those who were lost should be honored and revered. Those who were saved should be treasured and known. The disaster itself ought to be a warning to all ships and seamen traveling the same sea.

What use would the tale of *Carpathia* rushing to aid and risking endangerment add to the tale when more terrible things had happened?

But his conscience was clear, his heart at ease. He would have done the same again and again, and he was deeply grateful that his crew and his passengers had been so willing to follow him into that reckless action.

There was not a soul among them who had given less than his or her all, from the stokers in the bowels of the ship to the lookouts high above. Every stewardess had constantly served all around her, every joiner had tirelessly tended his work, every greaser had maintained his station, every engineer had monitored the ship, and every officer had done all that Arthur had asked of them. There could not have been a more dedicated, blessed, and loyal crew than the one he'd had that night, and the one he had with him now.

His thoughts turned to Harold Cottam.

The lad had indeed been required to stay in New York for additional questioning in the inquiry, but he would join them in England for the next journey, likely shuttled over with those of the *Titanic* who were also being interviewed.

How in the world would any of this have been possible without that man's dedication and skill? Without his consideration of relaying information to *Titanic* about something as simple as messages? If he had been less careful, less determined, or less alert, nothing remarkable would have happened on the *Carpathia* on April the fourteenth and fifteenth, and they would only have heard of the disaster long after the fact.

The world owed Harold Cottam greatly, and Arthur, though he might receive a great deal of attention in being *Carpathia*'s captain, would only ever consider Cottam as the one who made any of it possible.

With a final sigh as he took in the sea, he turned from the deck and returned to the bridge where his first officer stood at his post.

"Mr. Dean," Arthur said simply, "would you request that all crew present themselves to the deck, please? I wish to address them."

Dean did not seem entirely surprised by the order. "Of course, Captain." He moved away to have word sent, and Arthur waited, his hands clasped behind his back.

They still had a way to go before this particular journey could be closed, and he doubted any of them would forget anything they had seen or heard. Indeed, they would probably be asked to speak on the subject in some fashion for the rest of their lives, once their involvement was known.

Until one day, the world would no longer recognize the name *Carpathia* except as a footnote to another, larger story. The survivors of *Titanic* might have been loaded onto any ship that night, and one steamship was as good as any other in many people's minds. Time would scour the images from their minds, and the names of those who had done so much for so many. All would eventually be lost and forgotten except by those to whom the services had been rendered.

But what of the next generation? What of the one following? The disaster of *Titanic* would never be forgotten, but would future accounts truly grasp the magnitude of it all? The loss of life that was beyond imagination? The pain of each soul that had been brought aboard Arthur's ship and cared for in their hour of need? Would any of them understand the fear that had lingered in the minds of Arthur, of his officers, of any of his crew who truly understood what racing northbound in such conditions could mean?

Would anyone else understand the sort of death the victims of *Titanic* would have suffered?

The story would become simply a mark of history, something discussed with as much concern and respect as any given battle when it was too far removed to be appreciated.

No one would truly know. No one would see.

But here and now, he would. His crew and his officers would. His passengers would.

They would see and know and remember for as long as *they* lived. They would share their stories and live their lives forever changed.

History and posterity might never appreciate what they had endured, but Arthur Rostron certainly would.

"The crew are gathered, Captain."

Arthur nodded his thanks to Dean. "Shall we?" he invited with a gesture.

Dean nodded and followed him out to the deck.

His officers stood in line first, and he paused to shake hands with each one, considering the contribution each of them had made.

Mr. Hankinson and his unflappable calm. Mr. Dean and his dedication. Mr. Bisset with his keen eye. Mr. Rees doing anything and everything asked of him. Mr. Barnish overseeing each lifeboat's arrival and security.

Each of them had done his duty beyond the utmost that night and in the days following, and no captain could have wished for anything more than that. A fine company of officers he had, and their futures were undoubtedly promising indeed.

He shook hands with the heads of all departments: Chief Engineer Johnston, Purser Brown, Chief Steward Hughes. These men had come to his cabin in the middle of the night to receive his instructions and had then done everything they could to carry them out. There wasn't a fault among the lot of them, and a great deal instead to praise and admire.

His letter to the Cunard Company the day before might have been lacking in specific commendation for them, but he had been determined to include them as a whole.

His own words came back to him as he stepped back and looked out over this gathering.

"I beg to specially mention how willingly and cheerfully the whole of the ship's company have behaved throughout, receiving the highest praise from everybody, and I can assure you that I am very proud to have such a ship's company under my command."

Never had words been so true.

Arthur cleared his throat, suddenly overwhelmed by emotion he had not anticipated. "Men of the *Carpathia*," he began in a clear, ringing voice. "I have assembled you here to show you my sincere appreciation for what you have done for me and those that you saved some days ago. Your loyalty and obedience to every command and order has brought to you and your ship great praise."

The only sounds were the waves splashing against the ship and the flags snapping in the air; every eye was fixed upon him as he spoke. A few passengers had lingered to listen in, though the majority were at their midday meal.

"Some might say," Arthur went on, "that I, as captain, am to be commended for our actions. That I am deserving of praise. Indeed, you may have already heard and seen something of the sort, given the gifts and kind words our friends and associates bestowed upon us yesterday."

A few nods rippled through the group, but all expressions remained free of resentment.

"I tried to do my duty as a sailor," he told them, scanning as many faces as he could, "and to care for those suffering. But I will not take credit for the achievement of that night, when we went to the aid of the people of the *Titanic*. I do not deserve that credit. My crew deserves it, and to you I want to give my heartfelt thanks for your loyalty, valor, and fidelity to the trust that was imposed."

Thunderous whoops and applause sounded from the crew, whistles rending the air and a few cheers accompanying them.

The sight and sounds were stirring indeed, and Arthur found himself moved beyond words.

It took some time for the sound to abate, and each passing heartbeat brought his emotions closer to the surface.

And it appeared his were not the only eyes growing damp as he looked out across his crew.

No captain had ever had such a fine band aboard his ship, he was sure of it.

"I am proud to have such men under my command," he said, his voice rough and nearly hoarse with the depth of his feeling.

"Huzzah!" the crewmen cried with all their might. "Huzzah! Huzzah!"

Arthur smiled, and when the cheers faded, he pointed toward the fore of the ship. "You notice at the fore, the flag—the Stars and Stripes—which we have representing the people of the United States. Another flag, which I now have the honor to unfurl, is the blue ensign of His Royal Majesty's Naval Reserve, in which I have the honor to serve. The third flag is that of the Cunard Line, which you have honored."

His crewmen removed their hats to honor the flags, eyeing them with pride and appreciation.

"I want you men to remain with this ship," Arthur told them simply. "Do your duty. I shall always be just with you. I shall always be fair with you."

The attention of his crew returned to him, and it seemed that each set of shoulders seemed a little squarer, each chest puffed out a little more, and each chin was raised a little higher. These were sailors of sound character, whose confidence in each other and in him had been bolstered in the last few days. They had been tried and tested and emerged with a brilliance and strength that they had never previously known.

Therein might have lain the true miracle.

"Again, I wish to thank you for what you have done for me," Arthur told them, his voice filled with sincerity. "And again I say that I am proud to have such a crew as you serving under my command."

Silence again washed over the crew, the snapping of flags punctuating his speech as if offering a heavenly applause.

"That is all." He nodded and clasped his hands behind his back. "As you were."

Rather than depart, the men began to applaud, whistling and roaring proudly in the morning air. Some of them cheered for him, as their captain. Some for *Carpathia* herself. Some merely lent their voices and applause to the chorus of the rest.

Whatever the motivation, it was a beautiful sound, and one Arthur would not soon forget.

"As you were!" Dean called out with a broad smile. "To your posts! Quick as you can—look lively now!"

The men dispersed to their usual posts and tasks, clapping each other on the shoulders and shaking each other's hands.

Arthur watched them go, then strode back to the bridge, feeling a deep satisfaction in his soul.

There was no telling what his career would demand of him in the years ahead, nor what commands he might take. If any further disasters would cross his path, or if calm waters and smooth sailing would become his fate. If time would be his ally or if, like Captain Smith, the sea would take him soon.

But he would continue on, with his conscience and his faith to guide him as they always had. The sea would be his companion, the ship his instrument, and their song that of his heart.

"All hands ready, Captain," Dean informed him as he resumed his place by Arthur's side.

"Very good, Mr. Dean." Arthur nodded at the helmsman. "Take her to half speed. Steady on our course."

"Half ahead!" Dean called out. "Steady on our course."

Arthur turned to the other officers. "Thank you, gentlemen. About your duties, if you please."

"Yes, sir," they replied before dispersing to other parts of the ship.

Striding to the foremost part of the bridge, Arthur looked out at the waters, smiling with contentment.

"A fine day to be at sea, Captain," Dean said, coming to stand by his side.

Arthur nodded. "Yes, it is, Mr. Dean. Yes, it is."

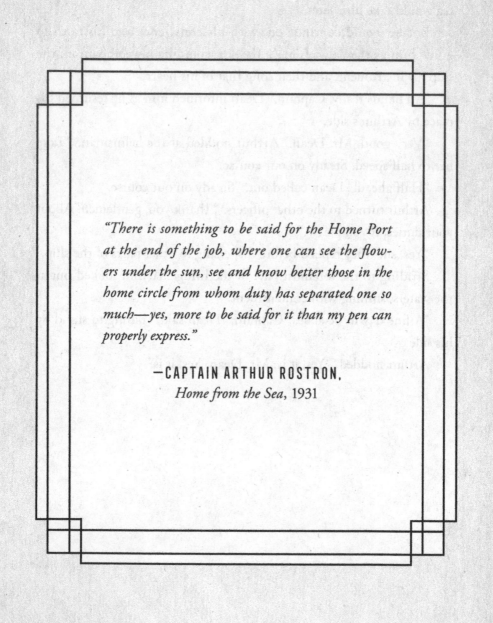

"There is something to be said for the Home Port at the end of the job, where one can see the flowers under the sun, see and know better those in the home circle from whom duty has separated one so much—yes, more to be said for it than my pen can properly express."

—CAPTAIN ARTHUR ROSTRON,
Home from the Sea, 1931

AFTERWORD

Captain Rostron and the crew of the *Carpathia* were hailed as heroes and celebrities. Honors, tributes, and awards were given, including medals and money from the survivors of *Titanic*.

At one tribute ceremony, John Temple Graves, editor of the *New York American* paper, said these words: "Other *Titanic*s may sail and sink. Other *Carpathia*s may go bravely out to rescue and to save. But the prompt courage with which they go and the wise and tender judgment they display will take lesson and inspiration from the Arthur Rostron way!"

Second Officer Charles Lightoller of the *Titanic* never received a command of his own. He retired from the sea in the early 1920s, but never lost his taste for adventure. In 1940, he took his yacht to Dunkirk, and despite being bombed by the Luftwaffe, managed to bring back 131 British soldiers. He died in 1952.

Fourth Officer Joseph Boxhall of the *Titanic* would spend another twenty years at sea. Over the years, the accuracy of the final position he had worked out for the *Titanic* would be questioned by critics, but he defended his work until the end of his days. After his death in 1963, his ashes were scattered over the North Atlantic, at the coordinates he originally calculated for the *Titanic*'s grave.

Harold Bride of the *Titanic* kept a low profile after the sinking. In August 1912, Bride was aboard the SS *Medina* as a Marconi operator. During World War I, Bride served as the wireless operator on the steamship *Mona's Isle*, and in 1922, he retired from the sea and became a salesman. He died in 1956 in Glasgow.

First Officer Horace Dean of the *Carpathia* went on to have a distinguished and active career at sea with Cunard and in the Royal Navy, working his way up to the rank of Lieutenant Commander. He remained on the *Carpathia* until 1913, then served on the *Mauretania* and *Franconia* as well. He retired from Cunard Line in 1938 and passed away in 1943.

Harold Cottam continued his career as a wireless operator, serving on one of the early ships to sail through the Panama Canal and traveling around the world. He retired from the sea ten years later, and over the years, gave the odd interview or two, recounting the night of the sinking. He passed away in 1984 at the age of ninety-three.

Katie McCarthy settled in her new home in Brooklyn and later met a fellow Tipperary man, John Croke, whom she married in 1914. In the early 1920s, Katie and John returned to their native Ireland where she still had family. Katie and her husband would remain childless and settled in Ballintemple, Dundrum, Tipperary. She passed away in 1948 at age sixty.

Mary McGovern remained in New York for a time but returned to her family in County Cavan, Ireland, before the close of the decade. Mary wed Peter McGovern, no relation, in 1921, just weeks before the partition of Ireland. Mary made her lifelong home on their farm in Tullytrasna, where she and Peter raised one son and one daughter. For the rest of her life, Mary kept the small parcel of Saint Mogue's earth that had accompanied her on *Titanic*. She died in 1957.

After recovering in the hospital in New York, Mary Glynn went on to Washington, DC, where she met her future husband, Patrick O'Donoghue. The couple were married in the US Capitol in 1917 and had six children. Mary died in 1955.

Julia Smyth developed scarlet fever not long after landing in New York. After her recovery, she soon found work as a domestic. She was married in Manhattan in 1917 to William Glover. After that marriage ended, Julia married Thomas White. Julia died in Manhattan in 1977.

Kate Connolly made her home in New York and was married there in 1916 to William Arkins, also from County Cavan, Ireland. They settled in Manhattan and had four sons. Kate applied for US citizenship in November 1924. She became a citizen in 1931. Kate Connolly Arkins died at age sixty, following a stroke, in Queens, New York, in 1948.

Captain Arthur Rostron was honored by the United States and Great Britain for his efforts in the *Titanic* disaster. He left the *Carpathia* in December 1912 and next captained the *Caronia*, the *Carmania*, the *Campania*, and the *Lusitania*. He was captain of the *Aulania* when World War I began; the ship was turned into a troopship, which Rostron continued to command.

In 1926, he was knighted by King George V for his service and became the Commodore of the Cunard fleet. After his retirement in May 1931, Rostron wrote an autobiography entitled *Home from the Sea*. In the dedication, he credited wireless operator Harold Cottam's alertness with making possible the rescue that "firmly planted my feet on the ladder of success."

He died of pneumonia in Wiltshire on November 4, 1940.

The *Carpathia* saw service in World War I and was involved in the rescue of Americans fleeing Naples, carrying cargo, munitions, and passengers and soldiers from North America to Europe.

On July 17, 1918, she was struck by a torpedo in the Celtic Sea from German U-Boat U-55, just four months before the Armistice.

In the words of her most famous captain: "It was a sorry end to a fine ship, yet it is a fitting end to my tale of her career. She had done her bit both in peace and war, and she lies in her natural element, resting her long rest on a bed of sand."

CAPTAIN ARTHUR ROSTRON,
R.D., R.N.R., while serving as master of the
Cunard liner RMS *Carpathia* in 1912

KATE CONNOLLY

AUTHOR'S NOTE

In the summer of 2015, I was on a tour of the British Isles with a good friend, indulging in our love of history as well as the beauty of those countries. One of our stops was the *Titanic* Museum in Belfast, Northern Ireland. My naivete in thinking I knew all about that ship and its tragedy, as so many others do, was quickly snuffed out, replaced instead by awe, by solemnity, and by inspiration.

Most moving of all to me was the communication room, the walls papered with images of messages sent out by *Titanic* as well as from other ships she was in communication with on that fateful night. One telegram caught my attention specifically—the last one of the collection.

It read simply "CQ—" and nothing more.

I stared at that telegram, the magnitude of the unfinished text sinking deep into my heart.

Around the next corner was a display about the rescue of the survivors, and there I learned two names that captured my interest: *Carpathia* and Captain Arthur Rostron.

There began my journey to learn the story of the *Carpathia* and her captain, and the years that followed have been full of research, of revelation, and of joy. I learned of a story of providence, of sacrifice, and of heroism that deserves to have its place restored in the minds of humankind.

Though this is a novel, I wanted to bring in as much of the history as I could.

The final and incomplete CQD message from *Titanic* was not heard by the *Carpathia*, but by the *Virginian*. For the purposes of this novel, I have given the receipt of that message to Harold Cottam and *Carpathia*.

Appearances of all characters were based on available historical photographs. For those characters where photographs were not available, the appearance was fictionalized.

There is no record of the hymns sung at the memorial service on board the *Carpathia*, so I selected from some popular hymns at the time.

The first *Titanic* survivor off the *Carpathia* in New York was an unidentified woman, but the tale of her being swept into loving arms, as depicted in the novel, is accurate from personal accounts. I took a liberty in identifying her as Sarah Roth, who was a *Titanic* survivor, and who married her fiancé in St. Vincent's hospital, New York, a week after the *Carpathia* docked.

The woman who was found in the water and pulled into lifeboat 13 was also unidentified in my research. Wanting to keep that part of the story in the narrative, I gave that character the identity of Helmina Josefina Nilsson, who boarded *Carpathia* with the rest of lifeboat 13.

Though she has no direct role in this book, I wanted to include the incredible example of Noël Leslie, Countess of Rothes, who truly did spend the entire return voyage to New York on *Carpathia* tending to the poor and needy of the survivors, despite being a survivor herself.

Such selfless service was an inspiration to me, and I felt she deserved to be honored.

There is no record that the "unsinkable" Margaret "Molly" Brown and Kate Connolly ever interacted while on the *Carpathia*. However, Molly Brown did go about helping her fellow survivors, collecting money and supplies, and she did a great deal to help the less-fortunate *Titanic* survivors and their families in the aftermath of the disaster. Perhaps it is not too great a stretch to think that the women might have crossed paths.

The discrepancy in the time of the disaster notification in Arthur Rostron's testimony to the US Senate Committee is true, and it is actually no discrepancy at all. Before 1920, all ships at sea used "solar time" as their time standard, which required setting clocks in the morning and evening so that, given the ship's direction and speed, it would be considered twelve o'clock when the sun crossed the ship's meridian. So, in solar time, the message was received at 12:35 AM, which was 10:45 PM the night before in New York.

There is still debate regarding the identity of the ship seen on the horizon after the rescue. Men of the *Carpathia* swear it was the *Californian*, and the *Californian* swears she was never close enough to help. Included in the various inquiries after the disaster, the captain and officers of the *Californian* were called upon to testify, and the captain was found to be at fault and was stripped of his position.

In the decades that followed, opinions have gone back and forth, and as technology improves, the real truth may someday be proven. This book is not designed to speculate on that issue, or offer the author's opinion, and is only to give the perspective of those on the *Carpathia* as recorded by those who were there.

I was deeply inspired by the removal of class distinctions on the decks of the *Carpathia*. First Class *Titanic* passengers helped other passengers of lower stations. *Carpathia* passengers of all stations, high and low, assisted in caring for the sick and the weary and brought comfort to those who had lost loved ones. Survivors of every station attended the funeral services for the four men buried at sea.

The tensions between Catholics and Protestants at the end of the nineteenth century and into the twentieth century were significant in some parts of the world, and particularly in Ireland.

Four years after the sinking of *Titanic*, the Easter Rising would take place in Dublin and the surrounding areas. Three years after that, war would break out in Ireland between the groups, dividing Ireland into two countries: The Republic of Ireland and Northern Ireland.

That did not end the trouble between the two religions, though, and decades of strife lay ahead for the Irish. Knowing that history, I found it moving that, on the *Carpathia*, services in both faiths were held for the men they buried, honoring each one with their respective religious beliefs.

I was attracted to the story of Kate Connolly purely because of our similar surnames, and by the fact that there were two women with the same name on board the *Titanic*. The story of the confusion between the two of them after the rescue is true, and that confusion extended to both sides of the Atlantic, though the exact details are unclear. At the time of the writing of this book, I can find no personal direct ties to either Kate Connolly though I continue to hunt for them. As a fun fact, I did find a man named John Connolly who worked on the *Carpathia*, but he was from Liverpool, England.

ACKNOWLEDGMENTS

Thanks go out to Heather Moore, Jen Johnson, Chris Bailey, and my father, Pat Connolly, all of whom read this book for me in its infancy and gave their valuable insight.

To Derek Hutchins for helping me bring the story to life in the earliest days.

To the Encyclopedia Titanica team for the mountains of research and work they've done over the years that made my task so much easier.

To Stephanie, Marilyn, and Jim for taking me along on the trip that started it all. It has been a journey, and I am in debt to each and every one of you.

Thanks to the amazing Lisa Mangum, Chris Schoebinger, Heidi Taylor Gordon, and the entire gang at Shadow Mountain for being as excited about this project as I am, and for making this dream come true.

SELECTED BIBLIOGRAPHY

Behe, George. *Voices from the Carpathia: Rescuing RMS Titanic*. Stroud, UK: The History Press, 2015.

"Burial of the Dead." *Episcopal Church*, 22 May 2012, https://www.episcopal church.org/glossary/burial-of-the-dead/. Accessed 8 November 2023.

"The Burial of the Dead: Rite II." www.bcponline.org/PastoralOffices /BurialII.html. Accessed 12 July 2020.

Butler, Daniel Allen. *The Other Side of the Night: The Carpathia, the Californian, and the Night the Titanic Was Lost*. Havertown, PA: Casemate, 2011.

Clements, Eric L. *Captain of the Carpathia: The Seafaring Life of Titanic Hero Sir Arthur Henry Rostron*. London: Conway, 2017.

"The Cunard SS Carpathia." *The Syren and Shipping: A Weekly Illustratede Journal*, Vol. XXVII, No. 349, 6 May 1903, pp. 250–55. *RMS Carpathia Ephemera Collection | GG Archives*, www.gjenvick.com/OceanTravel /ImmigrantShips/Carpathia.html. Accessed 27 July 2020.

Encyclopedia Titanica, 2019, www.encyclopedia-titanica.org.

Marshall, Logan, ed. *Sinking of the Titanic and Great Sea Disasters*. Philadelphia: J.C. Winston, 1912.

Map source: https://www.titanicinquiry.org/images/charts/Chart3.gif. Based on information from 1912.

Ottmers, Rob. "Titanic Inquiry Project—Main Page," 1997, www.titanic inquiry.org. Accessed 5 September 2020.

"Prayers." www.ibreviary.com/m2/preghiere.php?tipo=Rito&id=417. Accessed 12 July 2020.

Rostron, Arthur. *Titanic Hero: The Autobiography of Captain Rostron of the Carpathia*. Stroud, UK: Amberley, 2011. (Originally published as *Home from the Sea*, 1931.)

ABOUT THE AUTHOR

REBECCA CONNOLLY is the author of more than two dozen novels. She calls herself a Midwest girl, having lived in Ohio and Indiana. She's always been a bookworm, and her grandma would send her books almost every month so she would never run out.

Book Fairs were her carnival, and libraries are her happy place. She received a master's degree from West Virginia University.

Learn more about Rebecca and her books at rebeccaconnolly.com.

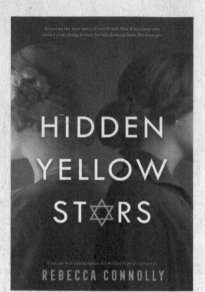

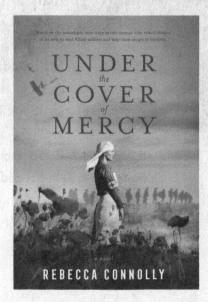